James Lee Burke is the author of thirty-one novels and two collections of short stories. He won the Edgar Award in 1998 for *Cimarron Rose*, while *Black Cherry Blues* won the Edgar in 1990 and *Sunset Limited* was awarded the CWA Gold Dagger in 1998. In 2009, the Mystery Writers of America presented him with the Grand Master Award. He lives with his wife, Pearl, in Missoula, Montana. Visit his website at www.jamesleeburke.com

# JAMES LEE BURKE

# THE LOST GET-BACK BOOGIE

An Orion paperback

First published in the United States in 1986
by Louisiana State University Press
First published in Great Britain in 2003
by Orion
This paperback edition published in 2012
by Orion Books,
an imprint of The Orion Publishing Group Ltd,
Orion House, 5 Upper St Martin's Lane,
London WC2H 9EA

An Hachette UK company

7 9 10 8 6

A CIP catalogue record for this book
is available from the British Library.

ISBN 978-1-4091-0953-2

Typeset by Deltatype Ltd, Birkenhead, Merseyside

Printed in Great Britain by
Clays Ltd, St Ives plc

The Orion Publishing Group's policy is to use papers that are natural,
renewable and recyclable products and made from wood grown in sustainable
forests. The logging and manufacturing processes are expected to conform
to the environmental regulations of the country of origin.

*For John and Judy Holbrook*
*Frank and Linda Loweree*
*and Dexter Roberts*

You know, the blues is something that's hard to get acquainted with. It's just like death. Now, I tell you about the blues. The blues dwells with you every day and everywhere. See, you can have the blues about that you're broke. You can have the blues about your girl is gone. The blues comes so many different ways until it's kind of hard to explain. But whenever you get a sad feeling, you can tell the whole round world you got nothing but the blues.

– Sam 'Lightning' Hopkins

# THE LOST
# GET-BACK BOOGIE

# chapter one

The captain was silhouetted on horseback like a piece of burnt iron against the sun. The brim of his straw hat was pulled low to shade his sun-darkened face, and he held the sawed-off double-barrel shotgun with the stock propped against his thigh to avoid touching the metal. We swung our axes into the roots of tree stumps, our backs glistening and brown and arched with vertebrae, while the chain saws whined into the felled trees and lopped them off into segments. Our Clorox-faded, green-and-white-pinstripe trousers were stained at the knees with sweat and the sandy dirt from the river bottom, and the insects that boiled out of the grass stuck to our skin and burrowed into the wet creases of our necks. No one spoke, not even to caution a man to step back from the swing of an ax or the roaring band of a McCulloch saw ripping in a white spray of splinters through a stump. The work was understood and accomplished with the smoothness and certitude and rhythm that come from years of learning that it will never have a variation. Each time we hooked the trace chains on a stump,

1

slapped the reins across the mules' flanks, and pulled it free in one snapping burst of roots and loam, we moved closer to the wide bend of the Mississippi and the line of willow trees and dappled shade along the bank.

'OK, water and piss it,' the captain said.

We dropped the axes, prizing bars, and shovels, and followed behind the switching tail of the captain's horse down to the willows and the water can that sat in the tall grass with the dipper hung on the side by its ladle. The wide, brown expanse of the river shimmered flatly in the sun, and on the far bank, where the world of the free people began, white egrets were nesting in the sand. The Mississippi was almost a half mile across at that point, and there was a story among the Negro convicts that during the forties a one-legged trusty named Wooden Unc had whipped a mule into the river before the bell count on Camp H and had held onto his tail across the current to the other side. But the free people said Wooden Unc was a nigger's myth; he was just a syphilitic old man who had had his leg amputated at the charity hospital at New Orleans and who later went blind on julep (a mixture of molasses, shelled corn, water, yeast, and lighter fluid that the Negroes would boil in a can on the radiator overnight) and fell into the river and drowned under the weight of the artificial leg given him by the state. And I believed the free people, because I never knew or heard of anyone who beat Angola.

We rolled cigarettes from our state issue of Bugler and Virginia Extra tobacco and wheat-straw papers, and those who had sent off for the dollar-fifty rolling machines sold by a mail-order house in Memphis took out their Prince Albert cans of neatly glued and clipped cigarettes that were as good as tailor-mades. There was still a mineral-streaked piece of ice floating in the water can, and we spilled the dipper over our mouths and chests and let the coldness of the water run down inside our trousers. The captain gave his horse to one of the Negroes to take into the shallows, and sat against a tree trunk with the bowl of his pipe cupped in his hand, which rested on the huge bulge of his abdomen below his cartridge belt. He wore no socks under his half-topped boots, and the area above his ankles was hairless and chafed a dead, shaling color.

He lived in a small frame cottage by the front gate with the other free people, and each twilight he returned home to a cancer-ridden, hard-shell Baptist wife from Mississippi who taught Bible lessons to the Sunday school class in the Block. In the time I was on his gang, I saw him kill one convict, a half-wit Negro kid who had been sent up from the mental hospital at Mandeville. We were breaking a field down by the Red Hat House, and the boy dropped the plow loops off his wrists and began to walk across the rows toward the river. The captain shouted at him twice from the saddle, then raised forward on the pommel, aimed, and let off the first barrel. The boy's shirt jumped at the shoulder, as though the breeze had caught it, but he kept walking across the rows with his unlaced boots flopping on his feet like galoshes. The captain held the stock tight into his shoulder and fired again, and the boy tripped forward across the rows with a single jet of scarlet bursting out just below his kinky, uncut hairline.

A pickup truck driven by one of the young hacks rolled in a cloud of dust down the meandering road through the fields toward me. The rocks banged under the fenders, and the dust coated the stunted cattails in the irrigation ditches. I put out my Virginia Extra cigarette against the sole of my boot and stripped the paper down the glued seam and let the tobacco blow apart in the wind.

'I reckon that's your walking ticket, Iry,' the captain said.

The hack slowed the truck to a stop next to the Red Hat House and blew his horn. I took my shirt off the willow branch where I had left it at eight o'clock field count that morning.

'How much money you got coming on discharge?' the captain said.

'About forty-three dollars.'

'You take this five and send it to me, and you keep your ass out of here.'

'That's all right boss.'

'Hell it is. You'll be sleeping in the Sally after you run your money out your pecker on beer and women.'

I watched him play his old self-deluding game, with the green tip of a five-dollar bill showing above the laced edge of his convict-made wallet. He splayed over the bill section of the wallet with his thick thumb and held it out momentarily, then folded it again in his palm. It was his favorite ritual of generosity when a convict earned good time on his gang and went back on the street.

'Well, just don't do nothing to get violated back to the farm, Iry,' he said.

I shook hands with him and walked across the field to the pickup truck. The hack turned the truck around, and we rolled down the baked and corrugated road through the bottom section of the farm toward the Block. I looked through the back window and watched the ugly, squat white building called the Red Hat House grow smaller against the line of willows on the river. It was named during the thirties when the big stripes (the violent and the insane) were kept there. In those days, before the Block with its lock-down section was built, the dangerous ones wore black-and-white-striped jumpers and straw hats that were painted red. When they went in at night from the fields, they had to strip naked for a body search and their clothes were thrown into the building after them. Later, the building came to house the electric chair, and someone had painted in broken letters on one wall: THIS IS WHERE THEY KNOCK THE FIRE OUT OF YOUR ASS.

We drove through the acres of new corn, sugar cane, and sweet potatoes, the squared sections and weedless rows mathematically perfect, each thing in its ordered and predesigned place, past Camp H and its roofless and crumbling stone buildings left over from the Civil War, past the one-story rows of barracks on Camp 1, then the shattered and weed-grown block of concrete slab in an empty field by Camp A where the two iron sweatboxes had been bulldozed out in the early fifties. I closed off the hot stream of air through the wind vane and rolled a cigarette.

'What are you going to do outside?' the hack said. He chewed gum, and his lean sun-tanned face and washed-out blue eyes looked at me flatly with his question. His starched khaki short sleeves were folded in a neat cuff above his biceps. As a new guard he had the same status among us as a fish, a convict just beginning his first fall.

'I haven't thought about it yet,' I said.

'There's plenty of work if a man wants to do it.' His eyes were young and mean, and there was just enough of that north Louisiana Baptist righteousness in his voice to make you pause before you spoke again.

'I've heard that.'

'It don't take long to get your ass put back in here if you ain't working,' he said.

I licked the glued seam of the cigarette paper, folded it down under my thumb, and crimped the ends.

'You got a match, boss?'

His eyes looked over my face, trying to peel through the skin and reach inside the insult of being called a title that was given only to the old hacks who had been on the farm for years. He took a kitchen match from his shirt pocket and handed it to me.

I popped the match on my fingernail and drew in

on the suck of flame and glue and the strong black taste of Virginia Extra. We passed the prison cemetery with its faded wooden markers and tin cans of withered flowers and the grave of Alton Bienvenu. He did thirty-three years in Angola and had the record for time spent in the sweatbox on Camp A (twenty-two days in July with space only large enough for the knees and buttocks to collapse against the sides and still hold a man in an upright position, a slop bucket set between the ankles and one air hole the diameter of a cigar drilled in the iron door). He died in 1957, three years before I went in, but even when I was in the fish tank (the thirty days of processing and classification in lockdown you go through before you enter the main population), I heard about the man who broke out twice when he was a young bindle stiff, took the beatings in solitary and the anthill treatment on the levee gang, and later as an old man worked paroles through an uncle in the state legislature for other convicts when he had none coming himself, taught reading to illiterates, had morphine tablets smuggled back from the prison section of the charity hospital in New Orleans for a junkie who was going to fry, and testified before a governor's board in Baton Rouge about the reasons that convicts on Angola farm slashed the tendons in their ankles. After his death he was canonized in the prison's group legend with a saint's aura rivaled only by a Peter, crucified upside down in a Roman arena with his shackles still stretched between his legs.

7

The mound of Alton Bienvenu's grave was covered with a cross of flowers, a thick purple, white, and gold-tinted shower of violets, petunias, cowslips, and buttercups from the fields. A trusty was cutting away the St Augustine grass from the edge of the mound with a gardener's trowel.

'What do you think about that?' the hack said.

'I guess it's hard to keep a grave clean,' I said, and I pinched the hot ash of my cigarette against the paint on the outside of the car door.

'That's some shit, ain't it? Putting flowers on a man's grave that's already gone to hell.' He spit his chewing gum into the wind and drove the truck with one hand over the ruts as though he were aiming between his tightened knuckles at the distant green square of enclosure by the front gate called the Block.

The wind was cool through the concrete, shaded breezeway as we walked toward my dormitory. The trusties were watering the recreation yard, and the grass and weight-lifting sets glistened in the sun. We reached the first lock and waited for the hack to pull the combination of levers that would slide the gate. The Saturday-morning cleaning crews were washing down the walls and floor in my dormitory with buckets of soap and water and an astringent antiseptic that burned the inside of your head when you breathed it. The dirt shaled off my boots on the wet floor, but no sign of protest or irritation showed on a man's face. Because the hack was there with me, there was some vague reason for them to redo part of their work, and they squeezed out their mops in the buckets, the ashes dropping from their cigarettes, and went about mopping my muddy tracks with their eyes as flat as glass.

'You can keep your underwear and your shoes,' the hack said. 'Throw your other clothes and sheets in a pile outside. Roll your mattress and don't leave nothing behind. I'll pick you up in the rec room when you get finished and take you over to Possessions.'

I pulled off my work uniform, put on my clack sandals, and walked down the corridor to the showers. I let the cold water boil over my head and face until my breath came short in my chest. One man on the cleaning detail had stopped mopping and was watching me through the doorless opening in the shower partition. He was a queen in Magnolia section who was finishing his second jolt for child molesting. His buttocks swelled out like a pear, and he always kept his shirt buttoned at the throat and never bathed.

'Take off, Morton. No show today, babe,' I said.

'I don't want nothing off you,' he said, and rinsed his mop in the bucket, his soft stomach hanging over his belt.

'You guys watch the goddamn floor,' I heard somebody yell down the corridor; then came the noise of the first crews who had been knocked off from the fields. 'We done cleaned it twice already. You take your goddamn shoes off.'

When I got back to my cell, the corridor was striped with the dry imprints of bare feet, and my cell partner, W. J. Posey, was sitting shirtless on his

9

bunk, with his knees drawn up before him, smoking the wet end of a hand-rolled cigarette between his lips without removing it. His balding pate was sunburned and flecked with pieces of dead skin, and the knobs of his elbows and shoulders and the areas of bone in his chest were the color of a dead carp. He was working on five to fifteen, a three-time loser for hanging paper, and in the year we had celled together, warrants had been filed for him in three other states. His withered arms were covered with faded tattoos done in Lewisburg and Parchman, and his thick, nicotine-stained fingernails looked like claws.

I put on the shiny suit and the off-color brown shoes that had been brought to my cell the night before by the count man. I threw my sheets, blanket, and the rest of my prison uniforms and denims into the corridor, and put my underwear, work boots, and three new shirts and pairs of socks into the box the suit had come in.

'You want the purses and wallets, W. J.?'

'Yeah, give them to me. I can trade them to that punk in Ash for a couple of decks.'

'Take care, babe. Don't hang out any more on the wash line.'

'Yeah. Write me a card when you make your first million,' he said. He dropped his cigarette stub into the butt can by his bunk and picked at his toenails.

I walked down the corridor past the row of open cells and the men with bath towels around their waists clacking in their wood sandals toward the roar of water and shouting in the shower stalls. The wind through the breezeway was cool against my face and wet collar. I waited at the second lock for the hack to open up.

'You know the rec don't open till twelve-thirty, Paret,' he said.

'Mr Benson said he wanted me to wait for him there, boss.'

'Well, you ain't supposed to be there.'

'Let him through, Frank,' the other hack on the lock said.

The gate slid back with its quiet rush of hydraulically released pressure. I waited in the dead space between the first and second gates for the hack to pull the combination of levers again.

Our recreation room had several folding card tables, a canteen where you could buy Kool-Aid and soda pop, and a small library filled with worthless books donated by the Salvation Army. Anything that was either vaguely pornographic or violent or, especially, racial was somehow eaten up in a censoring process that must have begun at the time of donation and ended at the front gate. But anyway, it was thorough, because there wasn't a plot in one of those books that wouldn't bore the most moronic among us. I sat at a card table that was covered with burns like melted plastic insects, and rolled a cigarette from the last tobacco in my package of Virginia Extra.

I heard the lock hiss, then the noise of the first men walking through the dead space, their voices echoing briefly off the stone walls, into the recreation room where they would wait until the dining hall opened at 12:45. They all wore clean denims and pinstripes, their hair wet and slicked back over the ears, combs clipped in their shirt pockets, pomade and aftershave lotion glistening in their pompadours and sideburns, and names like Popcorn, Snowbird, and Git-It-and-Go were Cloroxed into their trousers.

'Hey, Willard, get out them guitars,' one man said.

Each Saturday afternoon our country band played on the green stretch of lawn between the first two buildings in the Block. We had one steel guitar and pickups and amplifiers for the two flattops, and our fiddle and mandolin players held their instruments right into the microphone so we could reach out with 'Orange Blossom Special' and 'Please Release Me, Darling' all the way across the cane field to Camp I.

Willard, the trusty, opened the closet where the instruments were kept and handed out the two Kay flattops. The one I used had a capo fashioned from a pencil and a piece of inner tube on the second fret of the neck. West Finley, whose brother named East was also in Angola, handed the guitar to me in his clumsy fashion, with his huge hand squeezed tight on the strings and his bad teeth grinning around his cigar.

'I mean you look slick, cotton. Them free-people clothes is fierce. I thought you was a damn movie star,' he said.

'You've been sniffing gas tanks again, West.'

'No shit, man. Threads like that is going to cause

some kind of female riot in the bus depot.' His lean, hillbilly face was full of good humor, his mouth wide and brown with tobacco juice. 'Break down my song for me, babe, because I ain't going to be able to hear it played right for a long time.'

The others formed around us, grinning, their arms folded in front of them, with cigarettes held up casually to their mouths, waiting for West to enter the best part of his performance.

'No pick,' I said.

'Shit,' and he said it with that singular two-syllable pronunciation of the Mississippi delta: *shee-it*. He took an empty match cover from the ashtray, folded it in half, and handed it to me between his callused fingers. 'Now let's get it on, Iry. The boss man is going to be ladling them peas in a minute.'

Our band's rhythm-guitar man sat across from me with the other big Kay propped on his folded thigh. I clicked the match cover once across the open strings, sharped the B and A, and turned the face of the guitar toward him so he could see my E-chord configuration on the neck. The song was an old Jimmie Rodgers piece that began, 'If you don't like my peaches, don't shake my tree,' and then the lyrics became worse. But West was beautiful. He bopped on the waxed floor, the shined points of the alligator shoes his girl had sent him flashing above his own scuff marks, bumping and grinding as he went into the dirty boogie, his oiled, ducktailed hair collapsed in a black web over his face. One man took a small harmonica from his shirt pocket and blew a deep, train-moaning bass behind us, and West caught it and pumped the air with his loins, his arms stretched out beside him, while the other men whistled and clapped and grabbed themselves. Through a crack of shoulders I saw the young hack come through the lock into the recreation room, and I slid back down the neck to E again and bled it off quietly on the treble strings.

West's face was perspiring and his eyes were bright. He took his cigar from the table's edge, and his breath came short when he spoke. 'When you get up to Nashville with all them sweet things on the Opry, tell them the big bopper from Bogalusa is primed and ready and will be taking requests in six more months. Tell them I quit charging, too. I done give up my selfish ways about sharing my body. They ain't got to be Marilyn Monroe either. I ain't a snob, cotton.'

Everyone laughed, their mouths full of empty spaces and gold and lead fillings. Then the outside bell rang, and the third lock, which controlled the next section of the breezeway, hissed back in a suck of air.

'Got to scarf it down and put some protein in the pecker. Do something good for me tonight,' West said, and popped two fingers off his thumbnail into my arm as he walked past me toward the lock with the other men.

'Just leave the guitar on the table,' the hack said. 'The state car is leaving out at one.'

I picked up my box and followed him back through the lock. He held up my discharge slip to the hack by the levers, which was unnecessary, since the lock was already opened and all the old bosses along the breezeway knew that I was going out that day anyway. But as I watched him walk in front of me, with his starched khaki shirt shaping and reshaping across his back like iron, I realized that he would be holding up papers of denial or permission with a whitened click of knuckles for the rest of his life.

'You better move unless you want to walk down to the highway,' he said halfway over his shoulder.

We went to Possessions, and he waited while the trusty looked through the rows of alphabetized manila envelopes that were stuffed into the tiers of shelves and hung with stringed, circular tags. The trusty flipped his stiffened fingers down a row in a rattling of glue and paper and shook out one flattened envelope and brushed the dust off the top with his palm. The hack bit on a matchstick and looked at his watch.

'Check it and sign for it,' the trusty said. 'You got forty-three dollars coming in discharge money and fifty-eight in your commissary fund. I can't give you nothing but fives and ones and some silver. They done cleaned me out this morning.'

'That's all right,' I said.

I opened the manila envelope and took out the things that I had entered the Calcasieu Parish jail with two years and three months before, after I had killed a man: a blunted minié ball perforated with a hole that I had used as a weight when I fished as a boy on Bayou Teche and Spanish Lake; the gold vest watch my father gave me when I graduated from high school; a Swiss army knife with a can opener, screwdriver, and a saw that could build a cabin; one die from a pair of dice, the only thing I brought back from thirteen months in Korea because they had separated me from sixteen others who went up Heart Break Ridge and stayed there in that pile of wasted ash; and a billfold with all the celluloid-enclosed pieces of identification that are so important to us, now outdated and worthless in their cracked description of who the bearer was.

We walked out of the Block into the brilliant sunlight, and the hack drove us down the front road past the small clapboard cottages where the free people lived. The wash on the lines straightened and dropped in the wind, the tiny gardens were planted with chrysanthemums and rosebushes, and housewives in print dresses appeared quickly in open screen doors to shout at the children in the yard. It could have been a scene surgically removed from a working-class neighborhood, except for the presence of the Negro trusties watering the grass or weeding a vegetable patch.

Then there was the front gate, with three strands of barbed wire leaned inward on top and the wooden gun tower to one side. The oiled road on the other side bounced and shimmered with heat waves and stretched off through the green border of trees and second growth on the edge of the ditches. I got out of the car with my cardboard box under my arm.

'Paret coming out,' the hack said.

I knew he was going to try to shake hands while

the gate was being swung back over the cattle guard, and I kept my attention fixed on the road and used my free hand to look for a cigarette in my shirt pocket. The hack shook a Camel loose from his pack and held it up to me.

'Well, thanks, Mr Benson,' I said.

'Keep the rest of them. I got some more in the cage.' So I had to shake hands with him after all. He got back in the truck with a pinch of light in his iron face, his role a little more secure.

I walked across the cattle guard and heard the gate rattle and lock behind me. Four other men with cardboard boxes and suits similar to mine (we had a choice of three styles upon discharge) sat on the wooden waiting bench by the fence. The shade of the gun tower broke in an oblong square across their bodies.

'The state car ought to be up in a minute, Paret,' the gateman said. He was one of the old ones, left over from the thirties, and he had probably killed and buried more men in the levee than any other hack on the farm. Now he was almost seventy, covered with the kind of obscene white fat that comes from years of drinking corn whiskey, and there wasn't a town in Louisiana or Mississippi where he could retire in safety from the convicts whom he had put on anthills or run double-time with wheelbarrows up and down the levee until they collapsed on their hands and knees.

'I think I need to hoof this one,' I said.

'It's twenty miles out to that highway, boy.' And he didn't say it unkindly. The word came to him as

17

automatically as anything else that he raised up out of thirty-five years of doing almost the same type of time that the rest of us pulled.

'I know that, boss. But I got to stretch it out.' I didn't turn to look at him, but I knew that his slate-green eyes were staring into my back with a mixture of resentment and impotence at seeing a piece of personal property moved across a line into a world in which he himself could not function.

The dead water in the ditches along the road was covered with lily pads, and dragonflies flicked with their purple wings above the newly opened flowers. The leaves on the trees were coated with dust, and the red-black soil at the roots was lined with the tracings of night crawlers. I was perspiring under my coat, and I pulled it off with one hand and stuck it through the twine wrapped around the cardboard box. A mile up the road I heard the tires of the state car whining hotly down the oiled surface. They slowed in second gear alongside me, the hack bent forward into the steering wheel so he could speak past his passenger.

'That's a hot son of a bitch to walk, and you probably ain't going to hitch no ride on the highway.'

I smiled and shook the palm of my hand at them, and after the car had accelerated away in a bright-yellow cloud of gravel and dust and oil, someone shot the finger out the back window.

I threw the cardboard box into the ditch and walked three more miles to a beer tavern and cafe set off by the side of the road in a circle of gravel.

The faded wooden sides of the building were covered with rotted election posters (DON'T GET CAUGHT SHORT – VOTE LONG – SPEEDY O. LONG, A SLAVE TO NO MAN AND A SERVANT TO ALL), flaking and rusted tin signs advertising Hada-col and Carry-On and stickers for Brown Mule, Calumet baking powder, and Doctor Tichner's Painless Laxative. A huge live-oak tree, covered with Spanish moss, grew by one side of the building, and its roots had swelled under the wall with enough strength to bend the window jamb.

It was dark and cool inside, with a wooden ceiling fan turning overhead, and the bar shined with the dull light of the neon beer signs and the emptiness of the room. It felt strange to pull out the chair from the bar and scrape it into position and sit down. The bartender was in the kitchen talking with a Negro girl. His arms were covered with tattoos and a heavy growth of white hair. He wore a folded butcher's apron tied around his great girth of stomach.

'Hey, podna, how about a Jax down here?' I said.

He leaned into the service window, his heavy arms folded in front of him and his head extended under the enclosure.

'Just get it out of the cooler, mister, and I'll be with you in a minute.'

I went behind the bar and stuck my hand into the deep, ice-filled cooler and pulled out a bottle of Jax and snapped off the cap in the opener box. My wrist and arm ached with the cold and shale of ice against my skin. The foam boiled over the lip and ran down on my hand in a way that was as strange, at that

19

moment, as the bar chair, the dull, neon beer signs, and the Negro girl scraping a spatula vacantly across the flat surface of the stove. I drank another Jax before the man came out of the kitchen, then ate a poorboy sandwich with shrimp, oysters, lettuce, and sauce hanging out the sides of the French bread.

'You just getting out?' the man said. He said it in the flat, casual tone that most free people use toward convicts, that same quality of voice behind the Xeroxed letters from Boston asking for the donation of our eyes.

I put three dollar bills on the bar and walked toward the square of sunlight against the front door.

'Say, buddy, it don't matter to me what you're getting out of. I was just saying my cousin will give you a ride up to the highway in a few minutes.'

I walked down the oiled road a quarter of a mile, and his cousin picked me up in a stake truck and drove me all the way to the train depot in Baton Rouge.

# chapter two

I could have taken a bus home or hitchhiked, because it was only a three-hour trip to the coast, but I always loved trains, their rows of quiet, angular seats and the suck and rattle of the vestibule opening, and also, there is no dignity in hitchhiking when you are thirty years old. The clapboard general stores and taverns and oaks clicked by the window, and beyond the highway the grey trees of the marsh began. Negroes in flop straw hats cane-fished along the canal, and white cranes rose with their wings gilded in the sunlight above the dead cypress. The butcher boy swayed down the aisle with the roll of the train, his basket loaded with magazines, newspapers, cans of grape drink, and paper cones of plums. I bought a *Times-Picayune* from him and walked to the club car.

The porter brought me a Jax, and after I tired of the front page and its serious treatment of something the state legislature was doing, I sipped the beer and watched the fields of new sugar cane and black Angus roll past. But as we neared New Orleans, the country began to change. Somebody had been busy in the last two years; it was no longer a rural section of the delta. Land-development signs stood along the highway replacing the old ads for patent medicine and Purina feed, and great areas of marsh had been bulldozed out and covered with landfill for subdivision tracts. Mobile-home offices strung with colored flags sat on cinder blocks in the mud, with acres of waste in the background that were already marked into housing plots with surveyors' stakes. The shopping-center boys had been hard at work, too. Pecan orchards and dairy barns had become Food City, Winn-Dixie, and Cash Discount.

I had to change trains in New Orleans for the rest of the trip home. The train was an old one, with dusty seats and yellowed windows cracked on the outside of the double glass with bb holes. We crossed the Mississippi, and my head reeled when I looked down from the window at the wide expanse of water far below. The tugboats and Standard Oil barges and the brown scratches of wake off their hulls looked as miniature and flat as painted pieces on a map. The train clicked slowly across the bridge and the long stretch of elevated track above the levee and mud flats and willow trees, then began to gain speed and bend through the bayou country and the achingly beautiful dark green of the cypress and oak trees, covered with moss and bursting at the roots with mushrooms and cowslips.

Most of the passengers in my car were French people, with cardboard suitcases and boxes tied with string in the luggage rack. An old man in overalls and a suit jacket was speaking French to his wife in the seat behind me, and I listened to them with a violation of privacy that normally I would have walked away from. But in Angola the hacks, who came primarily from north Louisiana and Mississippi, never allowed anyone to speak French in their presence, and even back in the Block it wasn't used unless there was no non-French-speaking person within earshot, because it was considered to have the same clandestine quality as a private whisper between two snitches.

The train crossed Bayou Lafourche, and I leaned into the window and looked at the men in pirogues floating motionlessly against the cypress roots, their cane poles arched and beaten with light against the pull of a bull bream below the lily pads. Before the train moved back into that long corridor of trees through the swamp, I saw one man rip a large goggle-eye perch through a torn leaf and dip one hand quickly into the water with the cane bending in his other hand, the boat almost tilted into the shallows, and catch the line in his fingers and pull the fish slowly away from the lily pads.

Then we were back into the long span of track through the trees and the dead water in the irrigation canals and the occasional farmhouses that you could see beyond the railroad right-of-way. I walked up to the club car and had a bourbon and water while the train slowed into my hometown. The X signs and LOUISIANA LAW STOP warnings on the crossings moved by gradually with the decreased speed of the train, and then the uplifted

23

faces of the people on the platform stared suddenly at mine, then turned with a quick brightness of recognition at someone stepping off the vestibule.

There was an ice wagon on the loading ramp with a tarpaulin stretched across the ice blocks, and the evaporated coldness steamed on top of the canvas in the sun. Two taxicabs were parked in the shade of an oak that grew through the sidewalk in front of the depot.

'Do you know how to get to Robert Paret's place?' I said.

'Who?' The taxi driver's breath was full of beer through the window, and he smoked a filter-tipped cigarette in a gap between his teeth.

'It's up Joe's Shipyard road. You reckon you can take me there?'

'That's fifteen miles, podna. I'll turn the meter off for you, but it'll still cost you ten dollars and maybe some for the tires I bust on that board road up there.'

The town was changed. Or maybe it had been changing for a long time and I hadn't noticed it. Many of the old brick and wood-front stores had gone out of business, the hotel had a FOR LEASE sign in its dusty main window, and only a few cars were parked in front of the beer tavern and pool hall on the corner. The dime store, which used to be crowded with Negroes on Saturday afternoon, was almost empty. We passed the courthouse square and the lines of oak trees shading the wide sidewalks and wood benches where the old men used to sit, but it looked like a discarded movie set. The Confederate monument, inscribed at the base with the words THEY DIED IN DEFENSE OF A HOLY CAUSE, was spotted with pigeon droppings, and someone had stuffed trash paper in the barrel of the Civil War cannon next to it. Only one or two offices besides the bail bondsman's were open, and the corner bar that used to have a card game upstairs was now boarded over.

'Where did the town go?' I said.

'It just dried up after they put in that new highway,' the driver said. 'People ain't going to drive into town when you can get everything you need out there. You just getting out of the service or something?'

'I've been away awhile.'

'Well, there's lots of money to be made here. Like, I could be making twice what I'm getting today if that dispatcher didn't put me on call at the depot.' He belched down in his throat and loosened a can of beer from a six-pack on the seat. He pulled the ring, and the foam slid over his thumb. 'You can pick up fares at the airport and run them a half mile down to the motel, and what you get on tips is more money than I make all afternoon at the depot. Take one of them beers if you like.'

'Thank you,' I said. The can was hot, but I drank it anyway.

We drove out into the parish, crossed the wooden bridge over the bayou at the end of the blacktop, and bounced along the yellow, rutted road by the edge of Joe's Shipyard. Shrimp boats, rusted oil barges, and quarter boats used by seismograph companies were moored along the docks in the dead water, and Negro children were fishing with cane poles for bullheads and gars among the cattails. The driver was out of beer, and we stopped at a tavern filled with deckhands, fishermen, and doodlebuggers (seismograph workers), and I bought him a round at the bar and a carton of Jax to go.

The road followed along the edge of the bayou and the cypress trees that hung out over the water. The expanded swell of the trunks at the waterline was dark from the wake of passing boats, and white egrets were nesting in the sand, their delicate wings quivering as they enlarged the depression around them. I had fished for bream, sacalait, and mud cat under every cypress on that bank, because they always came into the shade to feed in the hottest part of a summer afternoon, and there was one tree that had rusted mooring chains nailed into the trunk with iron stakes that the bark had overgrown in stages until the chain looped in and out of the tree like a deformity. My grandfather said that Jean Laffite used to tie his boat there when he was blackbirding and that he had buried a treasure between two oaks on the back of our property. The ground around the two oaks was pitted with depressions and ragged holes that cut through the roots, and as boys my older brother and I had dug six feet down and scraped away the clay from around the lid of a huge iron caldron, hollowing out the hole like sculptors, to prize up the lid with our shovels and finally discover the bones of a hog that had been boiled into tallow.

We hit the section of board road that Shell Oil had put in three years before when the road had washed out again and the parish refused to maintain it any longer, since the only people who used it were my father and the two or three doodlebug companies that were shooting in that part of the parish. The boards twisted under the tires and slammed upward into the oil pan, and then I saw the mailbox by the short wooden bridge over the coulee.

I paid the driver and walked up the gravel lane through the oak trees. The house had been built by my great-grandfather in 1857, in the Creole architectural style of that period, with brick chimneys on each side and brick columns supporting the lattice-work veranda on the second story. The peaked roof was now covered with tin, and the foundation had sunk on one side so that the brick columns had cracked and started to shale. The decayed outlines of the slaves' quarters were still visible in the grass down by the bayou, and the original stone well, now filled with dirt and overgrown with vines, protruded from the ground at an angle by the smokehouse. My father had held on to forty-three acres since the Depression, when we lost most of the farm, and he had refused to lease the mineral rights to the oil companies (he called them Texas sharpers who destroyed your land, cut your fences, and gave you a duster in return), but in the last few years the only sugar cane had been grown by Negroes who worked on shares. His Ford pickup truck with last year's tag was parked in the shed, and there was an old Buick pulled onto the grass at the end of the lane.

27

The swing on the porch twisted slightly against the chains in the breeze. I tapped on the screen door and tried to see inside into the gloom.

'Hello!'

I heard someone at the back of the upstairs hallway, and I went inside with a strange feeling of impropriety. The house smelled of dust and a lack of sunlight. For some reason the only detail that caught in my eye was his guns in the deer-antler rack above the mantelpiece. The .30-.40 Kraig with the box magazine on the side, the lever-action Winchester, and the double-barrel twelve were flecked with rust and coated with cobwebs in the trigger guards and barrels.

'What you want here?'

I looked up the stairs at a big Negro woman in a starched nurse's uniform. Her rolled white hose seemed to be bursting around her black thighs.

'I'm Mr Paret's son.'

She walked down the stairs, her hand on the banister to support her weight. There were tangles of grey hair above her forehead, and I knew that she was much older than she looked.

'You Mr Iry?'

'Yes.'

'He figured you'd be home this week. I just give him his sedative, so he won't be able to talk with you too long. After he takes his nap and has his supper, he can talk a lot better to you.'

'How bad is he?'

'He ain't good. But maybe you better wait on the

28

doctor. He's coming out tonight with your sister. She stays with him on my night off.'

'Thank you.'

'Mr Iry, he talks funny because of that medicine. He's all right after his supper.'

I walked up the stairs into his room. It was dark, and the only light came from the yellow glow of sun against the window shade. Small bottles of urine were lined on the dresser, and there was a shiny bedpan on a stool at the head of the tester bed. His curved pipe and tobacco pouch rested against the armadillo-shell lamp on the nightstand. I didn't know that his face could look so white and wasted. The sheet was pulled up to his chin, and the knobs of his hands looked like bone against the skin. He ticked a finger on his stomach and squinted into the glare of light from the open door with one watery blue eye, and I saw that he couldn't recognize me in the silhouette. I eased the door closed behind me. He smiled, and his lips were purple like an old woman's. He moved his hand off his stomach and tapped it softly on the side of the bed.

'How'd they treat you, Son?'

'It wasn't bad.'

'I thought you might be in yesterday from your letter. I had that nigra nurse make up your room for you. Your guitars are on the bed.' His voice clicked when he spoke, as though he had a fishhook in his throat.

'How they been treating you, Daddy?'

'They like my urine. The doctor takes it away every two days after the nurse puts stickers all over

29

it.' He laughed down in his chest, and a bubble of saliva formed on the corner of his mouth. 'They must not have much to do down at the Charity except look at somebody's piss.'

'Daddy, did Rita and Ace put you in at Charity?'

'They got families of their own, Iry. It costs fifteen dollars a day to keep that nigra woman out here. They ain't got money like that.'

I had to clench my fingers between my legs and look away from him. My sister and brother had married into enough money to bring in the best of everything for him.

'Look at me, Son, and don't start letting those razor blades work around inside you. The one thing I regret is that my children never held together after your mother died. I don't know what they done to you in the penitentiary, but don't take your anger out on them.'

His watery blue eyes were starting to fade with the sedation, and he had to force his words past that obstacle in his throat. I looked at his white hair on the pillow and his thin arms stretched down the top of the sheet, and wondered at what disease and age could do to men, particularly this one, who had gone over the top in a scream of whistles at Belleau Wood and had covered a canister of mustard gas with his own body.

'Why don't you go to sleep and I'll see you later,' I said.

'I want you to do one thing for me this evening. Cut some azaleas by the porch and take them down by your mother's grave.'

'All right, Daddy.'

'I know you don't like to go down there.' The light in his eyes was fading away like a quick blue spark.

'I was going down there anyway,' I said.

His eyes closed, and the lids were red against the paper whiteness of his face.

I had heard stories about the effects of intestinal cancer and how fast it could consume a man and his life's energy, in spite of radiation treatments and the morphine shots to take away the pain, but you had to look at it to make it become real.

I walked down the hall to my room, which he had kept as it was the day I went on the road again with the band and ended up in the penitentiary. My over-and-under, with the .22 magnum and .410 barrels, was propped in the corner, my clothes hung limply in the closet, the creases on the hangers stained with dust, and my double guitar case that held the Martin flattop and the Dobro sat on top of the bed, with the gold-embossed inscription THE GREAT SPECKLED BIRD across the leather surface. I opened the case, which had cost me two hundred dollars to have custom-made in Dallas, and for a moment in the crinkled flash of the Confederate flag that lined the inside and the waxed shine off the guitars, I was back in the barroom with the scream of voices around me and the knife wet and shaking in my hand.

I stripped naked and dressed in a pair of khakis and a denim shirt and slipped on a pair of old loafers. I put everything from Angola inside the suit

31

coat, tied the sleeves into a hard knot, and pushed it down in the wastebasket.

Downstairs, I found the bottle of Ancient Age that my father always kept under the drainboard. I poured a good drink into a tin cup and sipped it slowly while I looked out the window through the oak trees in the yard and at the sun starting to fade over the marsh. Purple rain clouds lay against the horizon, and shafts of sunlight cut like bands of crimson across the cypress tops. I had another drink, this time with water in the cup, and took a butcher knife and the bottle outside with me to the azalea bushes by the side of the house.

I snipped the knife through a dozen branches covered with red flowers and walked down the slope toward the graveyard. It was close to the bayou, and ten years before, we had had to put sacks of cement against the bank and push an old car body into the water to prevent the widening bend of current from eroding the iron fence at the graveyard's edge. There were twenty-three graves in all, from the four generations of my family who were buried on the original land, and the oldest were raised brick-and-mortar crypts that were now cracked with weeds and covered with the scale of dead vines. The graves of my mother and sister were next to each other with a common headstone that was divided by a thin chiseled line. It was brutally simple in its words.

CLAIRE PARET AND FRAN
NOVEMBER 7, 1945

32

There was a tin can full of rusty water and dead stems on the grave, and I picked it up and threw it back in the trees, then laid the azaleas against the headstone in the half-light. It had been seventeen years, but I still had dreams about the fire and the moment when I raced around the back of the house and tried to break open the bolted door with my fists. Through the window I could see my mother's face convulsed like an epileptic's in the flames, the can of cleaning fluid still in her hand, while Fran stood with a halo of fire rising over her pinafore. Alcide, the Negro who worked for us, threw me backward off the porch and drove a pickax up to the helve into the doorjamb. But the wind blew the inside of the house into a furnace, and Fran plunged out of the flames, her clothes and hair dissolving and streaming away behind her.

I took a drink from the bottle and walked down the mud flat and skipped a stone across the bayou's quiet surface. The stone hit in the lily pads on the far side, and the water suddenly became dimpled with small bream. The light was almost gone from the trees now and as I sat back against a cypress and pulled again on the bottle, I had to wonder what I was doing there at all.

When I neared the top of the slope by the smokehouse, I saw a Cadillac parked by the front porch where the nurse's automobile had been. It must be Ace, I thought. Rita's preference would lean toward smaller expensive cars, something conservative enough not to make the wives of her husband's law partners competitive. Or maybe both of them at once, I thought, which was more than I was ready for at that moment.

I walked around the side of the front porch just as Ace was holding open the screen door for her. Ace's face had the formality of an undertaker's, with his mouth turned downward in some type of expression that he had learned for all occasions at a chamber of commerce meeting, and his wilted tie seemed almost glued to his throat. Rita saw me before he did, and she turned in the half-opened screen with her mouth still parted in the middle of a sentence and looked steadily at me as though her eyes wouldn't focus. She was pregnant, and she had gained a good deal of weight since I had seen her last. She had always been a pretty, auburn-haired girl, with small breasts and hips that were only slightly too large for the rest of her, but now her face was oval, her thighs wide, and her maternity dress was stretched tight over her swollen buttocks.

It wasn't going to be pleasant. Their genuine ex-convict was home, the family's one failure, the bad-conduct dischargee from the army, the hillbilly guitar picker who embarrassed both of them just by his presence in the area.

But at least Ace tried. He walked down the steps with his hand outstretched, as though he had been set in motion by a trip switch in the back of his head. He must have sold hundreds of ad accounts with the same papier-mâché smile.

Rita wasn't as generous. Her face looked like she had morning sickness.

We went inside and stood in the hall with the

awkwardness of people who might have just met at a bus stop.

'How about a drink?' I said.

'I could go for that,' Ace said.

I took three glasses from the cupboard and poured into the bottom of them.

'I'm not having any,' Rita said. She was looking in her handbag for a cigarette when she spoke.

'Take one. We don't get the old boy home much,' Ace said, and then pressed his lips together.

'I'll go look in on Daddy,' she said, putting the cigarette in her mouth as though it had to be screwed in.

'Have a drink, Reet. The nurse gave him sedation about a half hour ago,' I said.

'I know that.'

'So have one with us.' It was hard, and maybe there was just a little bit of bile behind my teeth.

She lit her cigarette without answering and dropped the match in the sink. Sometimes, without even trying, you can step in a pile of pig flop right up to your kneecaps, I thought.

'Do you have a finger on a job?' Ace said.

'Not a thing.'

'There's a lot of money being made now.'

'The taxicab driver told me.'

'I'm selling more accounts than I can handle. I might get into some real estate on the side, because that's where it's going to be in the next five years.'

'Do you know if any of the band is still around?' I said.

His face went blank, and his eyes searched in the air.

'No, I didn't know any of them, really.'

'We went to high school with most of them,' I said.

Rita put out her cigarette in the sink and went upstairs. I finished my drink and had another. The whiskey was starting to rise in my face.

'Between the two of us, you think you might want to get in on something solid?' Ace said. He could never drink very well, and his eyes were taking on a shine.

'I think I'm just going to roll, Ace.'

'I'm not telling you what to do, but isn't that how you got into trouble before?'

'I finished all my trouble as of noon today.' I poured another shot in his glass.

'What I'm saying is you can make it. I've got kids working for me that are bringing in ten thousand a year.'

'You're not offering me a public-relations job, are you?'

He started to smile, and then looked again at my face. Rita came back in the kitchen and opened the oven to check on the warmed plate of mashed potatoes and gruel that the nurse had left for my father. I shouldn't have started what came next, but they were drumming their nails on a weak nerve, and the whiskey had already broken down that polite line of restraint.

'Y'all really took care of the old man, didn't you?'

Rita turned from the oven, holding the plate in a hot pad, and looked at me directly for the first time. Her eyes were awful. Ace started to nod at what he thought was an automatic expression of errant-brother gratitude, but then that toggle switch in the back of his head clicked again and his face stretched tight.

'What do you mean, Iry?' The bourbon in his glass tilted back and forth.

'Like maybe Lourdes wants too much gelt to handle him, since they have the best doctors in southwest Louisiana.'

'I don't think you understand everything that was involved,' Ace said. His face was as flat as a dough pan.

'The emergency ward at Charity looks like a butcher shop on Saturday afternoon. I mean, just check out that scene. They deliver babies in the hallways, and the smell that comes off that incinerator is enough to make your eyeballs fall out. For Christ's sake, Ace, you could write a check to pay the old man's way a year at Lourdes.'

'That's very fine of you,' Rita said. 'Maybe there are some other things we've done wrong that you can tell us about. It was also good of you to contribute so much while you were in Angola.'

'All right, but you didn't have to put him into Charity.'

'You're really off base, Iry,' Ace said.

'Where did you learn that one? At an ad meeting?'

'Ridiculous,' Rita said.

'How do you think he feels being shoveled in with

every reject from the parish? He even defended you this afternoon.'

'If you think so much of his welfare, why don't you lower your voice?' Rita said.

And then Ace, the PR man for all occasions, filled my glass and handed it to me. I set it back on the drainboard, my head tingling with anger and the bourbon's heat and the strange movements of the day.

'It was a rotten thing to do,' I said. 'You both know it.'

I walked out the house into the twilight. I felt foolish and light-headed in the wind off the bayou, and there was a line of sweat down the front of my shirt. Through the kitchen window I heard them start to purge their anger on each other.

The trees were filled with a mauve glow from the sun's last light, and I went down to the shed where the pickup was parked, my legs loose under me and a bright flash of caution already clicking on and off in one sober part of my mind.

But the old reckless impulses had more sway, and I scooped some mud out of the drive and smeared it thickly over the expired plate. I turned the truck around and banged over the wooden bridge and roared in second gear down the board road, the ditches on each side of me whipping by the fenders like a drunken challenge.

I stopped at the beer joint by Joe's Shipyard, which contained about fifteen outlaw motorcyclists and their women. They wore grease-stained blue jeans, half-topped boots with chains on the side, and sleeveless denim jackets with a sewed inscription on the back that read:

DEVILS DISCIPLES
NEW ORLEANS

Their arms were covered with tattoos of snakes' heads skulls, and hearts impaled on bleeding knives. I didn't know what they were doing in this area, far from their usual concrete turf, but I found out later that they had come to bust up some civil-rights workers at a demonstration.

The bar had divided in half, with the doodlebuggers, deckhands, and oil-field roughnecks on one side and the motorcyclists on the other, their voices deliberately loud, their beards dripping with beer, and their girls flashing their stuff at the enemy.

I bought three six-packs of Jax and a carton of cigarettes at the bar and walked through the tables toward the door. Someone had turned the jukebox up to full tilt, and Little Richard screamed out all his rage about Long Tall Sally left in the alley. I was almost home free when one of them leaned his chair back into my stomach.

His blond hair hung in curls on his denim jacket, and a pachuco cross was tattooed between his eyebrows. There was beer foam all over his moustache and beard, and his eyes were swimming with a jaundiced, malevolent light at the prospect of a new piece of meat.

'Why don't you just watch it, buddy?' he said. His breath was heavy with the smell of marijuana.

I lifted my elbow and the sack of beer over his head and tried to squeeze by the chair, which was now pressing into a corner of my groin.

'Hey, citizen, you didn't hear the word,' he said.

Two of the girls at the table were grinning at him with a knowing expression over their cigarettes. A real stomp was at hand. One of the straights was going to get his butt kicked up between his ears. Or maybe, even better, he would shake a little bit and then run for the door.

The one advantage that an ex-con has in this kind of situation is that you have seen every one of them before, which is a very strong credential, and as physical people they are always predictable if you turn their own totems and frame of reference against them. In fact, sometimes you look forward to it with anticipation.

I pulled a beer loose from the top of the sack and set it down before him; then I leaned casually into his ear, the gold earring just a breath away from my lips, and whispered: 'Don't turn your head now, but a couple of those oil-field roughnecks are narcs, and they know your girlfriends are holding for you. One of them was talking in the head about stiffing you with a dealing charge. That's a sure fifteen in Angola, podna.'

He turned in his chair and stared at me with his yellow, blood-flecked eyes, and I walked out the door and got into the pickup before he could glue it all together in his brain.

The Point was thirty miles south of town, down a blacktop that wound through rows of flooded cypress and fishing shacks set up on stilts. The brackish water was black in the trees, and pirogues and flat-bottomed outboards piled with conical nets were tied to the banks. I drank one beer after another and pitched the cans out the window into the back of the truck while the salt wind cut into my face and the great cypress limbs hung with moss swept by overhead.

The Point extended into the bay like a long, flat sandspit, and the jetties and the collapsed fishing pier looked like neatly etched black lines against the grayness of the water and the sun's last red spark boiling into the horizon. The tide was out, and seagulls dipped down into the rim of white foam along the sand, and in the distance I could see the gas flares burning off the offshore oil rigs. There was a seafood place and dance pavilion by the dock where you could sit on the screened porch and drink draught beer in mugs thick with ice and feel the wind blow across the flat water. I ordered a tray of boiled crawfish and bluepoint crabs with a half bottle of wine and sucked the hot juice out of the shells and dipped the meat in a tomato sauce mixed with horseradish.

The pavilion was almost empty except for a few fishermen and some kids who had come in early for the Saturday night dance. The food had helped a little, but I was pretty drunk now, past the point of worrying about a DWI bust and what that would mean to the parole officer on my first day out of the bag, and I ordered another beer. There was only a thin band of purple light on the horizon, and I looked hard at the distant buoy that marked where a German submarine had gone down in 1943. Once, years ago, when a hurricane depression had drawn the tide far out over the flats, you could see just the tip of the bow breaking the water. The Coast Guard had tried to blow it up, but they managed only to dislodge it from the sand and send it deeper down the shelf.

Once I worked a doodlebug job out in the bay and we would ping it occasionally on the recorder's instrument, but it was never in the same place twice. It moved a mile either way in an easterly or westerly direction, and no one knew how far it went south into the Gulf before it returned again. And as I sat there on the screened porch, with my head in a beer fog, I felt for just a moment that old fear about all the madness everywhere. The crew was still in that crusted and flattened hull, those Nazis who had committed themselves to making the whole earth a place of concertina wire and guard towers, their empty eye sockets now strung with seaweed, and they were still sailing nineteen years after they had gone down in a scream of sirens and bombs.

The first musicians came in and set up their instruments on the bandstand. The Negro waiter took away my tray and brought me another beer, and I listened to the band tuning their guitars and adjusting the amplifiers. Bugs swam against the screen, trying to reach the light inside the porch, and as I ticked my fingernails against the glass and heard the musicians talking among themselves in their French accents, like on a hundred gigs I had played from Biloxi to Port Arthur, my mind began to fade through that bright drunken corridor to the one spot of insanity in my life, a return to the dream with all its strange distortions and awful questions that left me sweating in the middle of the night for two years at Angola.

We had picked up two weeks' work at a club by the air base in Lake Charles. It was like most roadhouses along that part of Highway 90, a flat, low-ceilinged ramshackle place built of clapboard and Montgomery Ward brick with a pink facade on the front and blue neons that advertised entertainment like Johnny and his Harmonicats. By ten o'clock the smoke always hung thickly against the ceiling, and the smell of the rest rooms reached out to the edge of the dance floor. The crowd was made up of airmen from the base, tough kids with ducktail and boogie haircuts, oil-field workers, people from a trailer court across the road, and sometimes the dangerous ones, who sat at the bar with their short sleeves turned up at the cuffs over their muscular arms, waiting to roll a homosexual or bust up anybody who would like to take his glance into the parking lot.

It was Saturday night, and because we didn't play Sundays, we were getting loaded on the bandstand and blowing up weed behind the building between sets. By two in the morning our lead singer couldn't remember the words to some of the songs, and he was faking it by putting his lips against the microphone and roaring out unintelligible sounds across the dance floor. I had my Dobro hung in a flat position like a steel across my stomach, with the strap pulled down tight against my arm, but when I slipped the bar up and down the frets, the marijuana singing in my head, I hit the nut and soundboard like a piece of loud slate and my finger picks were catching under the strings. One of the bad ones, who was sitting with a couple of prostitutes at the bar, kept returning to the bandstand to ask for 'The Wild Side of Life.' His hands were large and square, the kind you see on pipeline fitters; the fingers on one hand were tattooed with the word LOVE, the fingers of the other with the word HATE. His shirt was bursting with a cruel, animal strength, and a line of sweat dripped out of his hairline and glistened brightly on his jawbone.

Our singer, Rafe Arceneaux, our one real tea head, nodded at him a couple of times when he came back for his song, but on the third time the man put his hand around Rafe's ankle and squeezed just hard enough to show what he could do if he was serious.

'Hey, get fucked, man,' Rafe said. He kicked against the man's grip and fell backward into the drums.

The people on the floor stopped dancing and stared at us through the smoke. Rafe's electric Gibson was cracked across the face, and the wire had been torn loose from the electronic jack. He got up in a rumble of drums and a clash of cymbals with his guitar twisted around his throat. He wasn't a big man, and he had always been frightened of bullies in

**44**

high school, and there was sweat and humiliation all over his face.

'Get your ass out of here, you bastard,' he said.

Tables and chairs were already scraping and toppling across the floor, and the tattooed man had an audience that he would probably never get again. I heard some glass break in the front of the building; then the man raised himself in an easy muscular step, with one hand on the rail, onto the bandstand and threw Rafe headlong into the bar.

Rafe struck like a child thrown from an automobile. There was a deep triangular cut on his forehead, sunken in as though someone had pushed an angry thumb into the soft bone. He lay on the floor with one of his arms caught in the legs of an overturned barstool.

The bad man was still on the stand with us, and he had had just enough of somebody's blood in his nostrils to want some more.

He came for my Martin next, his face grinning and stupid with victory and the knowledge that there was nothing in his way.

'That's your ass if you touch it, podna.'

He got his hand around the neck and I hit him with my fist against the temple. He reeled backward from the guitar case with his eyes out of focus and put one elbow through the back window. I aimed for the throat with the second punch, but he brought his chin down and I hit him squarely in the mouth. His bottom lip broke against his teeth, and while I stood there motionlessly, looking at the blood and saliva run off his chin, he reached behind him in the windowsill and came up with a beer bottle in my face.

It was very fast after that. I had the Italian stiletto in my pocket, and it leaped in my hand with the hard thrust of the spring before I knew it was there. It had waving ripples on each side of the blade, and just as he brought the bottle down on my forearm, I went in under him and put all six inches right up to the bone handle in his heart.

When I would wake from the dream in my cell, with the screams still in my head, I would go through all the equations that would justify killing a man in those circumstances. I would almost be free of the guilt, but then I would have to face the one inalterable premise that flawed all my syllogisms: *I already had the knife in my pocket. I already had the knife in my pocket.*

# chapter three

My father died two weeks after the day I returned home. We buried him during a sun-spangled rain shower in the family cemetery by the bayou. The aunts and uncles were there in their print-cotton dresses and brushed blue suits, the old men from town who had grown up with him, and the few Negroes who lived on the back of our property. Rita and Ace kept their children in the car because of the shower, and an old French priest read the prayers for the dead while an altar boy held an umbrella over his head.

My relatives nodded at me, and two of the old men shook hands, but I could have been a stranger among them. After they were all gone and the last car had rumbled over the wood bridge, I stood under an oak tree and watched the two gravediggers from the mortuary service spade the dirt over the coffin. Their wet denims were wrapped tight across their muscles as they worked. One of them became impatient to get out of the rain, and he started to push the dirt off the mound into the hole with his boot.

'Do it right, buddy,' I said.

I walked back to the house, and the grass on the lawn was shining with water and light. I sat on the porch swing a while and smoked cigarettes with a glass of bourbon and listened to the tree frogs begin to sing in the swamp. The air was cool from the rain and the wind was blowing off the gulf, but it was all outside of me and the whiskey didn't do any good and one cigarette burned up between my fingers. I went upstairs and tried to sleep. The house was dark, and the tree frogs became louder in the twilight's stillness. I woke sometime in the middle of the night and thought I heard the count man click his stick on the bars at the same time a shovel scraped deep into a pile of dirt.

I had to roll, stretch it out, shake it down the road. I had put in for interstate parole to Montana with my parole officer two days after I got out of Angola, but it was very hard for an ex-convict with three years' time still ahead of him, particularly one who had been sent up for manslaughter (which had been a reduction from second-degree murder), to be accepted by the parole and probation office in another state. First, there had to be reason for the transfer, such as the presence of family, social reformers, psychologists, good guys of any description, who would aid the state in the rehabilitation of their product. Second, there was the problem of employment, which meant that you would hold a regular job sanctified by a machine-stamped payroll check each week, one that would not lead you into association with other ex-cons, boost artists, and the like. And in Louisiana, as in many other states, an ex-convict could violate his parole by quitting a job without due cause. Finally, a good part of your case depended on the whim of the parole officer.

Mine was a middle-aged man who had transferred from the welfare agency. He wore dark J. C. Higgins suits even in the summertime, and there were blue and red lines all over his cheeks and nose. His blunt hands were too large for the fountain pen and papers that he tried to handle, and his stomach pressed the flap of his fly outward as though he had a hernia. I had known him around town most of my life, in an indirect way, because he belonged to almost every civic organization in the parish, or at least you could always find him on the edge of newspaper photographs showing the sponsors of civic drives to promote American Legion baseball or a new park that would include areas for colored citizens.

My file perplexed him. He said he couldn't fully understand how a man who had been decorated with two Purple Hearts and a Bronze Star could also receive a bad-conduct discharge. Also, he didn't think it was a good plan for me to go to Montana. My family was in south Louisiana, and both my brother and sister could help me get started in business or whatever I would choose, since I had two years' college education at Southwestern Louisiana Institute. His thick thumb dented and creased the papers in my folder, and his eyes wandered over my face in his abstraction as he talked about the inadvisability of leaving home roots and the possibilities of working with my brother. He ignored my open smile at the thought of an ex-convict in the employ of a public-relations and advertising company.

I had put on a pair of slacks and a sport shirt and had gotten a shine at the newsstand before coming into his office, but as I looked at his well-meaning face and clear blue eyes that didn't fit the dark suit, and listened to the recommendations for my future, I wished that one of the bosses from Angola were there in his place, someone who had felt the same miserable touch of the prison farm that left a salty cut in the edge of your eye. Or at least someone whom you didn't have to con.

Because that was what he wanted. I had already talked with a state supreme court judge, a friend of my father's, who said he would push all the paper through Baton Rouge to get me an out-of-state parole. Also, Buddy Riordan, who had pulled time with me, had gotten his father to sponsor me with the Office of Parole and Probation in Missoula. But we still had to go through with the con.

The strange thing about conning a man who deliberately opens his vest to a series of lies is the fact that both of you have to protect him from knowledge of his own dishonesty. In this case my parole officer recorded every insult to his intelligence without an eyelid faltering over the movement of his pen, but occasionally the hand would pause and an eyebrow would lift off the paper to register some abstract discrepancy in my account, a small warning that would keep us both honest tomorrow.

So we went through it. I would like to do ranch work up in Montana, dig postholes in frozen ground, shave sheep with electric barber clippers, dehorn cows, wring the necks of chickens and shuck their feathers in pots of scalding water, shovel boxcar loads of green horse manure in one-hundred-degree heat.

Actually, most of what I told him was true. I did want to go to Montana and live on a ranch in the mountains with Buddy and buck bales on a new morning. But I couldn't tell him that most of all I just needed to roll, to flee the last two years of my life, to exorcise from my sleep the iron smell of jail and the clack of the count man's baton against my cell door.

I knew that the parole transfer might take weeks or longer to be approved in Baton Rouge, and I had only thirty-five dollars left from my discharge money. My father had left each of the children one-third of the farm, but he had borrowed against it twice, and an oil company was claiming that four acres of it was somehow part of a royalty pool. Which meant, in effect, that there was a legal cloud over the house and land title, and before the estate could be divided, we would have to settle in or out of court with Texaco as well as deal with the bank. Ace was the only one of us who had the combination of what it took to wait it through: money, a disregard for time, and an ambitious energy for the profits to be made in land development.

And Ace stayed right on top of it. Two days after my father was buried, he had his agency's lawyer draft a quitclaim settlement on the inheritance for Rita and me to sign. He drove his Cadillac up the front lane one afternoon while I was on the porch steps tuning my Dobro, and began explaining in his serious way the advantages of settling the estate now. I didn't feel like talking with him or listening to his practical statements of figures and legality. And his self-deluded attitude of magnanimity was more than I could stand at the moment.

He offered me five thousand dollars in exchange for the quitclaim and power of attorney. I drank out of my beer and set the can down on the step.

'I tell you what, Ace. Get your lawyer to draw up another one, and give me the old man's truck and four of the back acres by the bayou. You can have the rest of it, and I'll sign the oil rights over to you, too. But don't put any of your tract homes near my property.'

'You're cutting yourself short,' he said.

'That's all I need, Bro'.'

I had cut myself short, but I couldn't take any money from him, and I felt better at evening off any debt I owed for my father's care. And inside he was very happy because he had gone through his act of generosity and fairness and later would realize a fortune in the subdivision of the land.

So in a moment's irritation I had become an equal member of the family at a large cost: I was still broke and had taken to buying sardines and soda crackers with my six-packs of beer at the little store down the dirt road.

Sunday morning I drove to New Iberia and looked up Rafe Arceneaux, the tea-head singer in our band. He was married now, with twin boys, and working ten days on and five off as a radio man on an offshore oil rig. We sat on the wood porch of his small house and drank chicory coffee in the clang of church bells and the screams of his kids and the loud voice of his wife in the back of their house. The triangular scar from the barroom fight was raised like an inner-tube patch on his forehead.

'I wish I could say something helpful, man, but it's bad right now,' he said. 'Most of the old guys are gone. Bernard's wife got him locked up for nonsupport, Archie got busted for possession in Pascagoula, and the rest of us catch a gig when we can. They only want rock 'n' roll bands now, and they can get the colored guys to play cheaper than we do.'

'How about the Victory Club?'

'Some of the local punks burned it down while you were gone.'

His wife came through the screen door and put one of his diapered boys in his lap without speaking to either of us. The screen slammed shut after her. Rafe directed his embarrassed eyes at the line of dilapidated storefronts across the street. 'She's mad because I wouldn't take her to her mother's last night. It's one of those things you have to live with when you play it straight.'

I finished my coffee and started to leave, because

his wife's anger hadn't been directed at him but me, the ex-convict and bad influence out of his past.

'Hey, don't cut out yet, Iry. Look, I'm sorry about all this. It's just that things aren't the same anymore. I mean, ten years ago we all thought we'd be playing Nashville by this time. Sometimes it just doesn't work out. Let's face it, man – we're getting to be history.'

I finally found a job working four nights a week at a roadhouse outside of Thibodaux. They didn't really need a lead-guitar man, but when I opened my case and took out the Dobro, I had the job. A Dobro is a bluegrass instrument, inlaid in the sound box with a metal resonator and played flat with a bar like a steel guitar, and you don't see many of them outside the southern mountains. I had bought mine on order from El Monte, California, for four hundred dollars, and the thin neck and gleaming wood of the box was as light as an envelope of air in my hands.

I made twenty-five dollars a night and my share of the tips from the money jar on the bandstand. I worked in well with the band, which was made up of hillbillies who played only country and juke-joint music. My first night I played and sang six Hank Williams songs in a row, then went into 'Poison Love' by Johnny and Jack and 'Detour' and 'I'll Sail My Ship Along,' and the place went wild. They jitterbugged and did the dirty boogie, yelled from their tables, roared with some type of nostalgic confirmation when they recognized an old song, and dropped change and dollar bills into the money jar. Oil-field roughnecks with tin hats and beery faces and drilling mud on their clothes looked up at me with moist, serious eyes when I sang 'The Lost Highway.' I was good at imitating Hank Williams, and I could make the Dobro sound just like the steel that he had used behind him.

> *I was just a lad, nearly twenty-two*
> *Neither good nor bad, just a kid like you.*
> *Now when I pass by, all the people say*
> *Just another guy on the lost highway.*

I played there three weeks and picked up an afternoon job on Sundays at a club in St Martinville, which got me into trouble with the parole office. The St Martinville band had a thirty-minute television show on Sunday mornings, and as an aside into the microphone the singer decided that he would mention that their Dobro man, Iry Paret, would be at the club with them that afternoon.

So when I went in for my visit with the parole officer that week, I noticed first the stiffness of his handshake and then the rigidity of his elbows on the desk and the folded hands under his chin while he talked. We had to go around three corners before he got to it, but he did. And like most people who ask to be conned, he now felt that he had stepped too far over a line into a large hole.

'You didn't report that you were working in a nightclub,' he said.

'It's not much of a job. I'm just sitting in temporarily.'

It was an easy offering if he wanted to continue the con, but I could see the struggle in his face to turn the compromise around, and I knew that it was going to be at my expense.

'Your parole agreement stipulates that you won't return to any of the past associations that contributed to your crime. I know that's vague on a piece of paper, but in your case it means playing in beer joints and driving home drunk at four in the morning.'

'It's the only living I have, and I was flat broke.'

'Maybe we could have worked that out, but you should have reported in before you took the job. It would have cost you one telephone call.'

'Let's get the rest of it out of the way, too,' I said. 'I've got a gig over in Thibodaux for twenty-five bucks a night. There's no fights and the cop at the door doesn't let hookers in and I leave there sober after we finish.'

I felt like a child explaining his conduct to an adult.

'Why did you do that? Why did you decide that you couldn't trust me?'

'Mr Mouton, it wasn't a matter of trust. I was simply broke.'

'But you think the parole office is something to use evasion on.'

I had to catch my anger and humiliation in my throat before I spoke again. My unlit cigarette trembled in my fingers, and the other ex-convicts on metal waiting chairs and parole officers and secretaries in the room were listening to our conversation with an oblique, withdrawn enjoyment.

'I can't do anything else except hustle jugs on a doodlebug crew or carry hod, and they're not hot to hire ex-cons in the union,' I said.

He stroked lines with a ballpoint pen on his notepad.

'I don't know,' he said. He was taking out every ounce of blood that he could. 'I talked with your brother yesterday. He said he could get you a job on a well test in Opelousas.'

A well-test job in the oil field meant stringing flange pipe through a filthy sump hole for seventy-five cents an hour, and the job usually entailed only the day of the well's completion, which meant that it was no job at all.

'He didn't tell me about it,' I said.

'It's there if you want it.'

I lit the cigarette and leaned closer to him on my elbow with the butt touching against my brow. He didn't like the directness of the position, and he opened a side drawer in his desk as though he had forgotten a form or part of my file.

'Do I get violated back to Angola, or do we just play badminton awhile?' I said.

He wasn't good at that kind of encounter, and after he had pushed back the desk drawer with a slow, flat hand and ticked his thumbnail along the edge of my file, he said 'Your transfer will probably come through in a week. Everything I sent into Baton Rouge was positive, and I made a case for your war record. But you don't play in any more bars until you leave Louisiana, and then you're somebody else's responsibility.'

I looked at him blankly and sat back in the chair. 'That's it, Iry. You're cut loose,' he said.

The letter came from Baton Rouge three days later. I had four weeks to settle my affairs and report in to the parole and probation office in Missoula. Ace had transferred the title of the pickup to me, and I had $275 saved from my two jobs. I pushed my sleeping bag and tent with the wood supports wrapped inside the canvas behind the front seat and loaded a big box of canned stew meat, corned beef, bread, sardines, and soda crackers in the truck bed and stretched a tarpaulin over the sides.

The next morning I was rolling through the piney woods of east Texas, with the mist still in the trees and the red clay banked on each side of the road. By Dallas the radiator was blowing steam from under the hood, and a kid in a filling station had to knock the cap off with a broomstick. I pushed it on through the scorching afternoon to Wichita Falls, where the water pump went out and I had to spend five hours in a tin garage that enclosed the heat and humidity like a stove. I ate a can of stew meat cold and started chewing on No-Doze south of Amarillo. I should have pulled into a roadside park to sleep, but I was hooked on the highway and the combination of beer and No-Doze now, and I knew that I could roll it all the way to Denver.

The accents began to change in the filling stations and the truck stops, and then in the early dawn I saw the first mesa in the Panhandle. It rose out of the flat country like a geological accident, its edges lighted with a pink glow, the eroded gullies filled with purple shadow. The cotton and cornfields were behind me now, and also the patent medicine and MARTHA WHITE'S SELF-RISING FLOUR signs, the vegetables and watermelons sold off the backs of trucks along the roadsides, the revival tents set back in empty pastures, the South itself. It simply slipped past me over some invisible boundary that had nothing to do with geographical designation, and then it was Dalhart and Texline, where the grain silos stood grey against the hot sky and clouds of dust, and finally Raton, New Mexico.

I was in a stupor from the No-Doze and case of beer that I had drunk in the last twenty-four hours, and my eyes burned with the shimmer of heat off the blacktop. I put my head under a filling-station hose and let the water sluice down my neck and face and then ate a steak in the cafe. But I was finished. My hands, lined with the black imprint of the steering wheel, were shaking, my back ached when I walked, and I could still feel the truck's engine vibrating up through my legs.

The filling-station operator said I could park my truck behind the building overnight, and I unrolled my sleeping bag in the bed and used the tarpaulin and my shirt as a pillow. For a while in the softness of the sleeping bag I was aware of the semis hissing air on the highway and shifting down for the long pull up Raton Pass; then I felt myself drop down into the smell of the canvas and the cool air against my face and a quietness inside me.

The next morning was like an infusion into the soul, a feeling that you can only have after you dissipate all the mental and physical energy in yourself, to the point that you know you will never return from it. And on this morning it was really the West. The town lay flat against the mountains, which climbed steadily out of brown hills into the high, green timber of the Rocky Mountain range. The broken streets of the town were lined with stucco and adobe houses, outbuildings, chicken yards, and junker cars with weeds growing up through the frames. Mexican kids roared along the sidewalks in roller-skate wagons, Indians with creased faces like withered apples waited in front of the state labor office for the doors to open, and the sky was alive with a green-blue magic that was so hard and beautiful that I had to blink a little when I looked at it.

But it was the mountains and the early light in the pines more than anything else. As I shifted down to second for the two-mile grade up Raton Pass, the mountains seemed to tumble one upon another ahead of me, bluer in the distance, spread across the sky in a broken monolith that should have cracked the earth's edges. The needle on the temperature gauge was almost beyond the dash, and the gearshift was knocking in my palm when I crossed the Colorado state line at the top and rolled into the old town of Trinidad.

I bought two six-packs of Coors and pushed the

cans deep into a sack of crushed ice on the floor and highballed down the four-lane through Pueblo, a decaying, soot-covered town with plumes of ugly smoke rising from tin buildings, on up the steady incline toward Denver, with the mountains always blue and tumbling higher into the clouds on my left. Denver looked wonderful, filled with fir and spruce trees, green lawns and parks with tulip gardens. I ate Mexican food in a cafe north of town. Then it was Fort Collins and Cheyenne and a straight roll into the late red sun across the cinnamon-colored land of Wyoming toward the Montana line.

Deer grazed in the sparse grass, their summer coats almost indistinguishable in the fading purple light, and after dark I almost hit a doe and fawn that stood transfixed in my headlights by the side of the road. I picked up two drunk Indian hitchhikers, who both wore blue-jean jackets with two shirts underneath and sat pressed together in the cab in some type of isolation from me, passing a bottle of dago red back and forth. After we had driven fifty miles, they bothered to ask me how far I was going, and I told them I hoped to make it to Billings before I stopped. I saw their winestained teeth grin in the dashboard light.

'You better stay at my place tonight. You ain't going to make it to Billings,' one of them said, and he took a cigarette off the dash without asking.

'Why can't I make it to Billings?'

'Because you can't. You ought to know that, man,' he said.

I looked at him, but he had already lost attention

and was staring into the cigarette smoke with his flat, obsidian eyes.

The sound of the engine hummed in my head, and the headlights briefly illuminated the names chiseled into the concrete faces of the bridges over dried-out riverbeds, MEDICINE BOW, PLATTE, SHOSHONI, each a part of something old and thundering with war ponies.

I stayed at the Indian man's place that night, on the edge of the Bighorn Mountains. He had ten acres on the reservation and a Montgomery Ward brick house with a chicken yard and a few dozen rabbit hutches and the most beautiful Indian wife I had ever seen. They put blankets on the sofa for me and went to bed, but I couldn't sleep. The highway was spinning in my head, and I couldn't close my hands. I walked across the chicken yard to the outhouse and then sat on the edge of the sofa and smoked cigarettes in the dark. The solitary electric bulb screwed into the ceiling clicked on, and the Indian stood above me in his socks and jockey shorts, with a line of black hair running up out of the elastic over his metallic stomach.

'You can't sleep good, man?' he said.

'I just need to wind it down a little bit. I didn't mean to wake you up.'

'We'll go to the tavern and find you a girlfriend. Then we'll drink some beer together and you'll be all right.'

'I wouldn't be good company for anybody right now.'

'You got some snakes crawling around? That

ain't no big thing. Lots of people on the reservation is like that. Come down to the tavern. You'll see.'

'I'd better pass. But I appreciate it. I really do.'

'You got a race thing about Indian girls?'

'No, I'm not like that.'

'You're a nice-looking guy. You ain't a queer, either. You shouldn't be traveling around without no woman.'

Then I didn't know what to say. I put out my cigarette in an empty beer can and pushed my hand back through my hair, hoping that he would turn off the light and let it end there.

'I ain't one to poke in your business, but I think your insides is all stove in,' he said. 'I recognize it. Indians get like that before they kill themselves.'

'I was in the Louisiana pen. I guess I haven't gotten used to rolling around loose yet. They say it takes a while.'

'Get up, Irene,' he said through the curtain that hung from the bedroom door.

'You don't need to do that.'

'No, it's all right, man. We'll drink together and then you can sleep. I was in jail over in Deer Lodge. I got myself put in the hole so's I could sleep. People was always yelling and banging iron doors all night.'

His wife came out in a robe and sat silently at the table while he pulled out the beer from the icebox. Her eyes were brown and quiet, the dark skin of one cheek still lined with the creases of the pillow, and I could see the tops of her olive breasts below the V of her robe. While we drank beer and rolled cigarettes out of a large Half and Half can, she looked flatly through the back window as though she were at the table as a feminine duty. On the third six-pack I began to perspire, and the control in my conversation and mind started to slip away in the yellow electric light, the match blisters on my fingers, and the confused sentences and beer cans covered with cigarette stubs.

I popped a pill to stay alive. But instead all the wrong tubes lighted up, and I went in and out of the conversation and all the half-formed lingering and unspoken ideas and finally over the edge into the memory of that Indian girl's face. Her darkly beautiful eyes and the swirl of her black hair piled on her head flicked my mind, like the snap of a beer top, across the mountains and over the ocean to the soft clicking of bamboo shades and the dusky scent of a small Kabuki theater with the bottles of Nippon beer iced down in a bucket between me and the geisha waitress who dipped shrimp into a horserad-ish sauce with chopsticks and placed them in my mouth. I had been drinking for two days, my money was almost all gone, and I had three hours to report back to the hospital, but in my mind I had already resigned from the army, the war, and all the complexities that made it important for me to go back on the firing line. I finished the Nippon in the ice bucket, the mamasan sent the boy across the street for more, and the geisha girl heated sake for me in a cup over a candle flame while I watched the actresses in their white pancake makeup and red-painted eyes move across the stage in a whisper of flowered silk as though they were an extension of a drunken dream.

Then I realized that I hadn't yet accomplished what I had set out to do. The bamboo shades clicked in the breeze through the windows, and I could hear the MPs rousting someone at the street corner. I snapped the cap off a Nippon with my pocketknife, got to my feet, and almost fell through a paper partition.

'You no drink more now,' the mamasan said. Her teeth were rotted, and she held her hand over her mouth when she talked. 'You go back to hospital now.'

I ripped the shade off its fastening and leaned out the window. Two MPs had a drunk soldier pushed back against a wall on the corner with their sticks.

'No do that,' the mamasan said. 'This not whorehouse. No bring Mike and Pat in here.'

I lobbed the bottle at them and watched it burst into foam and brown glass all over their spitshines and bleached leggings. They forgot about the soldier and looked around with their sticks clenched in their hands.

'Over here, girls,' I said, and I let another one fly, except this time I curled it in an arc along the wall so that it hit directly between them in a fountain of foam that splattered their trousers.

'You son a bitch,' the mamasan yelled at me.

'Come on, you candy-ass shiteaters,' I said through the window. 'Get your balls fried in a skillet. We'll give you a bayonet right up the ass that you can haul all the way back to the stockade.'

I pitched the other full bottles one after another into the street while the mamasan and the geisha girls pulled at my belt and slapped at me with rolled pillow mats and their hands.

The first MP into the room parted the reed curtain with his stick and held up a pair of handcuffs on his index finger. In the half-light through the door they looked like a piece of chain mail spangled around his fist.

'You have a telephone call outside,' he said.

'Hey, man, you better not drink no more,' the Indian said.

'What?' I raised my head from my forearms in the weak yellow light.

'You was making some terrible sounds.'

'I'm sorry.' His wife's chair was empty, and the curtain to their bedroom was still swinging lightly back and forth. 'What did –'

'She just ain't used to white people. It ain't important.' He grinned at me and exposed a gold tooth next to an empty black space in his teeth. 'You got a long drive tomorrow.'

'Tell me what I did.'

'You was holding on to her hands. She couldn't make you turn loose.' His smooth leather face and obsidian eyes were both kind and faintly embarrassed.

I picked up my can of beer and tried to walk out the back door to my truck. I hit the doorjamb with my shoulder, and the can fell out of my hand on the porch. I felt the Indian touch me gently on the back and direct me toward the couch. Then while I sweated in my drunken pill-and-booze delirium on the edge of the cushions, with the sun turning the chicken yard and rabbit hutches purple in the new light, I heard the bugles blowing on a distant hill way beyond our concertina wire, and I knew that it was going to be a safe dawn because I was sitting out this dance and all the rest to follow.

# chapter four

I highballed the pickup all the way from the Little Bighorn River to Missoula, with stops only for gas and hamburgers in between. Montana was so beautiful that it made something drop inside me. At first there were only plains with slow, wide rivers and cottonwoods along the banks and the sawtooth edge of mountains in the distance, then I started to climb toward the Continental Divide and the Douglas fir and ponderosa pine country with chasms off the edge of the road that made my head reel. There was still snow banked deep in the trees at the top of the divide, and deer spooked out of my headlights in a flick of dirt and pine needles. I coasted down the other side of the grade and picked up the Clark Fork River the rest of the way into Missoula. The runoff from the snow in the high country was still heavy, and the river swelled out through the cottonwoods in the moonlight. The rick fences and long stretches of barbed wire and small ranch houses back against the foot of the mountains rolled by me in the whine of the pickup's treadless tires against the cement. Then I was in Hellgate Canyon, and Missoula suddenly burst open before me in a shower of lights among the elm and maple and fir trees and quiet streets with a ring of mountains silhouetted like iron all around the town.

I turned south into the Bitterroot Valley and followed Buddy's map to his father's ranch. The pasture land on each side of the road extended only a short distance into the mountains, which rose high and black into clouds torn with moonlight, and the Bitterroot River gleamed like a piece of broken mirror across the long sandbars and islands of willow trees. I got lost twice on rural roads, looking at names on mailboxes with a flashlight; then I found the right wire-trooped gate and cattle guard and rutted road up to his father's place.

Buddy Riordan was working on a five-to-fifteen for possession of marijuana when I met him in Angola. He was a good jazz pianist, floating high on weed and the Gulf breeze and steady gigs at Joe Burton's place in New Orleans, and then he got nailed in a men's room with two reefers in his coat pocket. As a Yankee, he was prosecuted under a felony rather than a misdemeanor law, and the judge dropped the whole jailhouse on his head. He pulled five years on the farm, and he was one of the few there who was considered an outsider, a man who didn't belong, by the rest of us who knew in the angry part of our souls that we had bought every inch of our time.

Buddy had strange Bird Parker rhythms in his head, and sometimes I couldn't tell whether he was flying on Benzedrex inhalers or just high on a lot of wild riffs stripping off inside him. The hacks put him in lockdown for three days when they found a tube of airplane glue in his pocket on a routine shake-down, but he was still clicking to his own beat when they sent him back to the dormitory, and after that they simply dismissed him as crazy.

What they didn't understand about Buddy was that he had turned in his resignation a long time ago: an 'I casually resign' letter written sometime in his teens when he started bumming freights across the Pacific Northwest. He didn't have a beef or an issue; he just started clicking to his own rhythm and stepped over some kind of invisible line.

And I guess that's the thing I sensed in him, like a flash of private electricity, when I first met him in the exercise yard after I got out of the fish tank. The wind was cold and wet, and I was trying to roll a cigarette out of the few grains left in my package of state-issue tobacco. He was leaning against the wall, one foot propped up behind him, with his chafed wrists stuck down deep in his pockets. His pinstripe trousers hung low on his slender hips, and he had his denim jacket buttoned at the collar. The sharp bones of his face were red in the cold, and the short cigarette between his lips was wet with saliva.

'Take a tailor-made out of my coat pocket, Zeno,' he said.

I pulled the pack of Camels out and put one in my mouth.

'Take a couple extra. You won't get any more issue until Saturday,' he said.

'Thanks.'

70

'Is this your first jolt?'

'I spent some time in an army stockade.'

'That don't count in here, Zeno. Come on over to my bunk in Ash after chow. I can give you some machine-made butts to tide you over.'

I had already started to regret accepting the cigarettes. I turned my face toward the wall and struck a match in my cupped hands.

'Look, man, I'm not a wolf,' he said. 'I read your file in records, and we need a guy to play electric bass in our jazz band. It's not a bad deal. We play over in the women's prison sometimes, and Saturdays we just wax the recreation room instead of scrubbing out toilets. Besides, somebody ought to teach you how to split matches. Those are worth almost as much as cigarettes in here.'

The ranch ran back to the face of a canyon, and the main house was a sprawling two-story place made of logs with a wide front porch and side rooms that had been built with clapboard. Every room in the house was lighted, and the cliffs of the canyon rose up steep and black in the back under a full moon. When I got out of the truck, the cold air cut into me, even though it was only early August, and I put on my army-surplus jacket that I had used for duck hunting in Louisiana. A girl stepped through the lighted screen onto the front porch and held her hand over her brow to shield her eyes against the glare of my headlights.

'I'm looking for Buddy Riordan, ma'am. I don't know if I have the right place. I got lost a couple of times.'

71

'He lives in the cabin where the road dead-ends by the trees. You'll see his porch light.' Her voice was thin in the wind, and her silhouette seemed to shrink when she stepped back from the screen.

I drove to the end of the road, where there was a flat log building on the edge of the pines with a porch and swing and a brick chimney. The smoke from the chimney flattened out under the trees and turned in the wind off the canyon, and two fly rods were leaned against the porch with the lines pulled tight into the cork handles. Buddy came through the door barefoot with a sleeveless nylon hunting vest on and a can of beer and a wooden spoon in his hand.

'Hey, Zeno, where the hell you been? I thought you'd be in yesterday.' He hit me on the shoulder with the flat of his hand like a lumberjack.

'I picked up some Indian guys in Wyoming and got sidetracked a while.'

'Those Indians are crazy people. Hey, you old son of a bitch, you pulled that last year okay. Not a dent on you.'

'I made an ass of myself in this Indian guy's home. I got a little saccharine with his wife.'

'We all do funny things when we make the street. Forget it. Come on in. I've had a rack of venison in the pot since yesterday.'

He had a wood stove in a small kitchen at the back of the cabin, and the iron lids glowed around the edges with the heat of the burning sap and resin in the sawed pine limbs. He took a beer from the icebox and put it in my hand. I sat at the table in the warm smell of the venison and felt the fatigue drain through my body. He finished slicing some wild mushrooms on a chopping board and scraped them into the pot with the knife.

'A few mushrooms and some wine and wow. You got a nickel and I got a dime – let's get together and buy some wine. And that's what we got to do. Bop it down to the tavern and get some vino for the pot and some more brew, and then we'll have dinner on the porch. No kidding, Iry, you look solid.'

'I feel like somebody kicked that highway up my butt.'

'Did you have any trouble your last year?'

'I made half-trusty six months before my hearing, so I was pretty sure on getting my good time. It wasn't a sweat. Just scratching off days and staying out of the boss man's eye.'

'I was sorry to hear about your father.'

I finished the can of Great Falls and lit a cigarette on one of the stove's glowing lids.

'Let's go get the brew,' I said. 'I don't think I'll be able to sleep tonight unless I put a case down.'

'You'll be able to sleep here, partner. We have the best damn air in the United States. It blows down the canyon every night, and you won't hear a sound except the creek behind the cabin and the pine cones hitting the roof. Look, it's too late for you to meet the family, but tomorrow we'll go up to the house for breakfast, and you can talk to the old man about work. You can make ten bucks a day bucking bales, and that's not bad money around here. We got the rent free, and I catch fish every day up Bass Creek or in the Bitterroot, and with the little truck garden I have and the game out of the freezer, it's a pretty cool way to live. I should have caught on to this when I was a kid, and I never would have built that five down there with you southern primitives. And speaking of that, man, you didn't bring any of that red-dirt Louisiana weed with you, did you?'

'What do you think, Buddy?'

'Well, it was just a question, Zeno. The kids up at the university in Missoula have got some new shit around called LSD, and it takes your brain apart in minutes and glues it back together one broken piece at a time. I mean you actually hear colors blowing sounds at you. I'm sorry, man. I didn't mean to run on about my obsessions. Let's travel for the brew and put some spotioti in the pot.'

I rubbed my palm into my eye, and a red circle of light receded back into my head.

'Yeah, I guess I was fading out,' I said. 'I still feel the truck shaking under me.'

'A little brew and a little food and you'll be cool. Come on, I'll introduce you to a Montana tavern. Meet the shitkickers. Pick up a little color your first night here. Something to expand that jaded southern gourd of yours. You know, I read an article once that said all you southern guys are sexual night-mares. That's why your rest rooms are always filthy and full of rubber machines.'

'Are we going to get the beer, Buddy?'

'Right. Let's take your truck, since I parked my car against a tree in the middle of the creek last night.'

We banged over the ruts in the corrugated road, with the truck rattling at every metal joint, until we bounced across the cattle guard onto the smooth gravel-spread lane that led back to the main highway through the Bitterroots. The moon had moved farther to the south, and I could see the dark water of the river cutting in silver rivulets around the willow trees on the edge of the sandbars. The mountains on each side of the valley were so large now in the moonlight that I felt they were crashing down upon me. The snow on the distant peaks was burning with moonlight beyond the jagged silhouette of the pines, and each time we crossed a bridge over a small creek, I could see the white tumble of water over the rocks and then the quiet pools hammered with metal dollars at the end of the riffle.

We pulled into the parking lot of a clapboard tavern next to a general store with two gas pumps in front. Pickup trucks with rifles and shotguns set in racks against the rear windows were parked in the lot, and the stickers on their bumpers were a sudden click of the eye back into the rural South: I FIGHT POVERTY – I WORK; PUT THE BIBLE BACK IN OUR SCHOOLS; DON'T WORRY, THEY'RE ONLY NINETY MILES AWAY.

Buddy and I went inside and had a beer at the bar and asked for a cold case to go and a small bottle of sauterne. A stone fireplace was roaring with logs at the far end of the pool table, and there were elk and moose racks on the walls and rusted frontier rifles laid across deer hooves. Most of the men in the bar wore faded blue jeans, nylon or Levi's jackets, scuffed cowboy and work boots, shirts with the color washed out, and beatup cowboy hats stained with sweat around the band. They all looked big, physical, with large, rough hands and wind-cut faces. The men at the pool table stamped down the rubber ends of their cues each time they missed a shot, and slammed the rack hard around the balls for a new game, and two cowboys next to me were shaking the poker dice violently in the leather cup and banging it loudly on the bar.

I didn't notice it at first, or I dismissed it as my natural ex-con's paranoia, but soon I started to catch a glance from a table or a man at the bar's elbow. Then, as I looked back momentarily to assure myself that there was nothing there, I saw a flick of blue meanness or challenge in those eyes, and I knew that I was sitting on top of something. I waited in silence for Buddy to finish his beer so we could go, but he ordered two more before I could touch him on the arm.

I felt the open stares become harder now, and I looked intently at the punchboard in front of me. At that moment I thought how strange it was that, even though I was a grown man, eyes could feel like a wandering deadness on the side of my face. I tried to compensate with a silly commitment to my cigarette and the details in the ashtray, and then I walked to the rest room with the instinctive con's slink across the yard, hands low in the pockets, cool, the shoulders bent just a little, the knees loose and easy.

But when I got back to the bar, the stares were

still there. No one seemed to realize that I was a Louisiana badass. And Buddy was on his third beer.

'Hey, what the hell is going on?' I said quietly.

'Don't pay any attention to those guys.'

'What is it?'

'It's copacetic, Zeno. By the way, you looked very cool bopping into the pisser.'

'Shit on this, Buddy. Let's get out of here.'

'Take it easy, man. We can't let a few hot faces run us off.'

'I don't know what it is, but I don't like fooling in somebody else's trouble.'

'Okay, let me finish and we'll split.'

Outside, I put the cardboard case of Great Falls in the back of the truck and turned around in the gravel parking lot. I shot the transmission into second gear and wound it up on the blacktop. One jagged piece of mountain cut into the moon.

'So what was that stuff about?'

'The old man has been pissing people off around here for years, and right now he's got them all on low boil.'

'What for?'

'He's trying to get the new pulp mill shut down, which means that about four hundred guys will lose their jobs. But forget it, man. It don't have anything to do with you. Those guys back there just like to snort with their virility when they have a chance.'

We crossed the cattle guard and passed the darkened main house on the ranch. The canyon walls behind the house were sheer and grey in the moon's reflection off the clouds.

'Tomorrow you got to meet my family,' Buddy said. 'They're unusual people. Sometimes I wish I hadn't burned them so bad.'

Then I realized that Buddy was drunk, because in the time I had known him, he had never indulged himself in private confession unless he was floating on Benzedrex inhalers or the occasional weed we got from the Negroes.

He poured the sauterne into the pot of venison and sprinkled black pepper and parsley on top of it, then replaced the iron lid and let it marinate for a half hour while we drank beer and I tried to retune my Dobro with fingers as thick and dull as a ruptured ear.

'I never did figure why you stayed with that hillbilly shot,' he said, 'but you do it beautiful, man. Did you ever finish that song you were working on?'

The blood had gone out of his face, and his cigarette had burned down close between his fingers.

'No, I've still got it running around in pieces.'

'Do "Jolie Blonde," man.'

I picked it out on the Dobro and sang in my bad Cajun French while Buddy turned the venison in the pot with a wooden spoon. His white face glowed in the heat of the stove, and for a moment he looked as preoccupied and solitary as the man I had met over two years before in the yard at Angola.

We dragged the kitchen table onto the porch and ate the venison out of tin plates with garlic bread and an onion-and-beet salad that Buddy had chopped into a wooden bowl. I hadn't had venison in a long time, and the mushroom and wine sauce was fine with the taste of the game, and as I watched the wind blowing snow off the top of the canyon, I knew that everything was going to be all right.

But I should have recognized it at the bar. Or at least part of it. It was there, and all I had to do was look at it.

In the morning the sun broke across the blue ridge of mountains, and the wet, green meadows shimmered in the light. The shadows at the base of the mountains were purple like a cold bruise, and as the morning warmed and the dew burned away on the grass, the cattle moved slowly into the shade of the cottonwoods along the river. Buddy and I fished with wet flies in the creek behind his cabin and caught a dozen cutthroat trout out of the deep pools that turned in eddies behind the rocks. I would crouch down on my haunches so as not to silhouette against the spangle of sunlight through the trees, and then I'd let the fly sink slowly to the bottom of the pool; a cutthroat would rise suddenly off the gravel, his brilliant rim of fire around the gills flashing in the sun, and the fly rod would arch down to the water with a steady, throbbing pull.

We cleaned the fish and took them up to the main house for breakfast. Piles of wood cut in round chunks with a chainsaw were stacked high next to the barn wall, and in the side lot there was the rusted-out skeleton of an old steam tractor with dark pigweed growing through the wheels. In back were at least fifty bird pens made with chicken wire and wood frames, and ducks, geese, and breeds of grouse and pheasant that I had never seen before wandered around the feed pens and watering pools located all over the yard.

'That's the old man's aviary,' Buddy said. 'It's probably the biggest in the state. He's got birds in there from all over the world, which is one reason why I live in the cabin. You ought to hear those sons of bitches when they crank up at four in the morning.'

We browned the trout in butter, and Buddy's mother cooked a huge platter of scrambled eggs and pork chops with sliced tomatoes on the side. The dining table was covered with an oil cloth thumb-tacked to the sides, and Buddy's father sat at the head, waiting quietly until each member of the family was seated before he picked up the first plate and started it around the table. Buddy's three younger brothers, all in high school, sat opposite me, their faces eagerly curious and yet polite about their brother's ex-convict friend. Their skin was tan, and there wasn't an ounce of fat on their bodies, and in their blue jeans and faded print shirts rolled over their young, strong arms, they looked like everything that's healthy in America.

Buddy's sister and her husband, an instructor at the university, sat at the far end of the table, and for some reason they made me uncomfortable. I had the teacher made for a part-time agrarian romanticist or an eastern college man on a brief excursion into the life of his wife's family. The smile and the handshake were too easy and open – and dismissing. She favored her mother, a well-shaped woman with clear skin and blue eyes that had a quick light in them, but none of the same cheerfulness was in the daughter's face. The daughter was pretty, with sun-bleached curly hair and beautiful hands, but there was a darkness inside her that marred the rest of it, and I could sense a resentment in her because I was someone whom Buddy had known in prison and had brought to their home.

But Buddy's father was the one who I realized instinctively was no ordinary person. His shoulders were square and hard, his neck coarse with sunburn and wind, and the edges of his palms were thick with callus and there were half-moon carpenter's bruises on his fingernails. He was a good-looking man for his age. He combed his thin, brown hair straight back over a wide forehead, and his grey eyes looked directly at you without blinking. He didn't have that soft quality to the edge of the bone structure in the face that most Irish have, and his back stayed straight in the chair and never quite rested against the wood. He took the silver watch on its chain from his blue-jeans pocket and looked at it a moment as though seeing it for the first time.

'I guess we ought to start getting the bales up on the wagon. You ready, boys?' he said.

The three younger brothers got up from the table and started to follow him through the kitchen; then he turned, almost as an afterthought, and looked back at me with those gray, unblinking eyes.

'I think I have something out in the lot that you might be interested in seeing, Mr Paret,' he said.

Buddy grinned at me over his coffee cup.

I walked with Mr Riordan and the three boys into the backyard. The whole expanse of the valley was covered with sunshine now, and the bales of green hay in the fields and the click of light on the Bitterroot River through the trees and the heavy shadows down the canyon walls were so heart-sinking that I had to stop and fold my arms across my chest in a large breath.

'Have you ever seen one of these fellows before?' Mr Riordan said.

He had opened a cage and picked up a large nutria. Its red eyes looked like hot bbs behind the fur, and its yellow buck teeth protruded from the mouth. The body was exactly like a rat's, except much bigger and covered with long fur that grew like a porcupine's quills, and the feet were almost webbed.

'I've never seen one outside of southern Louisiana,' I said. 'I didn't think they could live in a cold climate.'

'That's what most people say. However, no one has advised the nutria of that fact. How much do you know about them?'

I shook a cigarette out of my pack and put it in my mouth. I had the feeling that I was about to be taught the rules of a new game.

'The McIlhenny tabasco family brought them from South America about 1900,' I said. 'Supposedly, they were in cages on Marsh Island about twelve miles off the Louisiana coast, and after a storm smashed up their cages, they swam through waves all the way to land. Now they're in every bayou and canal in south Louisiana. They'll kill your dog if he gets in the water with them, and they can fill up a whole string of muskrat traps in a day.'

'I hope to eventually introduce them in the area. Do you think you'd like to help raise them?'

'At home they're a pest, Mr Riordan. They destroy the irrigation canals for the rice farms, and they breed like minks in heat.'

'Well, we'll see how they do in colder climates.' Then, without a change in the voice, he said, 'You murdered a man, did you?'

I had to wait a moment.

'That's probably a matter of legal definition,' I said. 'I went to prison for manslaughter.'

'I suppose those points are pretty fine sometimes,' he said.

'Yes, sir, they can be.'

'I signed for your parole transfer because Buddy asked me to. Normally, I stay as removed as I can from the dealings of the state and federal government, but he wanted you to come here. And so I've made some kind of contract with the authorities in Louisiana as well as in my own state. That involves a considerable bit on both of our parts. Do you understand me, Mr Paret?'

I drew in on my cigarette and flipped it toward the fence. I could feel the blood start to ring in my palms.

'I have three years' parole time to do, Mr Riordan. That means that on a whim a parole officer can violate me back to the farm for an overdrawn check, no job or just not checking in on the right date. Maybe he's got a little gas on his stomach, half a bag on from the night before, or maybe his wife cut him off that morning. All he's got to do is get his ballpoint moving and I'm on my way back to Angola in handcuffs. In Louisiana a P.V. means one year before you come in for a hearing again.'

'Did you ever do farm work outside of the penitentiary?' he said.

'My father was a sugar grower.'

'I pay ten dollars a day for bucking bales, and you eat up at the house for the noon meal. There's a lot of work in the fall, too, if you care to drive nails and butcher hogs.'

He walked away from me on the worn-out heels of his cowboy boots toward the flatbed wagon, where his three boys were waiting for him. I wanted to be angry at him for his abruptness and his sudden cut into a private area of my soul, but I couldn't, because he was simply honest and brief in a way that I wasn't prepared for.

I drove to Missoula that afternoon and checked in with the parole office. My new parole officer seemed to be an ordinary fellow who didn't think of me as a particular problem in his caseload, and after fifteen minutes I was back on the street in the sunshine, with my hands in my pockets and a whole new town and a blue-gold afternoon to explore. Missoula was a wonderful town. The mountains rose into the sky in every direction, the Clark Fork River cut right through the business district, and college kids in innertubes and on rubber rafts floated down the strips of white water with cans of beer in their hands, shouting and waving at the fishermen on the banks. The town was covered with elm and maple trees, the lawns were green and dug with flower beds, and men in shirtsleeves sprinkled the grass with garden hoses like a little piece of memory out of the 1940s.

I walked down the street with a sense of freedom that I hadn't felt since I went to the penitentiary. Even at my father's house the reminders were there: the darkness of the house, the ancestral death in the walls, the graveyard being eaten away a foot at a time by the bayou, that black vegetable growth across the brain that puts out new roots whenever you come home. But here there was sun all over the sidewalks, some of which still had tethering rings set in them.

I went into places that had names like the Oxford, Eddie's Club, and Stockman's Bar, and it was like walking through a door and losing a century. Cowboys, mill workers, lumberjacks, bindle stiffs, and professional gamblers played cards at felt tables in the back; there was a bar without stools for men who were serious about their drinking, a counter for steaks and spuds and draft beer, the click of billiard balls in a corner, and occasionally a loud voice, a scraping of chairs, and a punchout that sent a man reeling into the plasterboard partition of the rest rooms.

I was eating a steak fried in onions in the Oxford when a man without legs tried to raise himself onto a stool next to me. He had pushed himself along the street and into the bar on a small wooden platform that had roller-skate wheels nailed under it, and the two wood blocks sticking out from the pockets of his pea jacket looked like someone's beaten ears. One of the buckle straps on his stump had caught, and I tried to raise him toward the stool. His tongue clicked out across his bad teeth like a lizard's.

'He don't want you to help him, mister,' the bartender said.

'I'm sorry.'

'He can't hear or talk. He got all blowed up in the war,' the bartender said. He filled a bowl with lima-bean soup and placed it on a saucer with some crackers in front of the crippled man.

I listened to him gurgle at the soup, and I had to look at the far end of the counter while I ate. The bartender slid another draft in front of me.

'It's on the house,' he said, and then, with a matchstick in the corner of his mouth and his eyes flat, he added, 'You visiting in town?'

'I'm staying in the Bitterroot with a friend and looking around for work. I guess right now I'm going to be bucking bales for the Riordans awhile.' I couldn't resist mentioning the name, just like you put your foot in lightly to test the water.

The reaction was casual and slowly curious, but it was there.

'You know Frank Riordan pretty good?'

'I know his son.'

'What the hell is Frank up to with this pulp mill, anyway?'

'He's up to putting a lot of men out of work,' a

man farther down the counter said, without looking up from his plate.

Oh shit, I thought.

'I don't know anything about it,' I said.

'He don't know anything about it,' the same man said. He wore a tin hat and a checkered shirt with long-sleeved underwear.

The bartender suddenly became a diplomat and disinterested neutral.

'I ain't seen Frank in a long time,' he said. 'He used to come in here sometimes on Saturday and play cards.'

'He's got no time for that now,' a man eating next to the cripple said. 'He's too busy sitting on thirteen hundred acres of cows and making sure a dollar-fifty-an-hour man gets his pink slip. That's Frank Riordan for you.'

The bartender wiped the rag over the counter in front of me as though he were rubbing out a piece of personal guilt. 'Some people say that smokestack stinks like shit, but it smells like bread and butter to me,' he said, and laughed with a gastric click in the back of his throat, exposing his line of yellowed teeth.

I could feel the anger of the two men on each side of me, like someone caught between bookends. I put the fork and knife in my plate and lit a cigarette and smoked long enough to keep personal honor intact, then walked back into the sunshine. No more testing of reactions to names, I decided, and maybe I should have a more serious talk with Buddy.

Earlier in the afternoon a gyppo logger had told

me in a bar that I might get on with a country band in Bonner. I drove out of Missoula through Hellgate Canyon, a huge split in the mountains where the Salish Indians used to follow the Clark Fork and annually get massacred by the Crows and the Blackfeet (whence the name, because the canyon floor was strewn with skeletons when the first Jesuits passed through). I followed along the river through the deep cut of the mountains and the thin second growth of pine on the slopes until I reached the meeting of the Blackfoot and Clark Fork rivers, which made a wide swirl of dark water that spilled white and iridescent over a concrete dam.

Bonner was the Anaconda Company, a huge mill on the edge of the river that blew plumes of smoke that hung in the air for miles down the Blackfoot canyon. The town itself was made up of one street, lined with neat yards and shade trees and identical wood-frame houses. I hadn't seen a company town outside of Louisiana and Mississippi, and though there was no stench of the sugar mill in the air or vision through a car window of Negroes walking from the sugar press to their wood porches in the twilight with lunch pails in their hands, Bonner could have been snipped out of Iberia Parish and glued down in the middle of the Rocky Mountains.

I pulled into the parking lot of a weathered grey building by the railroad crossing that had a neon sign on the roof that read MILLTOWN UNION BAR, CAFE AND LAUNDROMAT. There were electric slot machines inside the bar, winking with yellow horseshoes, bunches of cherries, and gold bars. Over the front door was the head of a mountain sheep covered with a plexiglass dome, and mounted on the wall over the jukebox was an elk's head with a huge, sweeping rack. I talked with the owner at the bar about a lead-guitar job on the weekends, and while he pushed his coffee cup around in his saucer with a thick finger, I went to the truck and brought back my double case with the Dobro inside and the Confederate flag sewn into the lining. The metal resonator set in the sound hole swam with the silvery purple reflection of the lights behind the counter, and I pulled the steel picks across the strings and floated the bar down the neck into the beginning of Hank's 'Love-Sick Blues.'

The Dobro did it every time. It had paid for itself several times over in turning jobs for me. He said he would pay thirty-five dollars for Friday and Saturday nights and a three-hour session on Sunday afternoons, and I drove back through the Hellgate with the engine humming under the hood and the late sun red on the walls of the canyon and the deep current in the river.

The next day I went to work with Buddy bucking bales, digging postholes, and opening up irrigation ditches. The sky was immense over our heads, and the mountains were blue and sharp in the sunlight, and pieces of cloud hung in the pines on the far peaks. By midday our bare chests were running with sweat and covered with bits of green hay, and the muscles in my stomach ached from driving the posthole digger into the ground and spreading the wood handles outward. Buddy's sister, Pearl, brought out a pitcher of sun tea with mint leaves and cracked ice in it and poured some into two deep paper cups, and we drank it while we sat on the back of the flatbed wagon and ate ham sandwiches. Her curly hair was bright on the tips in the sunlight, and the sun halter she wore with her blue jeans showed enough that I had to keep my attention on the sandwich to be polite. She didn't like me, and I wished that Buddy had not tried to ignore that obvious fact.

'I'm going to visit the wife-o and kids Sunday, Jimmie's birthday scene, and why don't you and Melvin come along and we'll watch the hippy-dippy from Mississippi here do his Ernest Tubb act up at the beer joint in Bonner,' Buddy said.

She put the top on the iced-tea pitcher and set it carefully on the tailgate. Her eyes went flat.

'I'll have to ask Mel.'

'He's always good for Sunday afternoon boozing,' Buddy said. 'In fact, the only time he gets drunk is the night before he has to work. He goes roaring out of here to the college in the morning with a hangover that must fill up a whole classroom.'

I looked away at the cottonwoods on the river and put a cigarette in my mouth. I had a feeling that anything said next would be wrong. It was.

'You ought to hear this shitkicker, anyway,' Buddy said. 'Plays like Charlie Christian when he wants to, but for some reason my coonass pal is fascinated with the hillbillies and Okies. Loves Jimmie Rodgers and Woody Guthrie, imitates Hank

90

Williams, yodels and picks like Bill Monroe. It's gooder than grits.'

'Let's get on it, Buddy,' I said.

'He's also sensitive about his sounds.'

I folded the remaining half of my ham sandwich in the wax paper and put it back in the lunch pail.

'Your father said he wanted those holes dug up to the slough before we quit,' I said.

'He's loyal to employers, too. A very good man, this one,' Buddy said, hitting the wet slickness of my shoulder with his palm. I wanted to dump him off the tailgate.

'Hey, Pearl, wait a minute,' he said. 'Ask Melvin and maybe Beth can come along with us.'

She nodded without replying and walked across the hayfield, graceful and cool, her sun halter flashing a white line below her tan.

Buddy and I walked out to where the posts were laid at regular intervals on the ground along the fence line. I thudded the posthole digger in the hard dirt while he poured water out of a bucket into the hole.

'Man, I wish you wouldn't do that,' I said.

He tilted the bucket downward, sluicing water over the wooden handle and the mud impacted between the blades, as though he were preoccupied with a large engineering problem.

'No shit, Buddy,' I said.

'There were other things there, Zeno. You just didn't see them. I didn't mean to piss in your shoe with Pearl. She married this university instructor, and he's an all right guy, but he's got an eggbeater in his head most of the time, and she's trying to keep up with whatever mood he's in next. That means pack off to Alaska on snowshoes, join some sit-in deal in Alabama, or turn up Beethoven so loud on the hi-fi three nights in a row that it blows the old man out of his bedroom.'

I pulled the posthole digger out of the ground and knocked the mud from the blades.

'Well, that ain't exactly what was really going on there,' he said. 'You see, I'm trying to get back with the wife-o, which might seem like a bad scene, but the boys are nine and eleven now, and they're not doing worth a darn in school, and Beth is taking them to some kind of psychologist in Missoula. That's the only outside thing that bothered me in the joint. I cut out on them after the old lady got me locked up one night, and I kept on going all the way to New Orleans.'

I laid aside the digger and placed the fence post in the hole while Buddy shoveled in dirt and rocks on top of it. His thin back was glistening, and it rippled with bone and muscle when he spaded in each shovel-load.

'Maybe this is a bad time to ask you,' I said, 'but yesterday I was in a place called the Oxford, and I had the feeling that your father has declared war on everybody in this county.'

'Most of those guys have a log up their ass. You can't take that kind of barroom stuff too seriously.'

'I think they were pretty serious.'

'Here's the scene on that caper. They built this pulp mill on the river west of town, and some days the smell in the valley is so bad that you think an elephant cut a fart in your face. They make toilet paper or something up there. That's right, man. All those beautiful ponderosa pines eventually get flushed down somebody's commode in Des Moines. Anyway, the old man has got them in state court now, and if he wins his injunction, they shut down the whole damn thing. I guess I can't blame most of those guys for being pissed. They don't earn diddly-squat there, anyway, their union don't do anything for them, and the only other work around here is seasonal. Sometimes I even wonder if the old man sees the other end of what he's doing.'

He lit a cigarette while I started on the next hole. The leaves of the cottonwoods by the river flickered with sunlight in the breeze.

'But this is an old scene with him. He fought the Anaconda Company when they started polluting the Clark, and he helped stop a bunch over in east Montana that were catching wild horses and selling them to a dog-food company.' Buddy squatted down with the water can by the hole and puffed a minute on his cigarette. 'He's always got the right thing in mind, but he's one of these guys that draws a line in the dirt, and then that's it. He doesn't see anything in between.'

We dug the last hole by the slough in the late afternoon, and I looked back at the long straight line of fence posts, rigid and thick in the ground, and felt a pride in their geometric progression from the front of the ranch to the mud bottom we were standing in. The grass bent in the wind off the river, and the sun already had a black piece cut out of it by a mountain peak. We threw the tools into the wagon bed and walked back through the fields to the cabin. I felt physically tired and satisfied in the way you do when you have bent yourself to a right task. The shadows of the mountains were moving across the valley, over the log houses, the hay bales in the fields, the stone walls, and the cords of wood piled by the barns, as the light receded and gathered in the trees on the far side of the river.

We fished with worms in the creek behind the cabin during the twilight, then fired the wood stove and broiled the cutthroat trout in butter and garlic salt. I took a can of beer and the Martin out on the front porch while Buddy turned the fish in the pan. I dropped the tuning into D, clicked my thumb pick across the bass strings, and went up the neck into a diminished blues chording that I had learned from Robert Pete Williams in Angola. The strings rang with moonlight, and I felt the deep notes reverberate through my fingers and forearm as though the wood itself had caught the beat of my blood. I bridged over into 'The Wreck of the Ole 97,' hammering on and pulling off like A. P. Carter, the strings trembling with light and their own metallic sympathy.

*He was going down the grade making ninety*
  *miles an hour*
*When his whistle broke into a scream.*
*They found him in the wreck with his hand*
  *upon the throttle*
*He was scalded to death in the steam.*

Buddy walked out on the porch with a piece of trout between his fingers and drank out of my beer can on the railing.

'That sounded fine, babe,' he said. He sat on the railing, and the moonlight broke around his shoulders. I took the cigarette from between his fingers and put it in my mouth. The mountains were like a glacial blackness against the sky.

'I know what you're thinking about,' he said. 'You don't have to, man. It's going to be cool.'

That was Thursday.

# chapter five

On Sunday morning, Buddy, his sister, her husband, and I went into Missoula. It was a fine day for a birthday party in a green backyard, and Buddy had bought a claw mitt and spinning reel for his eleven-year-old boy, and a Swiss army knife full of can openers and screwdrivers for his younger son. I was surprised at how close Buddy was to his children. After we cracked away the rock salt and ice from the hand-crank ice-cream freezer, Buddy served each plate at the table under the maple tree, lit the candles in a glow of pink light and icing, and walked on his hands in the grass while the children squealed in delight.

He wasn't as successful with his wife, Beth. Her manner was quiet and friendly toward him, one of a shared intimate knowledge or perhaps an acceptance out of necessity. But I felt that if he had not been the father of her children, he wouldn't occupy even this small space in her life. I sat against the tree trunk and drank a can of beer, and as I watched Buddy talking to her, his arms sometimes flying in the air, his face smiling and his slacks and sport shirt ironed with sharp creases (and her eyes fading with a lack of attention and then quickening when one of the children spilled ice cream into his lap), I felt like an intruder in something that I shouldn't see, particularly with Buddy. He had always had a crapshooter's eye for any situation, but this time he was all boxcars, deuces, and treys.

She was certainly good to look at. Her hair was black with a light shine in it, and her white skin didn't have a wrinkle or freckle on it. She was a little overweight, but in a soft way, and she stood with her knees close together like a schoolgirl, and the smooth curve of her stomach and her large breasts brought back all my stunted sexual dreams and sleepless midnight frustration.

Later, Buddy insisted that she go with us to the bar in Milltown. She began clearing the table of paper plates and talking in an oblique way about the children's supper, and Buddy walked away to the neighbor's porch, knocked loudly on the jamb, then crossed the lawn again, his face set in a purpose, and started knocking on the other neighbor's door. I saw the anger in his wife's eyes for a moment; then her lips pressed together, and she patted the two boys softly on the shoulders and told them to finish cleaning the table.

She sat between us in the pickup, and Buddy's sister and her husband followed us through Hellgate Canyon along the river to Milltown. Because it was Sunday, yellow life rafts full of beer drinkers in swimming suits, their bodies glistening with tan, roared down through the riffle in a spray of water and sunlight and happy screams of terror against the canyon walls. One raft struck against a boulder, the rubber bow bending upward while the white water boiled over the stern; then it swung sideways into the current like a carnival ride out of control while the people inside tumbled over one another and sent ropes of beer foam into the air.

I looked into the rearview mirror and saw Melvin, Buddy's brother-in-law, driving with both arms folded on top of the wheel and a beer bottle in his hand while the car drifted back and forth toward the shoulder. He had started drinking early at the birthday party, and before we left, he had poured a boilermaker in the kitchen.

'I'd better pull off and let you take that fellow's wheel,' I said.

'Don't do that, man,' Buddy said. 'He'll want to fight. He's a real Irish drunk.'

'He's about to put himself and your sister all over those rocks.'

'You'd have to pull him from behind that steering wheel with a chain,' Buddy said. 'Right now he's probably talking about joining a revolution in Bolivia. You know, right after I got out of the joint' – Buddy stopped momentarily and touched a piece of tobacco on his lip, his eyes uncertain in front of his wife's stare through the windshield – 'I hadn't met the guy and he asked me how you burn a safe, because he had some friends who were going to peel one in California for the revolution and he didn't know if they could do it right. I mean he didn't blink when he said it.'

In the mirror I saw the car rip a shower of gravel out of the shoulder and float back toward the center stripe.

'Let's get some coffee and a sandwich at the truck stop,' I said.

'Go ahead. He'll be all right,' Beth said.

I glanced at her calm, lovely face in the cab, and for just a second I felt the touch of her thigh against mine and realized that I hadn't ridden close to a woman in a vehicle for over two years and had forgotten how pleasant it could be.

'Yeah, don't stop there, man,' Buddy said. 'They don't sell booze, and he'll make up for it by trying to get it on with the lumberjacks. Even the old man thinks he's got a lightning bolt in his head. He came into the house one night blowing some green weed and turned up his hi-fi until the plates were shaking in the cupboard. The birds were flapping in the pens, and the old man came up the stairs like a hurricane.'

I put the truck into second gear and slowed for the turn across the railroad embankment into the white shale parking lot in front of the bar. There was already a large afternoon crowd in the bar, and somebody was tuning an electric bass and blowing into the microphone over the roar of noise. Melvin bounced across the tracks, fishtailed on the back springs, and slid with his brakes in a scour of earth three inches from my front fender. His face was almost totally white, and he had a filter-tipped cigar in the middle of his mouth. He leaned toward the passenger's window to speak, and his wife averted her face from his breath.

'A little Roy Acuff this afternoon, cousin,' he said.

I nodded at him and rolled up the window.

'Say, Buddy, I've only played twice with these guys,' I said. 'It's a good gig and I want to keep it.'

'It's solid, babe. Just go in there and do the Ernest Tubb shot. We'll take care of this guy.'

'I'm not putting you on,' I said.

'Go inside. It'll be all right,' Beth said.

She was a princess inside the bar. After I began the first number on the bandstand, Melvin stood below the platform with a shot glass in one hand and a draft beer in the other, his face happily drunk. He swayed on his feet, talking with a fractured smile into the amplified sound; then she took him by the elbow and led him away to the dance floor.

I did the lead with my Martin on our second song, 'I'm Moving On,' and the bar became quiet while I held the sound box up to my chin and played directly into the microphone. I ran Hank Snow's chord progressions up and down the frets, thumping the deep bass notes of a train highballing through Dixie while I picked out the notes of the melody on the treble strings with my fingernail. I heard the steel try to get in behind me before I realized that I had been riding too long, and I moved back down the neck into the standard G chord on the second fret and tapered off into the rest of the band with a bass roll. The crowd applauded and whistled, and a man at the bar shouted out, 'Give 'em hell, reb.'

I saw Buddy in the rest room at the end of the set.

He was leaning over the urinal with one hand propped against the wall, and his eyes looked like whorls of color with cinders for pupils.

'I scored some acid from a guy out in the parking lot,' he said. 'You want to try some of this crazy mixture on your neurotic southern chemistry?'

'I got to work this afternoon, babe.'

'How you like my old lady? She's quite a gal, ain't she?'

'Yeah, she is.'

'I was catching your radiations in the truck there, Zeno,' he said. 'A little pulsing of the blood behind the steering wheel.'

'You better leave that college dope alone,' I said.

'Hey, don't walk out. After you get finished, we're going to Eddie's Club, and then I'm bringing a whole crew down to the place for a barbecue. Some bear steaks soaked overnight in milk. It's the best barbecue in the world. Puts meat in your brain and black hair all over your toenails.'

'Okay, Buddy.'

He drew in on his cigarette, the smoke and hot ash curling between his yellowed fingers, and squinted at me with a radiant smile on his face.

Eddie's Club was a place full of hard yellow light, smoke, wings, drunk Salish Indians, the clatter of pool balls, a hillbilly jukebox, college students, and some teachers from the university. One wall was lined with large framed photographs of the old men who drank in there, their mouths toothless and collapsed, their slouch hats and cloth caps pulled at an angle over the alcoholic lines and bright eyes of their faces.

'Boyd Valentine, the bartender, did all that,' Buddy said, his forehead perspiring in the smoke. 'You got to meet this guy. He's a Michelangelo with a camera. A real wild man. Your kind of people.'

Before I could stop him, Buddy had walked away into the confusion of noise and people, who were two-deep at the bar. I was left at the table with Beth, Pearl, and Melvin, who couldn't find the end of his cigarette with his lighter, and a half-dozen other people whose elbows rested in spilled beer without their taking notice of it.

'Try a Montana busthead highball,' Melvin said. 'Don't try to stay sober in this crowd. It's useless.'

He lowered a full whiskey jigger into a beer schooner with two fingers and pushed it toward me.

'I'd better pass,' I said.

He picked up the schooner with both hands and drank it to the bottom, the whiskey jigger rolling against the glass. I had to shudder while I watched him.

In the back two men began fighting over the pool table. A couple of chairs were overturned, a pool cue shattered across the table, and one man was knocked to the floor, then helped up and pushed out the back door. Few people paid any attention.

'What's on your mind?' Beth said, smiling.

'I wonder what I'm doing here.'

'It's part of Buddy and Mel's guided tour of Missoula,' Pearl said. She wasn't happy with any of it.

'You're a better man than I, Gunga Din,' Melvin said, toasting me in some private irony.

'We'll be leaving in a few minutes,' Beth said.

'Don't worry about me. I'll probably shoot on across the street to the Oxford and get something to eat.' Although I wouldn't admit the impulse to myself then, I was hoping that she would ask to go along.

'Hey,' Buddy shouted behind me. 'This is Boyd Valentine. Used to hang around New Orleans when I was making my cool sounds there. Got a '55 Chevy and blows engines out at a hundred and ten on the Bitterroot road. Outruns cops, ambulances, and fire trucks. Best photographer in the Northwest.'

Buddy held the bartender by one arm, a man with fierce black eyes and an electric energy in his face. One of his thumbs was missing, and the black hair on his chest grew out of his shirt.

'What's happening?' he said, and shook hands. There was good humor in his voice and smile, and a current in his hand.

'My man here is going to load up his hot rod with good people, and we're going to burn on down to the place and juice under the stars while I barbecue steaks that will bring you to your knees in reverence,' Buddy said. 'Then my other man will crank out his Martin and sing songs of Dixie and molasses and ham hocks cooked with grits in his mammy's shoe.'

We finally left the bar after Melvin turned over a pitcher of beer in an Indian woman's lap. She raised her dress over her waist and squeezed it out over her thighs and kneecaps, her husband tore Melvin's shirt, the bartender then brought three more pitchers to the table, and that was the end of that.

Buddy and I dropped Beth off at her house. He tried to convince her to come out to the ranch, but in her quiet woman's way she mentioned the children, their supper, school tomorrow, those arguments that know no refutation. We drove down through the Bitterroots with the river black and winding beyond the cottonwoods. Rain clouds had started to move across the mountain peaks, and there was a dry rumble of thunder on the far side of the valley. In the distance, heat lightning wavered and flickered over the rolling hills of pines. I opened the wind vane and let the cool air, with just the hint of rain in it, blow into my face.

Buddy took a reefer stub from his pocket and lit it, holding the smoke down deep, his teeth tight together. He let out the smoke slowly and took another hit.

'Where did you get that?' I said.

'An Indian girl at Eddie's. You want a snort?' He pushed in the cigarette lighter on the dashboard.

'Buddy, you've got enough shit in you now to make a time bomb out of your head.'

'Forget that crap, man. The only thing I could never pull down right was coke.' He placed the stub on the hot lighter and held it under his nose, sniffing the curl of smoke deeply into his head. 'Look, I struck out with her back there, didn't I?'

'I don't know.'

'Hell yes, you know.'

'I never met your wife before. She said she had to take care of the kids.'

'That's not what I mean, man, and you know it. Don't give a con the con.'

'I was on the bandstand. I don't know what went on between you.'

'But you *know*.'

'Come on, Buddy. You're pulling me into your own stuff.'

'That's right, Zeno. But you got an eye for looking into people. You tool around the yard, throwing the handball up against the wall, cool walk under the gun hack, but you're clicking right into somebody's pulse-beat.'

He knocked the lighter clean against the wind vane and rubbed it clean again on his shoe. There were red flecks in the corners of his eyes. This was the first time I had seen a bit of meanness come out in Buddy when he was high.

'Hell, Iry, I read your action when you first came in. All that southern-country-boy jive works cool on old ladies, but you *know*, man, and you're digging everything I say.'

I was in that position where there is nothing to say, with no words that wouldn't increase an unpleasant situation, and silence was equally bad. Then the bartender's 1955 Chevrolet passed us in a roar of twin exhausts, a quick brilliance of head-lights, and a scorch of black rubber as he shifted up and accelerated in front of us. The back draft and vacuum pushed my truck toward the shoulder of the road.

'Damn,' I said. 'Does that fellow drive in demolition derbies or something?'

'That's just Boyd Valentine airing out his gourd.'

'You have another stick?' I thought it was better that I smoke it and dump it if he had any more.

'That was the last of the souvenirs from the reservation. It was green, anyway. Think they must grow it in hog shit. Makes you talk with forked brain. Pull into the bar up there and I'll buy a little brew for our crowd.'

The neon sign reflected a dull purple and red on the gravel and the cars and pickups in the parking lot. It was the same bar where we had gone my first night in Montana.

'Let's pass, man,' I said. 'We have some in the icebox, and I can go down the road later.'

'Pull in, pull in, pull in. You got to stop worrying about all these things.'

'I don't think it's too cool, Buddy.'

'Because you've got your head in the parole office all the time. Wait just a minute and I'll bop on out with the brew.'

I parked the truck on the edge of the lot by the road and Buddy walked inside, his balance deliberate like a sailor's on a ship. I smoked a cigarette and watched a few raindrops strike against the windshield. A long streak of lightning quivered in the blackness off a distant mountain, and I flicked my cigarette out into the moist, sulfurous air. *Well, to hell with it*, I thought, and went inside after him.

It was crowded, and the barstools were filled with cowboys and mill workers bent over into the poker dice, punchboards, and rows of beer bottles. Buddy was standing in front of a table with a beer in his hand, talking with three rawboned men and their wives, who were as bovine and burned with wind and sun as their husbands. They had empty steak plates in front of them, streaked with gravy and blood, and while Buddy talked, they tipped their cigarette ashes into the plates with a kind of patient anger that they kept in with only the greatest stoicism. Buddy must have played the Ray Charles number on the jukebox, because I didn't think anyone else in the place would have, and his speech was already full of hip language that raised up and down with the song while his hand tapped against the loose change in his slacks. He was on the outer edge of his high, and Bird Parker rhythms were working in his head, and it couldn't have come at a worse time.

'Well, that's your scene, man, and that's copacetic,' he said. 'And the old man has got his scene, too. And that's cool. He just turns over his action a little different. It's a matter of understanding what kind of scene you want to build and which kind of cats you want in on it –'

I went to the bar and asked if Buddy had put in an order to carry out.

'That's it waiting on the end of the counter when you're ready to leave, mister,' the bartender said.

I picked up the cardboard case of beer from the bar and walked over to Buddy with it.

'My meter's running overtime,' I said.

'Just a minute. There's a delicate metaphysical point involved here.'

'What's involved is our ass.'

'Set it down. Let's clear this question up. Now, if that stink plant down there invested some money in a purification system, the valley wouldn't smell like it just had an enema, and they could supply all kinds of copacetic toilet paper all over the world.'

One man, with a bull neck, iron eyebrows, and his shirt lapels pressed and starched flat, looked at Buddy with a stare that I would never want to have turned on me. The thick veins in his neck and brow were like twisted pieces of cord. He breathed deeply in his chest, almost clicking with a stunted anger, and his thumb knuckle rubbed back and forth on the oil cover of the table. He blinked and looked at a far spot on the wall.

'You better tell your old man that four hundred working men are going to lose their jobs because he thinks there's a little bit of smell in the air,' he said.

'Well, that's the way the toilet flushes sometimes, Zeno,' Buddy said.

I picked up the case of beer and headed for the door. I had to wait for a drunk cowboy to kiss his girl good night and stumble out ahead of me; then I walked across the parking lot in the light rain and threw the beer in the back of the truck. Buddy followed me in the frame of yellow light from the open door.

'Get in,' I said.

'Why the fire drill, man?'

'The next time, you charge your own hill. Collect Purple Hearts when I'm not around.'

'You're really pissed.'

'Just get in. I'm burning it down the road in about five seconds.'

We pulled onto the blacktop, and I revved it up all the way in first and slammed the gearbox into second. The oil smoke billowed out of the truck's tailpipe.

'What the hell are you doing?' he said. He still had the beer bottle in his hand, and he drank the foam out of the bottle.

'Don't you know what you're fooling with back there? Those people have blood in their eye. For a minute that man wanted to ice you.'

'Iry, you don't know the scene around here. It's not like rednecks opening up a shank in your face. This kind of crap goes on all the time. Besides, I can't stand the righteousness of those bastards. They bitch about the federal government, the Indians, farm control, niggers, college kids, anything that's not like them. You get pretty tired of it.'

'Haven't you learned to leave people like that alone?'

'You're really coming on like gangbusters tonight.'

'Yeah, well, quick lesson you taught me my first week in the population: walk around the quiet ones that look harmless.'

'Okay, Zeno.'

I put a cigarette in my mouth and popped a kitchen match on my thumbnail. The rain turned in the headlights, and I breathed in on the cigarette and let the smoke out slowly.

'Buddy, I just don't like to see you fade the wrong kind of action,' I said.

'I know all that, man.'

'You got to ease up sometimes and let people alone.'

'Forget about it. I'm cool. Do I look like I'm worried? I'm extremely cool on these matters.'

I looked into the rearview mirror as I slowed to turn into the side road that led to the ranch. A pair of headlights was gaining on me through the rain as though the driver couldn't see that I was slowing. I shifted into second and accelerated into the gravel turnoff, the truck body bouncing hard against the springs. The trees were black by the side of the road, and the rocks pinged and rattled under the frame. The headlights turned in after us, and I pushed the accelerator to the floor.

'Hey, you trying out for the hot-rod circuit or something?' Buddy said. 'Come on, you're going to rip a tire on these rocks.'

I didn't answer him. The driver behind us had on his brights, and they reflected in my eyes like a shattered white flame. I wound the truck up in second, shot it into third, with the gas all the way down, and popped the clutch. It slipped momentarily until it could grab, the speedometer needle quivered in a stationary place like part of a bad dream, and the headlights suddenly loomed up close enough to the tailgate so that I could see the hood and outline of a large yellow truck.

'Pull over and let those drunk sons of bitches pass,' Buddy said.

Then they hit us. The back end of my pickup fishtailed toward the ditch, and I spun the steering wheel in my hands and shifted down in a spray of rocks. Then they hit us again, and I heard the metal tear like someone was ripping strips out of a tin roof. The headlights beat against the dark line of trees and wavered up into the sky, and I couldn't pull the pickup to the center of the road again because either a fender had been crumpled against a tire or the frame had been bent. Buddy was looking backward through the cab window, his face brilliant in the headlights' illumination.

'Another mile, man,' he said. 'I'm going to get the old man's shotgun and blow these assholes all over the road.'

They closed on us and caught my back bumper as a snowplow might, with a heavy superior thrust of engine and weight that pushed the pickup forward as though it had no momentum of its own, the transmission shearing into filings, the wheels locked sideways and scouring ruts out of the rock road. I held on to the steering wheel with one hand and tried to put an arm in front of Buddy as the edge of the ditch cut under the front tire and we went over. The pine saplings slashed against the windshield, and the bottom of the ditch came up blackly and smashed the radiator into the fan. Buddy's head spiderwebbed the glass, and he recoiled backward into the seat, a brilliant jet of blood shooting from a small raised split like a crucifix in the skin. My

111

stomach had gone hard into the steering wheel, my breath rushed out of a long collapsing place in my throat, and I fought to bring the air back in my lungs.

Then I heard their truck stop and back up on the road. Their doors slammed, and three big men skidded down the side of the ditch through the underbrush, their boots digging for balance in the wet dirt. I pulled the tire iron from under the seat and opened the door just before the first one got his hand on it. Before I could turn into him and swing, he brought a nightstick down on my arm. It was the type used by policemen and barroom bouncers, drilled out on the end and filled with lead, and I felt the bone crack like a piece of plate. My hand opened as though the tendons were severed, and the tire iron fell foolishly to the ground.

'That other one's Riordan,' a second man said. They were all dressed in blue jeans, work boots, and washfaded flannel shirts, and their large bodies were bursting with a confident physical power.

They pulled Buddy from the cab and knocked him to the ground, then held him up against the tire well and drove their fists into his face. They discounted my presence as they might have a stray limb that was in their way. The blood was already swelling up in a blue knot under the skin on my arm, and my fingers were quivering uncontrollably. Buddy's hair was matted against the split in his forehead, and his face had gone white from the blows. I picked up the tire iron with my left hand and stumbled around the front of the truck in the brush, the headlights bright in my eyes, and threw it as hard as I could into a man's back. His shoulders straightened abruptly, and his arm flickered in the air behind his spine, his body frozen as though some awful pain was working its way into his groin.

They didn't take long after that. They had finished beating Buddy, streaking his clothes with blood, and now they turned their attention to me. The man I had hit leaned against my truck with one arm, arching his back and kneading his fist into the vertebrae. I could see the pain in his eyes.

'Give that son of a bitch his buckwheats,' he said.

The first punch caught me in the eye. I felt the man's whole weight lift into it, and I spun backward off the fender with a corridor of purple light receding into my brain. I must have held on to the fender, because the second blow came downward across my nose, and for just an instant I knew that he had a ring on. There was mud all over my hands and knees, the rain ticked in my hair, and I heard one man say, 'You ought to know when to stay in Louisiana, bud.' Then he kicked me between the buttocks, and I thought I was going to urinate.

I heard their truck doors slam, and as they turned around in the road, the headlight beams reflected off the tree trunks, and I saw the words on the side of the cab: WEST MONTANA LUMBER COMPANY. I got to my feet and started over toward Buddy, who was bent on his knees in the undergrowth. My back felt cold and wet, and I realized that half my shirt had been torn away from one shoulder. Then I saw the thin ribbon of fire curling up the twisted strip of

113

cloth into the open gas tank. I ran to Buddy and grabbed him under the arm with my good hand, and we tripped along the bottom of the ditch with the pine branches whipping back across our faces and arms.

A red finger of light leaped down the gas hole, and there was a whoosh and a brilliant illumination like strobe lights in the ditch. The truck body steamed and constricted, and the paint burst into blisters; then the fire suddenly welled up through the wooden bed and shot into the air in an exploding yellow scorch against the pine boughs high over-head. The heat burned my face and made my eyes water. The tires became ringed with fire, and the grease in the rear axle boiled and hissed through the seals, and the hood sprang open from its latch as though it were part of some isolated comic act. I heard the Martin and Dobro start to come apart in the cab. The mahogany and spruce wood, the tapered necks and German silver in the frets, gathered into a dark flame cracking through the windshield, and the strings on the Dobro tightened and popped one by one against the metal resonator, ringing out through the woods as though they were being pulled loose by a discordant pair of pliers.

I heard the rain on the windowsill and pulled the sheet up over my eyes. It was cool under the sheet, and I rolled back into that strange, comfortable world between sleep and wakefulness. On the edge of my mind I heard my father moving around downstairs in the early dawn, breaking open the shotguns to see that they were empty and dropping the decoys with their lead-anchor weights into the canvas duffel bag. I knew that it was going to be a fine day for duck hunting, with an overcast sky and enough rain to bring them sailing in low, denting the water with their feet and wings before they landed. It had been a good year for mallard and teal, and on a grey day like this one they always came in right above our blind on their way to feed in the rice field.

'*Allons aller*,' I heard my father call up the staircase.

And I could already feel the excitement of the outboard ride across the swamp to the blind, with the shotgun and the shells under my raincoat, knowing that we could take all the ducks we wanted simply because that part of the swamp was ours – we had earned it, the two of us. They would dip suddenly out of the sky when they saw our decoys while we sat motionlessly in the reeds, our faces pointed toward the ground, our camouflaged caps pulled down on our foreheads; then, as they winn-owed over the bayou, we would rise together and the sixteen-gauge would roar in my ears and recoil into my shoulder, and before the first mallard had folded in the air and toppled toward the water, even before the dogs had splashed through the reeds after him, I was already firing again with the empty shell casings smoking at our feet.

But the swamp and my father's happy voice over the piled ducks in the blind didn't hold in my mind. I felt the gun go off again against my shoulder, but this time I was looking through the peep sight on my

M-1 at a concrete bunker on the edge of a frozen rice field. The bunker was covered with holes, as though it had been beaten with a ball peen hammer, and the firing slit was scoured and chipped with ricochets. I let off the whole clip at the slit, the concrete shaling and powdering away like wisps of smoke in the grey air, and then I pulled back into the ditch and pressed in another clip with my thumb. The bottom of the ditch was filmed with ice and covered with empty shell casings. My hands were shaking with the cold inside my mittens, and my fingers felt like sticks on the bolt. I raised up and let off three rounds across the crusted snow on the edge of the ditch. Then I heard the sergeant behind me.

'All right, he's dead in there. Save what you got.'

The other seven stopped firing and pulled away from the top of the ditch. The moisture in their nostrils was frozen, and their faces were discolored from the wind and the crystals of snow on their skin.

'So here's the deal,' the sergeant said. 'We got about one hour to get around that hill or there ain't going to be anybody to meet us there.'

'He's under a mattress in there. They put a whole pile of them in every one of them things,' another man said.

'Well, we can take our choices, and it's a finger any way you look at it,' the sergeant said. He had a knitted sweater tied around his ears under his helmet, and two fingers of his left hand had started to swell with frostbite. 'We can sit on our ass here and shoot everything we got on one gook, and in the meantime we're going to get left, because those other fuckers aren't going to wait on us, and we ain't going to have nothing except a frozen pecker to stick out of this hole when they send their patrols through here tonight.'

There was no answer, but each of us was thinking of that hundred yards of wind-polished snow that at least four of us would have to cross before we would be beyond the angle of the machine gunner behind the slit in the bunker.

'OK, it's Paret, Simpson, and Belcher,' the sergeant said. 'Paret, you stay on my ass. We're going around behind him and blow that iron door open. What you got left in the Browning, Roth?'

'A half clip and four in the bag.'

'Put it in his face until we get all the way across the field.'

The BAR man started firing, and we went over the top of the ditch in a run, our shoulders crouched, our boots like lead weights in the snow. The two other men headed toward the left side of the bunker, their breath laboring out in a fog before them. I followed hard on the sergeant, as though I were trying to run in a dream, and then the sun broke through the overcast and turned the snowfield into a brilliant white mirror. Our tracks looked sculptured, like a dark violation of the field's whiteness.

The snow became deeper and softer, and the sergeant and I pushed for that safe imaginary angle beyond the range of a machine gun's swivel. Then the slit burst open with flame, and I saw the bullets clip in a straight pattern toward me in the snow. For a moment I saw the sergeant's face turn and stare at me over his shoulder, as though he had been disturbed in an angry mood. I fell forward on my elbows, my boots still locked in their deep sculptured depressions, and heard the snow hiss and spit around me.

The whiteness of the snow ached like a flame inside my eyelids.

*Where are you hit?*

*I don't know.*

*Jesus Christ, his back is coming off.*

*Get up over the rise and tell them to wait. Shoot out their tires if you have to.*

*They better have plasma. Look at the snow.*

I felt the nurse rub salve with a piece of cotton over my back and pull the gauze back into place. The rain broke on the windowsill in dimples of light, and I could see the dark green of the elms and maples waving in front of the old brick buildings across the street. I raised up on my elbows and felt the skin burn on my back. The plaster cast on my forearm was like a thick, obscene weight.

'Don't turn over. You have some pretty bad blisters there,' a man's voice said.

Buddy's father was bent forward in a leather chair at the foot of the bed, his square, callused hands folded between his legs. His gold watch chain glinted against his faded Levi's, and his wide forehead looked pale in the room's half-light. His gray eyes were staring straight into mine.

'They put you under before they set your arm.

**118**

The doctor said it might hang on a while after you woke up.'

My arms and bare chest were damp against the sheet, and I wiped my face with the pillow. The pressure sent a sudden touch of pain along my eyebrow and the bridge of my nose. I heard him pull his chair to the side of the bed.

'They really did a job on us,' I said.

He nodded with his eyes squinted, and I saw that he was looking over my face rather than at me. I propped myself on one elbow and softly touched the hard row of stitches under the strip of gauze bandage on my eyebrow. There were flecks of dried blood on my fingertips. When I moved, my back burned as though it had been scalded.

'How's Buddy?'

'He's asleep in the next room.'

'His head hit the glass when we went over in the ditch. Then they really hit him,' I said.

'He'll be all right. He was awake earlier and we talked, and then he wanted to sleep for a while.'

'How bad is he?'

'He has a concussion, and they put twenty stitches in his forehead.'

Outside, the rain was dripping from the trees, and I could hear someone punting a football in a front yard.

'I tried to stop it,' I said. 'I got one of them with the tire iron, but they had already broken my arm.'

He rubbed his coarse palms over his knuckles and looked momentarily at the floor, then at me. There was a thin part line in his graying brown hair, and his eyelids blinked as though he were keeping some idea down inside himself.

'I didn't press Buddy this morning, but I want to know what happened. Was it something that grew out of an argument in a saloon, or was it more involved than that?'

I reached over to the nightstand where someone had placed my package of Lucky Strikes beside my billfold, and put one in my mouth. He took a book of matches from his denim shirt and lit it. I wanted to avoid his face and the private question that was there beyond the wind-burned skin, the short growth of whiskers, and those intense gray eyes.

'It started with Buddy at the bar, Mr Riordan. I was outside most of the time. You'd better ask him about it later,' I said.

'And what was it exactly about?'

'Maybe too many drunk men in a bar on Sunday night.'

'What was said?'

I drew in on the cigarette and placed it in the ashtray. The wind blew the rain off the windowsill into the room. His big hands were pressed on his knees, and the veins stood up like twists of blue cord under the skin.

'You've got me in a hard place, and I think you know that,' I said.

'Yes, I guess I do. But I'd like to have it now.'

'Buddy was talking with some people at a table about the pulp mill. I don't know who the men were who followed us out. Buddy thought they were just drunks until they smashed into the back of my truck.'

'I see,' he said.

I heard the wet slap of the football again and then the heavy rattle of leaves in a tree.

'It looks like we've gotten you into some of our family's trouble, Mr Paret,' he said.

'No, sir, that's not true. I usually make a point of finding my own.'

He took a package of tobacco from his shirt pocket and rolled a cigarette, wet the glue neatly, and pinched the ends down.

'What did you kill that man for?' he said.

'I don't know.'

'It never came to you in those two years?'

'No.'

'I shot at a man once. I would have hit him and maybe killed him if he hadn't jumped from the cab of a combine when he did. I shot at him because I'd thought for a long time about something he had done.'

'I formally resigned from my war a long time ago, Mr Riordan.'

He cleared his throat quietly, as though there were a piece of bad air in it, and put out the rolled cigarette in the ashtray. This is one that's hard to read, I thought.

'I'll be back this evening,' he said. 'The doctor said you two should be able to leave in the morning. Do you want anything?'

'I'd like a half pint of bourbon.'

'All right.'

'Wait,' I said, and gave him three dollars from my billfold.

After he had gone, I tried to sleep in the cool sound of the rain and fall back into the dream about the duck hunt with my father, but the perspiration rolled off my back onto the sheets, and when I kept my eyes closed too long, I saw the headlights roaring up out of the dark road into my tailgate. I turned on my side, with the ooze of salve thick against my skin, and stared at the wooden crucifix on the wall with two withered palms stuck behind it. I got up from the bed and found my slacks and shoes in the closet, but no shirt, and then I remembered the curl of flame climbing into the gas tank. It took me ten minutes to get on my trousers with one hand, and even with my buttocks against the bed the room kept tilting sideways from the square of pale light through the window. Sweat dripped out of my hair onto the cast, and my good hand was shaking as I tried to pop a match with my thumb and light a cigarette.

After I rang for the nurse, I looked across the room at my image in the dresser mirror. *Oh man*, I thought.

A nun in white pushed open the door softly, and then her quiet, cosmetic-free face dilated with a red hue.

'Oh, no, you shouldn't do that,' she said. 'Please don't do that. You mustn't.'

'I think I should leave this evening, Sister, but I need a shirt. I'd appreciate it if you could find any old one you have around here.'

'Please, Mr Paret.'

'I have to check out, and I guess I'm going to. I just hate to ride the bus in a pajama shirt. You'd be doing me a great favor, Sister.'

Just then the nurse came in, and she could have been a matron in a women's reformatory. Her face was at first a simple bright piece of cardboard and irritation at an annoyance on her floor; then after a few sentences were exchanged between us, the anger clicked in her eyes, and I was sure that she would have enjoyed seeing me collapse on the floor in a spasm that would require heart surgery with a pocketknife.

The nun came through the door again with a folded checkered shirt in her hands, brushed past the nurse in a swirl of white cloth over her small, polished black shoes, and put the shirt next to me, quickly, with just a flash of her concerned pretty face into mine.

I buttoned the shirt so I could rest my limp hand and the weight of the cast inside it and walked down the corridor to the desk in the waiting room. I could hear the leather soles and etched voice of the nurse echo behind me, and evidently she had enough command in the hospital to make the interns and the resident doctor look around walleyed and full of question marks at the strange man walking toward them a little off-balance.

I told the lady at the desk my name and asked for the bill.

'You ought to go back to your room, fella,' the resident said.

'Got to catch air, doc, and stretch it out a little bit tonight.'

He looked at me steadily for a moment.

'All right, that's fine,' he said, and motioned the nurse away. 'But we're going to give you a sling and some pills for infection and pain. You come back in tomorrow to have your bandages changed.'

I sat down in a metal chair while another nurse tied a sling around my neck and placed my elbow carefully into the cloth and clipped safety pins into the folds. She stuck a brown envelope full of pills into the pocket of the checkered shirt, and I stood up to walk to the desk again. I could feel the stitches drawing tight against my eye, and I felt that there was a large blood blister swelling up on the bridge of my nose. My eyes couldn't focus on the grey dimpling of rain on the concrete outside.

I asked again for my bill and was told that Mr Riordan had asked that it be sent to him. I took out twenty-five dollars from my billfold and said that I would be back in to pay the rest.

I walked through the wet streets under the overhang of trees toward the bus depot. The wind swept the rain in gusts into my face. Clouds hung like soft smoke on the peaks of the mountains, and the neon signs over the bars were hazy red and green in the diminishing grey light.

So you showed everybody at the hospital you're a stand-up guy, I thought. Isn't that fine? Then I had to think about the rest of it. My truck and my Martin and Dobro burned up, a broken arm that put me out of work, and living at a strange family's

124

place as a bandage case because there wasn't another damn thing I could do. And deeper than any of it was just a sick feeling, a humiliation at being beaten up by men who had done it with a lazy form of physical contempt. I'd had the same feeling only once before, when a bully in the eighth grade had caught me after school and pinned my arms into the dust with his knees and slapped my face casually back and forth, then spit on his finger and put it in my ear.

# chapter six

In the morning the sun was all over the Bitterroot Valley, the grass had become a darker green from the rain, and the irrigation ditches were flowing high and muddy through the pigweed along the banks. I fired the wood stove and set the coffeepot to boil on an iron lid with the grinds in the water and went out back to see if I could start Buddy's old Plymouth. He had driven it through the creek and smashed one headlight and fender into a cottonwood when he was drunk, and white water had boiled over the front axle into the wires and distributor. But I finally turned it over on three cylinders and left it knocking and drying in neutral in front of the cabin while I drank coffee out of the pot and ate some smoked trout from the icebox.

Buddy's father and his younger brothers looked up at me from their work in the hayfield as I drove slowly with one arm up the dirt road toward the cattle guard. The ignition wires I had tied together swung under the dashboard and sparked whenever they clicked against the metal. Out of my side vision I saw Mr Riordan raise his checkered arm in the sunlight, but I slipped the transmission into third and thumped across the cattle guard onto the gravel road. I passed the burned wreck of my truck and the large area of blackened grass around it. The windows hung out on the scorched metal in folded sheets, and the boards in the bed were collapsed in charcoal over the rear axle. Through the broken eye of one window I thought I could see the silver wink of the twisted resonator from my Dobro.

I drove into Hamilton, the Ravalli County seat, and parked in front of the jail. As I walked up the sidewalk toward the building, a man behind the wire screen and bars of a cell window blew cigarette smoke out into the sunlight, then turned away into the gloom when I looked into his face.

I talked to the dispatcher in the sheriff's office, then waited for thirty minutes on a wood bench with the salve oozing out of my bandages into my shirt before the sheriff opened the door to his office and nodded his head at me.

His brown sleeves were rolled back over his elbows, and there was a faded army tattoo under the sun-bleached hair on one forearm and a navy tattoo on the other. His fingers on top of the desk pad were as thick as sausages, the nails broken down to the quick and lined with dirt, and there was a rim of dandruff around the bald spot in the center of his head. He didn't ask me to sit down or even look at me directly. He simply clicked his fingernail against a paper spindle, as though he were involved in an abstract thought, and said:

'Yes, sir?'

'My name is Iry Paret. Buddy Riordan and I got run off the road by Florence the other night, and I got my truck burned up.'

'You're Mr Paret, are you?' he said.

'That's right.'

He clicked his finger against the spindle again.

'I sent one of my deputies up to the hospital in Missoula after I heard about it. You fellows sure put it in the ditch, didn't you?'

'I had two guitars in that cab that were worth around seven hundred dollars,' I said.

'What would you like us to do?' He looked up at me from his finger game with the spindle. There was a blue touch in his eyes like something off an archer's bow.

'I want to get the three men that burned my truck.'

'I talked with a few people in the tavern later that night. They said you and Buddy Riordan were drunk.'

'We weren't drunk. We were knocked off the road, and somebody used my shirt to set fire to the gas tank.'

'I looked at your truck, too. There's one pair of skid marks going off into the ditch.'

I took a cigarette from my shirt pocket and tried to light a match from the folder with one hand.

'Look, Sheriff, a yellow truck with a West Montana Lumber Company sign on the door ran right over my tailgate, and then they really went to work. I don't know who those guys are, but they owe me for a 1949 pickup and two guitars and a broken arm.'

'Well, I guess you're saying you just got the shit beat out of you,' he said, and popped his thick index finger loose from his thumb on the desk blotter. He opened his desk drawer and pulled out a folder with three sheets clipped together inside. He turned over to the second page and folded it back and looked hard at one paragraph.

'Was it a colored man you killed down there?' he said.

I lit the cigarette and looked beyond him through the open window at the soft blue roll of the mountains.

'I mean, you got off with two years for murdering a man. In Montana, you'd get ten in Deer Lodge, even if it was an Indian.'

In that moment I hated him and his wry smile and the private blue glint in his eye.

'I got three years' good time, Sheriff. I imagine that's in your folder, too.'

'Yes, sir, it is. It also says you could get violated back to that place in Louisiana without too much trouble.'

I drove back to the ranch with my hands tight on the steering wheel. I had wanted to say something final to him when I left the office, something that would crack into that blue glint in his eyes, but I had simply walked out like someone who had been told his bus was gone.

Buddy was sitting on the front porch of the cabin with a cup of tea in one hand and a cigarette in the other. His face was puffed with yellow and purple bruises, and a thick band of gauze was wrapped around his head. He tried to grin, but I could see the pain in his mouth.

'I didn't know when you'd be back, so I wired it up,' I said.

'I'm just going to guess, Zeno. The sheriff's office,' he said.

'Do you import these bastards out of the South?'

'A couple of quick lessons from Uncle Zeno. Around here the law won't do anything about barroom brawls or any variety of Saturday night cuttings or swinging of pool cues. It don't matter if it's one guy against the whole Russian army – he's on his own. Number two, the name Riordan is like the stink on shit down there at Hamilton.'

'In the meantime we got stomped, partner,' I said. 'I'm out my truck and my guitars, and I don't know when I can work again.'

'We got this place, man. You don't have to worry about money.'

His acceptance made me even angrier than I had been in the sheriff's office.

'That's not my kind of caper.'

'Maybe you don't like to hear this, but you got to mark it off.'

'Damn, Buddy, those guys are out there somewhere.'

'Yeah, man, and maybe you'll recognize them somewhere, but what are you going to do then? Call the same dick that just threw you out of his office?

Get a beer out of the icebox and sit down. I'm going to go fishing in a little while.'

'That's real Kool-Aid, babe. I have to give it to you,' I said.

'You haven't taken the wood plugs out of your ears yet. You talk like a fish with part of his brain still outside. You know better.'

I walked out of the sun's glare into the shade of the porch and went inside. My suitcase was opened beside my bunk bed, and I wanted to throw my clothes into it and hitch on down the road, but I was broke and stuck here with my parole. I opened a can of beer and leaned back against the wood ceiling post and drank it. I could hear the creek through the back window.

'Come on out here, Iry,' he called through the screen door.

I drank the bottom of the can slowly, and then I felt my throat and chest begin to relax and the blood slow in my temples. I took another can from the icebox and went back outside. The ridge of mountains behind the main house was dark blue and honed like a knife against the sky.

'You see what I mean, don't you?' Buddy said. 'I know you got brass cymbals going off in your head all the time. What's the name of that guy you celled with, the one with all the whorehouse stories? He told me how you used to sweat all over the bunk at night and sometimes just sit up till morning bell. But, man, on a deal like this we just lose. That's all. You just draw a line through it and flush it on down.'

'All right, Buddy, no therapy. I'll watch you fish for a while, and then I want to borrow your car again.'

'Like what kind of action do you have planned, Zeno?'

'I need to call my brother in Louisiana, and I'm supposed to stop by the hospital.'

'There's a phone up at the house.'

'Can I use the car?'

He took the keys from his pocket and dropped them in my palm. I followed him into the woods with my can of beer and watched him fish with wet flies for cutthroat in the turning pools behind the boulders. After he had moved farther up the stream into the deeper shade of the trees' overhang, I finished my beer against a pine trunk, whistled at him softly and waved, and walked back to the cabin.

I had one good suit, a gray one that I wore when I played at good clubs, and I put it on with my half-topped black boots and a blue-and-white, small-checked cowboy shirt with pearl snap buttons. It took me almost a half hour to dress with one arm, and it was impossible to get the necktie into a knot.

I drove the thirty miles to Missoula and stopped at a beer joint with no cars in front to phone Ace. I got change for five dollars at the bar. Then it struck me what type of conversation I was about to have, and I ordered a vodka and ice to take to the telephone.

After his secretary whispered something hurriedly, like 'I think it's your brother, Mr Paret,' Ace was on the line, and I could almost see his stomach swell up

132

in satisfaction in that reclining leather chair. 'Hello, Iry,' he said, 'how do you like it up there with the Eskimos? Just a minute. I've got about three people on hold. . . . Go ahead. . . . Well, I don't know if I want to buy just the two acres. Your four run all the way back to the bayou, and that's going to leave a strip that anybody can move in on later. . . . I mean, if you decide later on to sell to a boatyard or let that oil company build a dock there, what I've got invested in the development isn't going to be worth spit on the sidewalk. That's the way it is, Bro'. . . . What the hell went wrong up there? I thought you had a job with that friend of yours. . . . Well, I don't want to be the one that told you about latching the gate too quick behind you, but that's the deal. All four acres or I can't use it.'

So I took it at $250 an acre and gave up any mineral rights or future land-lease agreements for oil exploration, and Ace said he would have the deed transfer and check in the morning's mail.

I walked back to the bar and finished the vodka. For a thousand dollars I had quitclaim forever to any of the Paret land, and if I knew Ace, I would not want to see the farm or the bamboo and cypress and oaks along the bayou ever again, even in memory.

I drove west of town through the green, sloping hills along the Clark. The sun was bright on the green riffles in the water, and insects were turning in hot swarms over the boulders that stood exposed in the current. Ahead I could see the huge plume of smoke that curled up against the sky from the pulp mill, and then I caught the first raw odor in the air.

It smelled like sewage, and the wind flattened the smoke across the valley and left a dull white haze low on the meadows. I cleared my throat and spat outside the window, but my eyes started to water and I tried to breathe quietly through my mouth. The only thing I had ever smelled like it, on a scale that could cover a whole rural area, was the sugar mill back home in winter, which produced a thick, sick-sweet odor that seemed to permeate the inside of your skull.

I turned through the gate and parked in the employees' lot. A new shift was going in, and men in Levi's clothes and work boots and tin hats with lunch pails were walking into the side of the building. Log trucks piled with ponderosa pines, the booming chains notched tightly into the bark, were lined up in back to unload, the tractor engines hammering under the hoods. Someone told me later that the leather boots the men wore eventually turned black and rotted from the air inside the mill and the chemicals on the floor and I thought their lungs must have looked like a pathologist's dream.

I asked a foreman where the management was, and he looked at me with a sweaty, questioning eye from under his tin hat.

'There's no jobs right now,' he said.

'I just want to see the timekeeper or somebody in personnel.'

His eyes moved over my face; then he pointed at a door.

'Over there. There's some glass doors at the end of the hall,' he said.

The hallway was dark and hot, and it smelled much worse than the outside of the mill. Someone had painted the walls green at one time, but the paint was blistered and peeling in flakes on the baseboards. Behind the glass doors I could see an air-conditioning unit with streamers blowing off the vents, a big-breasted secretary who sat in her chair as though she had an arrow in her back, and three men in business suits behind their glass-topped desks, each of them concerned with typed papers that brought on knitted brows, a sweep of the hand to the telephone, a quick concentration on some piece of thunder hidden in a figure.

The secretary wanted to know who it was exactly that I would like to see or if I could explain exactly what I wanted.

'It's about an accident, actually,' I said. 'I haven't talked with a lawyer yet. I thought I'd come down here and see what y'all could tell me.'

Her eyelashes blinked, and she looked sideways briefly at the man behind the next desk. There was a pause, and then the man glanced up from his papers and nodded to her.

'Mr Overstreet can talk with you. Just have a seat,' she said. (All of this in a room where each of us was within five feet of the other.)

I sat in the chair in front of Mr Overstreet's desk for possibly two minutes before he decided that I was there. He looked like a working man who had gotten off the green chain years ago, worked his way up to yard foreman, and finally slipped through a side door into a necktie and a place in front of an air-conditioning unit. There were still freckles on the backs of his hands, and thin pinch scars on his fingers that come from working with boomer chains, and he had the rigidity and habitual frown of a man who was afraid of his own position every day. He pushed the papers to the side of the glass desktop, then looked up flatly into my eyes.

'Sunday night my pickup was knocked off the road by one of your trucks down by Florence,' I said. 'There were three men in it, and they burned my pickup and musical instruments and left me and another guy a hospital bill to pay. I'm not after your company. I just want those three guys.'

He stared at me, and then his eyes flicked angrily at the secretary. He rubbed the back of one hand into his palm.

'What are you saying?'

'There's a truck out in your lot that probably has red paint all over the front bumper. Also, you must know who drives a company truck out of here at night.'

The other two men behind the desks had stopped work and were looking blankly at us. I could hear the secretary squeak the rollers of her chair across the rug.

'That doesn't have anything to do with the mill,' he said. 'You take that up with the sheriff's department in Ravalli County.'

'It was your truck. That makes you liable. If you protect them, that makes you criminally liable.'

'You watch what you say, fella.'

'All you've got to tell me is you'll come up with the men in that truck.'

'Who the hell you think you are talking to me about criminal charges?'

'I'm not asking you for anything that's unreasonable.'

'Yeah? I think you stopped using your reason when you walked in here. So now you turn around and walk back out.'

'Why don't you flick on your brain a minute? Do you want guys like this beating up people out of one of your trucks?'

'You don't understand me. You're leaving here. Now.'

'You ass.'

'That's it.' He picked up the telephone and dialed an inner office number. His free hand was spread tightly on the glass desktop while he waited for an answer.

'All right, bubba,' I said. 'Go back to your papers.'

But he wasn't listening. 'Send Lloyd and Jack down here,' he said.

I walked out the office and down the dark hallway; then the outer door opened in a flash of sunlight and two big men in tin hats moved toward me in silhouette. One of them had a cigar pushed back like a stick in his jaw, and he wiped tobacco juice off his mouth with a flat thumb and looked hard at me.

'Better get in that office,' I said. 'Some crazy man is in there raising hell.'

They went past me, walking fast, their brows wrinkled intently. I was across the parking lot when I heard the door open again behind me. The man with the cigar leaned out, his tin hat bright in the sun, and shouted, 'You keep going. Don't ever come around here again.'

I drove back to Missoula and stopped at the tavern where I had called Ace earlier. I started drinking beer. Then from among the many wet rings on the bar I lifted up a boilermaker, and I guess it was then that an odd tumbler clicked over in my brain and it started.

In the darkness of the tavern, with the soft glow of the mountain twilight through the blinds, I began to think about my boyhood South and the song I never finished in Angola. I had all the music in my mind and the runs that bled into each chord, but the lyrics were always wooden, and I couldn't get all of the collective memory into a sliding blues. I called it 'The Lost Get-Back Boogie,' and I wanted it to contain all those private, inviolate things that a young boy saw and knew about while growing up in southern Louisiana in a more uncomplicated time: the bottle trees (during the Depression people used to stick empty milk of magnesia bottles on the winter branches of a hackberry until the whole tree rang with blue glass), the late evening sun boiling into the green horizon of the Gulf, the dinners of crawfish and bluepoint crabs under the cypress trees on Bayou Teche, and freight cars slamming together in the Southern Pacific yard, and through the mist the distant locomotive whistle that spoke of journeys

138

across the wetlands to cities like New Orleans and Mobile.

There was much more to it, like the Negro juke joint by the sugar mill and Loup-garous Row, the string of shacks by the rail yard where the whores sat on the wood porches on Saturday afternoons and dipped their beer out of a bucket. But maybe that was why I didn't finish it. There was too much of it for one song or maybe even for a book.

I kept looking at the clock above the neon GRAIN BELT sign, and I was sure that I had my thumb right on the pulse of the day, but each time I focused again on the hour hand, I realized that some terrible obstruction had prevented me from seeing that another thirty or forty minutes or hour and a half had passed. When I walked to the rest room, my cast scratched along the wall with my weight, and when I came back out, the tables, the row of stools, and the people all seemed rearranged in place.

'You want another one, buddy?' the bartender said.

'Yeah. This time give me a draft and a double Beam on the side.'

He brought the schooner dripping with foam and ice and set a shot jigger beside it.

'You want to throw for the washline?' he said.

'What do I do?'

He picked up the leather cup of poker dice and set it down in front of me with his palm over the top.

'You roll me double or nothing for the drinks. If you roll five of a kind, you get everything up there on the line.'

There was a long string of wire above the bar with one-dollar bills clipped to it with clothespins.

'What are my chances?' I said.

'Outside of the drinks, bad.'

'All right.' The whiskey was hot in my face, and I could feel the perspiration start to run out of my hair. There was a dead hum in my head, and behind me I heard Kitty Wells's nasal falsetto from the jukebox: 'It wasn't God who made honky-tonk angels.'

I rattled the dice once in the leather cup with my hand tight over the top and threw them along the bar.

'I'll be damned,' the bartender said.

I had to look again myself, in the red glow of the neon beer sign, at the five aces glinting up from the mahogany bar top.

The bartender pulled twenty one-dollar bills from the clothespins and put them in front of me, then took away my beer glass and jigger and brought them back filled. He chewed on the flattened end of a match and shook his head as though some type of mathematical principle in the universe had just been proved untrue.

'You ought to shoot craps at one of them joints over in Idaho, buddy,' he said.

'I've shot lots of craps. They keep you off night patrol.'

He looked at me with a flat pause in his face, the matchstick motionless in a gap between his teeth.

'You can throw the bones for high point right down at the end of the blanket and the other guy

140

has got to go up through their wire. Him and fifteen others.' Then I knew that I was drunk, because the words had already freed themselves from behind all those locks and hasps and welded doors that you keep sealed in the back of your mind.

'Well, I guess you got good luck, buddy,' he said, and wiped the rag over the bar in front of me before he walked down to a cowboy who had just come in.

I drank the whiskey neat and chased it with the beer, then smoked a cigarette and called him back again.

'Give me a pint of Beam's Choice and a six-pack. While you're getting it, give me a ditch.'

'Mister, I ain't telling you nothing, but you ain't going to be able to drive.'

Outside, the stars were bright above the dark ring of mountains around Missoula, and the plume of smoke from the pulp mill floated high above the Clark Fork in the moonlight. My broken arm itched as though ants were crawling in the sweat inside my cast. I fell heavily behind the steering wheel of Buddy's Plymouth, and for just a second I saw my guitars snapping apart in the truck fire and heard that level, hot voice: *Give that son of a bitch his buckwheats.*

As I drove back down the blacktop toward Lolo, with the bright lights of semis flashing over me and the air brakes hissing when I swerved across the center line, I remembered again the bully putting spittle in my ear, reenacted in my mind being thrown out of a pulp mill that manufactured toilet paper, and studied hard upon the sale of my inheritance to the cement-truck and shopping-center interests.

Bugs swam around the light on the front porch of Buddy's cabin and his fly rod was leaned against the screen door, but he must have been up at his father's house. I walked unsteadily to the back room, where he kept the '03 Springfield rifle with the Mauser action on two deer-antler racks. I put the sling over my shoulder and filled the big flap pockets of my army jacket with shells from a box on the floor. Even as drunk as I was, even as I caught my balance against the doorjamb, I knew that it was insane, that every self-protective instinct and light in my head was blinking red, but I was already in motion in the same way I had been my first day out of prison when I covered the license plate of the pickup with mud and went banging down the road drunk into a possible parole violation.

I put the rifle on the back floor with my field jacket over it and drove back toward the cattle guard. The wind off the river bent the grass in the pasture under the moon, and the cows were bunched in a dark shadow by the cottonwoods. I saw a flashlight bobbing across the field toward me and heard Buddy's voice call out in the dark. I stopped and let the engine idle while the sweat rolled down my face and my own whiskey breath came back sharp in my throat. He jumped across the irrigation ditch on one foot, and one of his younger brothers jumped in a rattle of cattails behind him.

'Where are you going, man?'

An answer wouldn't come, and I just flicked an index finger off the steering wheel toward the road.

'What have you been drinking?' he said.

'Made a stop down the highway.'

'You really look boiled, Zeno. Turn it around and go fishing with us. We're going to try some worms in a hole on the river.'

I got a cigarette out of my shirt pocket and pushed it in my mouth. It seemed that minutes passed before I completed the motion.

'I got lucky at craps today. There's a lady in a beer joint that wants to help me drink my money.'

'Where?'

'Eddie's, or one of those places of yours.'

'I'll go with you,' he said, and clicked off the flashlight. 'Joe, go down to the river with the old man, and I'll try to meet you later.'

'That's no good, Buddy. She's a one-guy chick, and I'm the guy that faded all the bread this afternoon.'

'I don't give a shit about the car,' he said, 'but you're going to get your ass in jail tonight.'

'Never had a ticket, babe.'

'That's because those coonass cops don't know how to write. Move it over and let's go down and investigate it together.'

'You want the car back?'

'No, I want to keep you from going back on P.V.'

'I got to catch air. If you want the car, I'll thumb.'

He stepped back from the door and bowed like a butler, sweeping his arm out into the darkness.

'It's your caper, Zeno,' he said. 'I ain't got money for bond, so you take this fall on your own.'

I thumped across the cattle guard, and in the rearview mirror I saw Buddy and his brother swing the gate closed and pull the loop wire over the fence post.

The drive back to the pulp mill was a long blacktop stretch of angry headlights, horns blowing in a diminishing echo behind me, gravel showering up under the fender when I hit the shoulder, and a highway-patrol car that kept evenly behind me for two miles and then turned off indifferently into a truck stop. I opened a can of beer and set it beside me on the seat and sipped off the bottle of Beam's Choice. I picked up a radio station in Salt Lake that was advertising tulip bulbs and baby chicks sent directly to your house, C.O.D., in one order, and the announcer's voice rose to the fervor of a southern evangelist's when he said, 'And remember, friends and neighbors, just write "Bulb." ' B-U-L-B. That's "Bulb." '

There was a wooden bridge over the Clark Fork just below the pulp mill, and then a climbing log road against the mountain that overlooked the river, the sour, mud-banked ponds where they kept their chemicals before they seeped out into the current, and the lighted parking lot full of washed and waxed yellow trucks. The Plymouth slammed against the springs and dug rocks out of the road with the oil pan as I pushed it in second gear up the grade, and the dense overhang from the trees slapped across the windshield and top like dry scratches on a blackboard. When I reached the top of the grade and drove along the smooth yellow strip of road among the pines, the heat indicator was quivering past the red mark on the dash, and I could hear the steam hissing under the radiator cap. I pulled the car into a turnaround at the base of a curve on the mountain and slipped the sling of the Springfield over my shoulder and picked up the field jacket with my good hand.

I walked down through the timber, with the brown pine needles thick under my feet, and found a clear place where I could lean back against a pine trunk and cover the whole parking lot with the iron sights. There were white lights strung up the sides of both smoke stacks, against the dark blue of the far mountain, and the parking lot ached with a brilliant electric glow off the asphalt.

I opened the breech of the Springfield and laid it across my lap, then counted out the shells on a handkerchief and cut a deep X with my pocketknife across each soft-nose. I pushed the shells into the magazine with my thumb until the spring came tight, then slid the bolt home and locked it down. I readjusted the sling and worked it past the cast so I could fire comfortably from a sitting position and aim across my knee without canting the sights.

The first round broke through a front windshield and spiderwebbed the glass with cracks, and I drove two more shots through the top of the cab. The bullets against the metal sounded like a distant metallic slap. I couldn't see the damage inside, but I figured that the flattened and splintered lead would tear holes like baseballs in the dashboard. I shifted my knee and swung the iron sights on the next truck and let off three rounds in a row without taking my cheek from the stock. The first bullet scoured across the hood and ripped the metal like an ax had hit it, and I tore the grill and radiator into a wet grin with the other two.

I suppose that in some drunken compartment of my mind I had only planned to pay back in kind, on an equal basis, what had been done to me, but now I couldn't stop firing. My ears rang with a heady exhilaration with each shot, the empty casings leaped from the thrown bolt and smoked in the pine needles, and then there was that whaaappp of the bullet flattening out into another truck. I took a long drink from the pint of Beam's Choice, then reloaded and fired the whole clip all over the parking lot without aiming. I was now concentrated on how fast I could let off a round, recover from the recoil and throw the bolt, then lock another shell in the chamber and squeeze again.

On the last clip I must have bit into something electrical on an engine, either the battery or the ignition wiring, because the sparks leaped in a shower from under the hood. Then I could see the yellow-and-blue flame wavering under the oil pan and the paint starting to blister and pop in front of the windshield.

I slipped the sling off my shoulder and began to pick up the shell casings with one hand while I watched it. The casings were hot in my hand, and I put them clinking into the flap pocket of my field jacket. The fire sucked up through the truck cab, then caught the leather seat over the gas tank in earnest, and then it blew. The flame leaped upward into one cracking red handkerchief against the dark, and the truck body collapsed on the frame and the tires roared with circles of light.

I drank again from the bottle and watched it with fascination. The heat had already cracked the glass on the next truck, and the fire was whipping inside the cab. The red light reflected off the river at the foot of the hill, and the dark trunks of the pines were filled with shadows. Out on the highway beyond the mill, I saw the blue bubblegum light of a police car turning furiously in the darkness. I put the bottle in my pocket and felt around for any shells that I hadn't picked up, then shoved my hand under the pine needles and swept it across a half circle on my right side. The whiskey was throbbing behind my eyes, and I lost my balance when I tried to get to my feet with the sling across my chest.

For the first time that night I became genuinely aware that I was in trouble. My mind couldn't function, I didn't know anything about the back roads, and I stood a good chance of being picked up on the highway for drunk driving. My heart was beating with the exertion of climbing to the top of the rise with the Springfield slung on my shoulder, and sweat ran in rivulets out of my hair into my eyes. I sat behind the wheel of the Plymouth and tried to think. I could take the log road over the mountain and possibly drive off the edge of a wash into five hundred feet of canyon (provided that the road went anywhere) or return across the log bridge into a good chance of a jolt in Deer Lodge plus an automatic violation back to Angola. I started the engine but kept the lights off and let the car roll down the road in neutral, braking heavily all the way down the grade. The pines began to thin toward the bottom of the hill, and then I saw the brown sweep of the river with the thick eddies of sawdust along the banks. The bridge stood out flat and hard in the reflection of lights from the mill, and there was a police car parked at the other side with the airplane headlights turned on and the bubble-gum machine swinging on the roof.

I cut on my lights and eased the Plymouth into second as I came off the incline; then I remembered the Springfield propped like an iron salute against the passenger's door. It was too late to dump it or even throw it over into the backseat. The sheriff's deputy was already by the wooden bridge rail, winking his flashlight at me.

Oh boy. And you rolled right into it, babe.

I slowed the car and looked over at the bright flame in the parking lot and the two men who were spraying it with fire extinguishers in silhouette. Then the deputy began to sweep his flashlight impatiently, and it took a second, like a beat out of my heart, to realize that he was waving me past. I rattled across the board planks, and the headlights suddenly illuminated his brown uniform, the wide gun belt and cartridges, and the Stetson pushed low over his eyes. I nodded at him and slowly depressed the accelerator.

I hit the highway and opened up the Plymouth with the rods knocking, the frame shaking, and the moon rising over the mountain like a song. I opened the wind vane into my face and felt the sweat turn cold and dry in my hair, and then I drank the last of the whiskey in a long swallow and sailed the bottle over the roof. I had walked right out of it with the kind of con luck that drops on your head when you're sure that this time they're going to weld the cell door shut.

I bought a six-pack of Great Falls to drink on the way back to the ranch, and I felt a light-headed, heartbeating sense of victory and omniscience that I had known only in the infantry after moving all the way to the top of a Chinese hill without being hit. The fact that I weaved across the white center line or ran through an intersection at seventy seemed unimportant; I was flying with magic all over me, and the alcohol and adrenaline worked in my heart with a mean new energy.

The next morning I felt the sun hot and white in my eyes through the window. There was an overturned can of beer by the bed, and my shirt was half off and tangled around my cast. I walked into the back room where Buddy was sleeping and saw the Springfield back on the rack, though I had no memory of having put it there. I could still taste the mixture of beer, whiskey, and cigarettes in my mouth, and I worked the pump on the sink and cupped the water up in my hand. When the coldness hit my stomach, I thought I was going to be sick.

My hands were shaking, the blood veins in my head had started to draw tight with hangover, and my eyes ached when I looked through the window into the bright light and the dew shimmering on the hay bales.

I tried to light the kindling in the wood stove to make coffee, but the paper matches flared against my thumbnail, and as I stared at the split chunks of white wood, the whole task suddenly seemed enormous. I took a beer out of the icebox and sat on the edge of the bed while I drank it. The sickening taste of the whiskey began to dissipate, and I felt the quivering wire in the middle of my breast start to dull and quieten. I finished the beer and had another, and by the bottom of the second can that handkerchief of flame in the parking lot became removed enough to think about. Then I saw Buddy leaning against the doorjamb, naked to the waist, his blue jeans low on his flat stomach, grinning at me.

'Are you getting in or getting up, Zeno? Either way, you look like shit,' he said.

'What's up?' I said. My voice sounded strange, distant and apart from me, a piece of color in the ears.

'Did you get bred last night?'

'Get me a can out of the icebox.'

'Man, I can hear those hyenas beating on their cages in your head.'

'Just get the goddamn beer, Buddy.'

'My car ain't in the pound, is it?'

I hadn't thought yet about the car or what

condition it might be in. My last memory of the Plymouth was winding it up out of Lolo after some drunk discussion in a bar about steelhead fishing over in Idaho. Then I remembered the tack-hammer rattle out of the crankcase that meant a burnt bearing and maybe a flattened crankshaft.

I heard Buddy click off the cap from a bottle of beer and the foam drip flatly on the floor. He pushed the bottle inside my hand.

'What did you get into last night?' he said.

He struck a match on the stove. Then I smelled the flame touch the reefer.

'It's a real bag of shit, man.'

He pulled a chair out from the table and sat down, his eyes focused and serious over the joint in his mouth.

'Like what?'

'I really went over the edge and hung one out.'

'What did you do?'

'I took your Springfield and shot the hell out of the parking lot in that pulp mill.'

'Oh man.'

I couldn't look at him. I felt miserable, and the absurdity of what I had done ached inside my hangover like an unacceptable dream.

'How bad?'

'I left about three trucks burning and probably blew the engine blocks out of a half-dozen others.'

'Wow. You don't fool around, do you?'

It was silent for a moment, and I heard him take a long inhale on the reefer and let it out of his lungs slowly.

'Iry, what's in your head? They're going to pour your ass in Deer Lodge.'

'I got out of it. There was a dick at the log bridge but he must have thought the damage was done inside the lot.'

'Forget that. You were in the sheriff's office yesterday, and maybe these cowboys ain't too bright, but they're going to put the dice together and waltz you right into the bag. And believe me, buddy, they hand out time here to outsiders like there's no calendar.'

He set the reefer on the edge of the table and walked back to the bedroom.

'What are you doing?' I said.

He unlocked the bolt of the Springfield, and an unfired cartridge sprang from the magazine.

'Really cool, man. What do you think I'm going to do?'

He walked out the screen door, and then I heard a shovel crunching in the earth behind the cabin. I wanted to argue with him about his rifle, but I knew he was right. I wet a towel under the pump and held it to my face and neck. I couldn't stop sweating. Buddy dropped the shovel on the porch and came back through the door with grains of dirt in the perspiration on his arms. He was grinning again, with that crazy light in his eyes that used to get him into isolation at Angola.

'You're sure a dumb son of a bitch,' he said.

'That's the smartest thing you've said since I got out here.'

'But we're in a real hardball game now, partner.'

Fifteen minutes later we heard a car rumble over the cattle guard. Buddy looked through the window, then back at me.

'That's your taxi, Zeno,' he said. 'Don't say anything. Little Orphan Annie with empty circles for eyes. You were juicing in the saloon at Lolo, and you were too drunk even to drive into Missoula.'

'Get rid of the roach.'

He went to the sink and peeled the reefer, then pumped water over it.

'This is a crock, ain't it?' he said.

'Give me all the cigarettes you have.'

'Look at that pair of geeks. They love making a bust on the old man's place.'

He handed me two packs of Lucky Strikes and a paper book of matches.

'I ain't got the bread for a bondsman, so you're going to have to sit it out, Zeno,' he said.

'I should have a check by tomorrow or the next day. Bring it down to the jail and I'll endorse it.'

The deputy didn't knock. He opened the screen door and pointed one thick finger at me.

'All right, Paret. Move it up against the car,' he said.

He held the screen open while I walked past him to the automobile. The other deputy leaned against the fender with his palm resting on the butt of his .357. Both of them were over six feet, and their wide shoulders were stiff and angular against their starched shirts.

'Lean on it,' the first deputy said.

I spread my legs and propped my hands against

the roof of the automobile while his hands moved inside my thighs, then dug inside my pockets and turned them inside out. He pulled my arms behind me and snipped on the handcuffs, and the other deputy held open the door into the wire-mesh segregated backseat.

'Are you going to give us any trouble on the way back, or do you want me to sit with you?' the first deputy said.

I didn't answer, and he locked both back doors from the outside. As the car rolled along the rutted lane, I leaned back against the handcuffs and felt the metal bite into the skin. I tried to raise myself forward to keep the pressure off my wrists, but each chuckhole in the road sent me back into the seat and another dig into my skin. The mountains had taken on a deeper blue and green from the rains, and the boulders in the creeks under the bridges were wet and shining and steaming in the sunlight at the same time. But at that moment, in my comical effort to sit rigid in the back of a sheriff's car, I remembered a Negro kid at Angola who was handcuffed and taken down to the hole and beaten with a garden hose for stealing a peanut-butter sandwich. He spit on a hack, and so they sweated him five more days and took away his good time.

At that time, what bothered me was meeting him out on the yard after he got out of lockdown. There were still blue gashes on the insides of his lips, and while he smoked a cigarette, he told me he didn't mind pulling the extra three years because he knew that eventually he would fall again anyway.

# chapter seven

The holding cell was dull yellow with a crisscrossed door of flat iron strips that were coated with thick white paint. Names had been burned on the walls and ceiling with cigarette lighters, and there was a small, round drain in the center of the floor to urinate in. I sat on the concrete against the wall and smoked cigarettes and listened in my preoccupation with my own troubles to all the jailhouse complaints, stories of bum arrests, wives who should have had their teeth kicked in, and advice about how to deal with each screw on the day and night shifts. The area around the drain was covered with wet cigarette butts and reeked with a stench that made your eyes water when you had to stand over it. Two Flathead Indians were still drunk and waiting for the reservation police to pick them up; a check-writer who was already wanted in Idaho kept calling the sergeant back to the cell to ask about his wife, who was in the lock upstairs; a deranged old man, whose toothless gums were purple with snuff, sat by the drain, hawking and spitting through his knees; and then the one dangerous man, a twenty-five-year-old tar roofer, with square callused hands that had no fingernails and were dark with cinders, leaned against the wall on a flexed arm waiting for his wife to bring the bondsman down to the jail.

He asked me for a cigarette; then he wanted to know if I had ever pulled time. He paused a minute, lighting the cigarette with his thick, dark fingers, then asked what for.

After I told him, his muddy eyes looked at me for a moment, then stared off into the smoke. He sat down beside me and pulled his knees up before him. His white athletic socks were grimed with dirt. I said nothing to him, made no inquiry about his crime, and I could feel the sense of insult start to rise in him.

'What they got you for, podna?' I said.

'This guy give me some shit at Stockman's last night. Like he was going to whip my ass with a pool cue. I put him once through the bathroom door. Then he learned what real shit smells like. And he ain't going to press no charges, either, believe me.'

An hour later his wife, a vacuous and pathetic-looking blond girl in a waitress's uniform, was at the jail with the bondsman. As I watched them through the grated door, holding hands in front of the property desk, I could see the humiliation in her face and the fear of another night and all the others to follow. They would pay out their lives in installments to bondsmen, guilty courts, finance companies, and collection agencies.

At seven that evening a deputy sheriff stood in front of the door with a pair of handcuffs hung over his index finger and waited for the sergeant to turn the lock.

'Get rid of the cigarette and put them behind you,' he said.

I flicked the butt toward the drain and waited for him to snip the cuffs around my wrists. He ran his hands under my armpits and down both sides of my trousers, then caught me under the arm with his hand. The cell door clanged behind us, and we walked down a corridor with spittoons on the floor toward the back of the building. Our shoes sucked against the damp mopping on the wooden floor, and a frosted yellow square of light shone from an office by the exit sign.

'Before we go in, tell me what the hell you thought you were going to get out of it,' he said.

'What?'

'Your parole officer said you were straight and probably wouldn't do time again. You must have had some real ingrown hairs in your asshole, buddy.'

Inside the office the deputy took off the cuffs, and I sat down in a wood chair in front of the sheriff's desk. The room was poorly lighted and smelled of cigars, and the desk lamp shone upward into the red corpulence of the sheriff's round face. There was a tangle of grey hair above the V of his shirt, and the roll of fat on his stomach hung heavily on his gun belt. The red stone on his Mason's ring glinted when he moved the wet stub of his cigar in the ashtray.

'It looks like you can't stay out of a sheriff's office,' he said. 'Yesterday you tried to file a complaint down in Ravalli County, and today I get to meet you after you did some target practice at the mill.'

I looked him back in the eyes, but because of the lamp's glare, I couldn't tell yet how hard he was ready to turn it on. He took a sandwich out of his drawer and unfolded the wax paper.

'Go down to the cooler for me, John,' he said.

While the deputy was gone, he ate the sandwich and didn't speak, and I thought, Watch out for this one. The deputy returned with a beaded can of beer and set it on the blotter. The sheriff sucked out half of it with one quick upward turn of the hand, the sandwich bread thick and white in his mouth.

'Now,' he said, 'this shouldn't take either one of us long. You know all the rules, so we don't have to explain a lot of things. We'll take a statement from you, you can look over it and add or change anything, and I'll get you into court within a week and then off to Deer Lodge.'

'I don't even know what you're charging me with, Sheriff.'

'Son, you weren't listening too good. I don't have time for a game. I can charge you with any one or all of a half-dozen things. I guess about the worst one down on your sheet might be arson.'

'I don't know what we're talking about.' Our eyes locked together and held until he picked up his cigar.

'I see,' he said, and turned his swivel chair partly into the shadow, obscuring his face. 'Well, tell us what you were up to last night.'

'I was boozing in a couple of beer joints in Lolo and another place just south of Missoula.'

'Did you meet any interesting people who might remember you?'

'Ask them. I don't remember. I was drunk.'

'Maybe you had a little trouble with a cowboy or knocked over some chairs.'

'Don't recall a thing.'

He turned his big, oval face abruptly back into the light.

'You're lying, son. Yesterday you were out at the mill raising hell about your pickup and your guitars, and last night you had Buddy Riordan's Plymouth up on that mountain, and you drilled holes in those trucks like an infantry marksman. Some of my men ain't the brightest in the world, or you wouldn't have gotten back across that bridge. But the deputy made you, and that's going to get you at least a two-spot. Now, if you want to piss around with us, we'll see how much time we can add on to it.'

My con's antennae quivered for the first time with a sense of hope. His eyes stared confidently into mine, but he had come on too strong and too soon. Also, I hadn't been booked yet, and I realized that I might still have another season to run.

'I was at the mill yesterday afternoon, and I was driving Buddy's car last night, but I don't know a thing about your deputy or a bridge.'

'Why don't you use your head a minute? You're still a young man. You can be out with good time in nine months, and maybe Louisiana will waive on you if you get a strong recommendation from here.'

'Number one, I'm not going to take the fall for some local crap with that toilet-paper factory. Number two, you know the parole authority doesn't work that way, Sheriff. They'll send me straight back to the joint.'

He looked at me steadily and held the flattened wet end of his cigar to his mouth. Then his gaze broke and he finished the rest of his beer.

'I don't know what to tell you, then, son. It looks like you have things pretty well figured out for yourself.'

Without thinking, I put my fingers in my shirt pocket for a cigarette. The deputy behind me put his hand on my arm.

'That's all right, John,' the sheriff said. 'Tell me, what's your connection with Frank Riordan?'

'I did time with his boy.'

'That's right. Buddy was in the Louisiana pen, wasn't he?' He lit his cigar again, and the red stone on his ring glowed with fire. 'Tell me another thing, since you got it all tucked in your watch pocket. How far away from this jail do you think your life's going to be?'

I kept my face expressionless and looked at his massive weight leaning into the desk.

'I mean, do you believe you're just going to walk out of it? That you can come into this county as a parolee and destroy fifteen thousand dollars' worth of machinery and go back to your guitar?'

'You don't have anything, Sheriff.'

'Before you go back to the tank, let me give you something to roll around. How do you think you

**160**

got five the first time? And believe me, son, you're just about to become a two-time loser.'

The deputy walked me in the handcuffs back to the front of the building, then pointed me toward a spiral metal stairs.

'My coat's in the holding cell,' I said.

'You'll get it later.'

'Do I get booked?'

'Don't worry about it.'

He locked me in a four-man cell upstairs with a wire-mesh and barred window that looked out on a brick alley. I could hear heat thunder and dry lightning out in the mountains, and momentarily the alley walls would flicker with a white light. There was a rolled tick mattress and a blanket on one empty iron bunk, and I sat down and rested the weight of my cast on my thigh and began to take off my shoes with one hand. Then a large black head, glistening like shoe polish in the gloom, leaned over the bunk above me, and before I could even look into the wine-red eyes, the odor of muscatel and snuff and jailhouse funk washed over me.

'Hey, blood,' the man said, 'do you got a cigarette for a brother? I been up here a whole day with this white whale that's got money stuck up his ass but won't give the screw two bits for some cigarettes.'

I handed up the pack, but the Negro dropped off the bunk with one arm, and then I saw the black, puckered stump on his other shoulder. He picked a cigarette out with his fingernails and pulled down his white boxer undershorts and squatted on the seatless toilet. I unrolled the mattress and lay down

161

with my head pointed toward the door and the draft of the corridor, then looked across the cell at the white whale. He lay on his back with his trousers and shoes on, and his stomach rose up like a mountain under his dirty white shirt. The fat in his cheeks hung back against his bones, and his eyes stared like burnt glass into the bottom of the bunk overhead.

I heard the Negro cracking wind into the toilet, and I turned on my stomach and lit a cigarette.

'Now catch this,' the Negro said. 'They grabbed this cat on a morals charge. Eleven-year-old boy in a hotel room. The screw says all he's got to do is pick up the phone and he's out. But he just lays there and says "Jesus, forgive me."'

'You shut up,' the white man said quietly.

'He says that, too,' the Negro said. 'Every time I tell him to loosen up with some change. You ain't crazy, too, are you, brother?'

'I don't think so,' I said. Then I wondered, *Good Lord, am I?*

'He won't eat his food, and now they don't even bring him none.'

The cell was hot from the heat rising in the building, but I folded the blanket over my head and tried to close the sickening odors, the Negro, and the sad man out of my consciousness. The thunder echoed across the mountains like rows of distant cannon, and as I lay with my forehead damp against my wrist and the mothball smell of the blanket enveloping me, I slipped away through the concrete floor and the resonating clang of iron through jail

162

corridors, melting with the softness of a morphine dream into yesterday when I could still turn the dial a degree in either direction and reshape the day into sunlight on trout streams, blue shadows on the pines in the canyons, or just a glass of iced tea on a lazy porch.

I awoke sometime in the middle of the night to the rain falling on the windowsill. The drops sprayed inside on the concrete floor, and I could smell the cool wetness blowing through the air shaft. I felt a sick ache in my heart, and I lay on my back and smoked, waiting for it to pass, but it wouldn't. In the darkness I felt the beginnings of a new awareness about myself, one that I had always denied before. When I was in Angola, I never thought of myself as a real con, a professional loser who would always be up before some kind of authority. I was just a juke-joint country musician who had acted by chance or accident in a beer and marijuana fog without thinking. But I realized now that I killed that man because I *wanted* to. I had shot people in Korea, and when I put my hand in my pocket for the knife, I knew exactly what I was doing.

Now I had run right back to jail, just like every recidivist who is always sure he will stay on the street but works full time at falling again. And maybe you got your whole ticket punched this time, I thought. Yes, maybe this is the whole shot, and you never saw it during those two years you waited for that cosmic mistake in time and place to correct itself.

'Put the board up in the window, blood,' the Negro said.

I got off the bunk and picked up the piece of shaped plywood that fitted into the frame against the bars. The mist blew into my face, and I looked at the glistening brick of the alley wall and heard a train whistle blow in the distance.

'Come on, man. I feel like somebody pissed on my mattress,' the Negro said.

In the morning an Indian trusty and a deputy opened the cell and handed us two tin plates of cold scrambled eggs and bread and black coffee in paper cups.

'Is he going to eat today?' the Indian said.

The Negro touched the white whale on the knee. He lay in the bunk with his face toward the wall, and the black hair on his buttocks showed above his trousers.

'Better eat now. The man don't bring it back again till two o'clock,' the Negro said.

The whale didn't answer, and the Negro held his palm up in a gesture of failure in trying to reason with a lunatic.

'If you want any candy or cigarettes from the machine, give me the money and I'll bring it back to you this afternoon,' the Indian said.

I reached in my pocket and felt a wadded dollar bill with a quarter inside.

'Forget about him,' the deputy said, and locked the cell door.

'Hey, man, what these cats got down on you?' the Negro said.

'I don't know. I haven't been booked yet.'

'I mean, you got in the man's face last night or something?'

'I didn't read it like that. Maybe I did.'

'Let me have a smoke.'

There were two cigarettes left, and I gave him one and lit the other. He sat on the floor in his white undershorts, his knees splayed, and ate the eggs with one hand and held the cigarette in the back of his knuckles. His skin was absolutely black.

'I got a hundred and eighty to do,' he said. 'But I don't do nothing except wash cars. The judge says he'd send me to the joint, but you can't cowboy with one arm.'

He laughed, and the dried eggs fell from his bad teeth back into the plate. 'I'll tell you why they ain't put me in Deer Lodge, brother. Because they won't take no niggers up there. That's right. There ain't a colored man in that whole joint.'

I sat on my bunk and drank the coffee from the paper cup. It tasted like iodine.

'You a paperhanger?' he said.

'No.'

'I ax you this because, you see, this is my living place, and they bring in this white whale that moans at night and makes gas every fifteen minutes. I don't like jailing with no queer, either.'

'His family will come for him eventually,' I said.

'Which means me and you, brother.'

'OK, let me give it to you. Five in Louisiana for manslaughter. Maybe another jolt here for shooting up some people who leaned on me.'

He pressed the scrambled eggs into the spoon with his thumb and dropped them into his mouth, then took a puff off his cigarette and laughed again.

'What they putting you badasses in with me for?'

'I think the man wants to talk with me,' I said.

I heard the deputy's keys and leather soles in the corridor.

'They ain't bad guys,' the Negro said. 'Most of them work another job in town. Just don't stick your finger in the wrong place.'

The deputy who had brought breakfast with the Indian trusty turned the key and opened the cell door.

'Let's get it, Paret,' he said.

He didn't have the handcuffs out, nor did he catch me under the arm, which I waited automatically for him to do.

'Down the stairs,' he said.

'What's going on?'

'Just walk.'

We went down the spiral metal staircase to the first floor, and I had to squint at the sudden light off the yellow walls. I looked over at the door to the booking room, the box camera on its tripod, and the ink pad, rollers, and cleansing cream on the counter.

'Sign for your stuff at the property desk,' he said.

I turned and stared at him, but his attention was already locked on the holding cell, where a man in a suit was shaking the door against the jamb.

I walked to the property desk and gave my name. A woman in a brown uniform smiled pleasantly at me, pulled a manila envelope from a pigeonhole and placed it, my folded coat with one wet sleeve, and a release card in front of me. I slipped on my watch, put my billfold in my pocket, and in a signature I was back on the street, in the sunlight, into a cool morning with a hard blue sky and the brilliant whip of Indian summer in the air.

I didn't have enough money to ride the bus back to the ranch, and I didn't feel like hitchhiking, so I walked toward the Garden District by the university, where Buddy's wife lived. It didn't seem an unreasonable thing to do, and I didn't allow myself to think deeply on it, anyway. The air was so clear and bright from the rains and the touch of fall that I could see college kids hiking high up on the brown mountain behind the university and the line of green trees that began on the top slope. I crossed the bridge over the Clark and looked down at the deep pools where large rainbow hung behind the boulders, waiting for food to float downstream. The sidewalks in the Garden District were shaded by maple and elm trees, and overnight the leaves had started to turn red and gold.

Buddy's boys were playing catch in the front yard, burning each other out with the baseball. I started to walk up on the porch, and then I felt a sense of guilt and awkwardness at being there. I paused on the walk and felt even more stupid as the two boys looked at me.

'Did your old man ever show you how to throw an inshoot?' I said. 'It's the meanest pitch in baseball. It leaves them looking every time.'

I wet two of my fingers, held the ball over the

stitches, and whipped it out sidearm at the older boy's claw mitt. He leaped upward at it, but it sailed away into the trees.

'I've been having trouble with my arm since I threw against Marty Marion,' I said.

'That's all right. I'll get it,' the boy said, and raced across the lawn through the leaves.

You're really great with kids, Paret, I thought. I heard the screen door squeak on the spring.

'Come in,' Beth said. She wore white shorts and a denim shirt, and she had a blue bandana tied around her black hair.

'I was trying to get back to the ranch, and I thought Buddy might be around,' I said.

'I haven't seen him, but Mel ought to be by later. Come on in the kitchen.'

I followed her through the house, which was darkened and furnished with old stuffed chairs and a broken couch and mismatched things that were bought at intervals in a secondhand store. She pulled a pair of dripping blue jeans from the soapy water in the sink and then rubbed the knees against one another. Her thighs and stomach were tight against her white shorts and when she leaned over the sink, her breasts hung heavily against her denim shirt.

'What are you doing in town?' she said.

'I managed to get put in the bag yesterday.'

'What?'

'I just got out of the slam.'

'What for?' She turned around and looked at me.

'Some trucks were shot up down at that pulp mill.'

She went back to her washing in silence, then stopped and dried her hands on a towel.

'Do you want a beer?'

'All right.'

She took two bottles from the icebox and sat down at the unpainted wood table with me.

'Do they want Buddy?'

'They were just interested in me because I'd been out there about my pickup being burned.'

The younger boy came in perspiring and out of breath for a glass of water from the sink faucet. She waited until he finished and had slammed the screen behind him.

'Buddy can't go to jail again. Not here,' she said.

'It doesn't have anything to do with him.'

'There're many people here who would like to destroy Frank Riordan, and they'll take Buddy as a second choice. I had five years of explanation to his children about where he was, and we're not up to it again.'

I wanted to explain that he wasn't involved, that it was my own drunken barrel of snakes and southern barroom anger that had put me up on the mountain with a rifle. But I had stepped across a line with a heavy, dirty shoe into her and her children's lives, and I felt like an intrusive outsider who had just presented someone with a handful of spiders. I drank down the bottle and set it lightly on the tabletop.

'I guess I'd better catch air,' I said. 'I can probably hitch a ride pretty easy out by the highway.'

'Wait for Mel. He comes by after class for coffee.'

'Buddy's probably junking his Plymouth for bond, and I have to go by the hospital anyway.'

She got up from her chair and took another beer from the icebox. The V in the tail of her denim shirt exposed the white skin above her shorts. She clicked the cap off into a paper bag and put the bottle in front of me.

'Buddy says you could make it as a jazz musician if you wanted to. Why do you play in country bands?'

'Because I'm good at what I do, and I have the feeling for it.'

'Do you like the people you play for?' She said it in a soft voice, her eyes interested, and I wondered why Buddy had ever left her.

'I think I understand them.'

'The type of men who beat you up and burned your truck?'

'Not everybody in a beer joint is a gangster. We wouldn't have had that scene if Buddy –'

'I know. Buddy's favorite expression: "That's the way the toilet flushes sometimes, Zeno." He has a way of saying it when somebody is already thinking about killing him.'

'Well, it was something like that. But when you cruise into it with your signs on, somebody is going to try to cancel you out.'

'I read the story in the paper. Did you really do that much damage from across the river?' Her dark eyes were dancing into mine.

'What do you think, kiddo?'

'That you don't understand the sheriff you're dealing with or Frank Riordan either.'

'Ever since I came here, people have been telling me I don't understand something. Does that happen to everybody who wanders into Montana?'

'Pat Floyd might look like a fat Louisiana redneck behind his desk, but he's been sheriff for fifteen years, and he doesn't let people out of his jail for something like this unless he has a reason. I think you're going to find, also, that Buddy's father can be a strange man to deal with.' She went to the sink and pulled the rubber plug in the drain, then began squeezing water out of the jeans and T-shirts. 'Excuse me. Take another beer. I have to get this on the line before it rains again.'

I took a Grain Belt from the icebox and looked at the motion of her shoulders while she twisted the water out of her boys' clothes. I was never very good with women, possibly because I had always thought of them simply as women, but this one could reach out with an intelligent fingernail and tick the edge of your soul and walk away into a question mark.

I waited three minutes in the silence, drinking the beer and looking out through the screen at the green trees in the backyard.

'So why is Mr Riordan a strange man to deal with?' I said.

'He doesn't recognize anything outside of his idea of the world and the people who should live in it. He might be a good person, but he's always determined to do what he calls right, regardless of the cost to other people. You might not have thought about it yet, but to his mind you probably created something very large for him when you shot up those trucks.'

'I don't create anything for anybody. I've tried to announce in capital letters that somebody's fight with the pulp mill or the lumberjacks isn't part of my act. So far I've gotten my arm broken and lost my job just for being around. So I don't figure I owe anybody.'

'Why did you come here?'

'Sometimes you got to roll and stretch it out.'

'You should have stayed in Louisiana.'

'Do I get a bill for that?' I smiled at her, but her face stayed expressionless.

'If the pulp mill shuts down because of Frank Riordan, you won't want to see what the people in this town will be like.'

'I've met some of them.'

'No, you haven't. Not when they're out of work and there's no food in the house except what they get from the federal surplus center. There's nothing worse than a lumber town when the mill closes down.'

'Why don't you leave?' Then I felt stupid for my question.

'I could probably wait tables at the bus depot in Billings or a truck stop in Spokane. Do you recommend that as a large change?'

'I'm sorry. Too much beer in the morning.'

She dried her hands and pushed her hair back under her blue scarf.

'Tell me another thing,' she said. 'Do you believe Buddy is going to stay out of jail?'

'Sure.'

'You don't think that someday he'll go back to prison for one thing or another? For dope or a drunk accident or a bottle thrown across a bar or any of the things that he does regularly and casually dismisses?'

'Buddy's not a criminal. He fell in Louisiana because he was holding some weed at the wrong time. If he wasn't a Yankee and had had some money, he could have walked out of it.'

'That wasn't the first time he was in jail.'

'He told me about that.'

'What?' she said.

I felt uncomfortable again under her eyes, and I took a sip from the beer.

'He said you had him locked up once.'

'That's wonderful. He drove his car through the lawns all the way down the block and ran over the front steps, then stuck a matchstick in the horn. Every neighbor in the block called the police, and the next day we were evicted from the house. While he spent ninety days in jail, we lived in a trailer without heat in East Missoula.'

I heard the front screen slam back on the spring. Melvin walked through the hallway into the kitchen, chalk dust on the back of his brown suit coat, his face bright and handsome, and poured a cup of coffee off the stove. He began talking immediately. He didn't know it, but at that moment I would have enjoyed buying him a tall, cool drink.

He talked without stopping for almost fifteen minutes. Then he set down the empty coffeepot on the stove and said, 'You ready to roll, ace?'

'Yeah, let's get it,' I said.

'Jesus Christ, you blew the hell out of that place, didn't you?'

'No.'

'Well, all right. But I drove past the mill last night, and they were still scraping up a melted truck from the asphalt. Partner, that was a real job.'

'Let's hit it if you're going.'

We walked through the hallway to the front with Beth behind us. I paused at the screen door.

'I should have a check in the mail today if you and the kids would like to go on a barbecue or something,' I said. 'Maybe Melvin and his wife would like to come, and Buddy can take along his little brothers, and we'll find a lake someplace.'

She smiled at me, her blue-black hair soft on her forehead. Her dark eyes took on a deeper color in the sunlight through the trees.

'I used to make the second-best sauce piquante in southern Louisiana,' I said.

'Ask the others and give me a call,' she said.

I winked at her and walked across the shady lawn to the car.

Winking, I thought. Boy, are you a cool operator.

'You want to stop at Eddie's Club for a beer?' Melvin said.

'I'd like to get this jailhouse smell off me, and I'll buy you one this afternoon.'

We rolled across the bridge over the river, and I looked at the deep flashes of sunlight in the current.

'Did you use Buddy's Springfield?' he said.

'I was pretty drunk that night, and I don't remember much of anything.'

'OK. But you ought to throw it in the river.'

'That's a good idea,' I said.

The wind was blowing up the Bitterroot Valley, and the leaves of the cottonwoods trembled with silver in the bright air. I watched the fields of hay and cattle move by, and the log ranch houses chinked with mortar, and the drift of smoke from a small forest fire high on a blue mountain. The creek beds that crossed under the road were alive with hatching insects, and the pebbles along the sandy banks glistened wet and brown in the sun. Damn, Montana was a beautiful part of the country, I thought. It reached out with its enormous sky and mountains and blue-green land and hit you like a fist in the heart. You simply became lost in looking at it.

Buddy got up from his chair on the porch of the cabin and spread his arms in the air when he saw the automobile. Melvin let me down and drove up the rutted road toward the main house, and I saw Buddy flip away a hand-rolled cigarette into the wind. His shirttail was pulled out, and his stitched and bruised face was grinning like a scarecrow's as he walked disjointedly across the lawn.

'One night in the bag and Zeno has made the street,' he said. 'That's what I call accelerated.'

I could smell the marijuana on his clothes when I was five feet from him.

'I can see you've been sweating out your podna's poor ass being in jail.'

'I knew you were going to walk late last night. I did a ding-a-ring on the ring-a-ring after the old man said he would go a property bond. But they said there was no bail because Zeno hadn't been charged, and you would be sent home safely in the morning.'

'What time was this?'

'About midnight.'

'That's great, Buddy. So I spent the night with one of your local homosexuals and a one-armed Negro psychotic while everything was cool on the farm. I'm relieved as hell to know that I didn't have anything to worry about.'

'I couldn't get you out that late. They don't hire a night jailer, and I don't think they liked you down there too much anyway. Look, man, I got something for you inside. Also, you got to see the rainbow I took this morning.'

We walked up on the porch, and Buddy went through the screen door in front of me.

'I got it on credit, so don't worry about it. I got credit out my winky hole, and I just send them a hubcap from the Plymouth when they threaten to take my property.'

On my bunk was a new Gibson guitar with a Confederate flag wrapped around the sound box. The blond, waxed wood in the face and the dark, tapered neck and silver frets shone in the light through the window.

'They ain't got Dobros in Montana, and I couldn't find a Martin,' he said.

'Well, hell, man.'

'But this has got a lifetime guarantee, and the guy says he'll sell us a case for it at cost.'

'Well, you dumb bastard.'

He folded a torn match cover around a roach and lit it, already grinning into the smoke before he spoke.

'I tried to get you a Buck Owens instruction book but they didn't have it,' he said.

I sat down on the bed and clicked my thumbnail over the guitar strings. They reverberated and trembled in the deep echo from the box. I tried to make an awkward E chord, but I couldn't work my cast around the neck.

'Can you figure that scene down at the jail?' I said.

'You got me. I thought they had you nailed flat.'

'What do you know about the sheriff?'

'Look out for him. He's an old fox.'

'Yeah, Beth told me.' Then I regretted my words.

'What were you doing over there?' he said.

'I didn't have any bread to catch the bus, and I thought you might be around.'

He looked at me curiously. I took a flat pick out of my pocket and began tuning the first string on the guitar. The room was silent a moment.

Then he said, 'Take a look at the rainbow I got on a worm this morning,' and lifted a twenty-inch trout out of the sink by the gill. The iridescent band of blue and pink and sunlight was still bright along the sides. 'I had the drag screwed all the way down, and I still couldn't horse him out. I had to wade him up on a sandbar. If you can keep your ass out of jail today, we'll go out again this evening.'

'My check ought to be here today. What if I pick up the tab for a beerbust and a picnic this afternoon?'

'That sounds commendable, Zeno. But I already went to the mailbox, and your check ain't here. Also, before we slide into anything else, the old man wants to talk with you.'

He opened up the trout's stomach with a fish knife and scooped out the entrails with his hand.

'How involved is that going to be?' I said.

'It's just his way. He wants to talk a few minutes.'

'Say, I know I'm getting free rent here, and maybe becoming an instant sniper is pretty stupid, but like you said, it's my fall.'

'You are the most paranoid bastard I've ever met. Look, he was going to go a property bond for you. I mean put the whole place on the line. OK, big deal. But give him his innings. He's all right.'

This was the first time I had seen Buddy become defensive about his father.

'OK,' I said.

Buddy worked the iron pump over the trout and scraped out the blood from the ridge of bone on the inside with his thumbnail.

'All root, all reet,' he said, and lit the kindling in the stove. 'A few lemon rings and slices of onion, and we'll dine on the porch and do up some of this fine Mexican laughing grass.'

'Your father came to my room while we were in the hospital and said he tried to shoot someone once.'

'I'm surprised he would tell you about that.'

'He was pretty intent on making a point.'

'That's something he keeps filed away in a dark place. But by God, he tried to do it, all right. When I was a kid, we used to live over by Livingston, and every day I climbed over this guy's barbed wire to fish in his slough. I climbed over it enough until it was broken down on the ground, and thirty of his cows got out on the highway. The next morning he caught me at the slough with a horse quirt. It only took him about a dozen licks, but he cut through the seat of my overalls with it. I had blood in my shoes when I walked into the house, and that's the only time I've ever seen the old man look the way he did then.'

The trout broiled in the butter inside the pan, and Buddy squeezed a lemon along the delicate white-and-pink meat.

'So do I march up to talk with your father or wait around?' I said.

'No, you take a beer out of the icebox, and then we eat. If you want to boogie down the road then, and not blow five minutes with the old man, that's OK. We'll catch a couple of brews and worm fish along the river. Don't fret your bowels about it. Everything's cool.'

We ate out on the front porch, with the breeze blowing up through the pines from the river. It was almost cold in the shade of the porch, and Mr

Riordan's four Appaloosas and his one thorough-bred and Arabian stood like pieces of sunlit stone in the lot next to the barn. Beyond the house, the edges of the canyon and the cliffs were razor blue against the sky.

I was eating the last piece of trout with a slice of onion when I heard Mr Riordan step up on the side of the porch. He had slipped his overalls straps down over his shoulders so that they hung below his waist, and the red handkerchief tied around his neck was wet with perspiration. He reached into the bib of his overalls and took out a small cigar that was burned at the tip. Buddy's face became vacant while he cleaned off the tin plates.

'I guess you get pretty serious when you decide to do something,' he said.

He lit his cigar, and his grey eyes looked through the smoke and lighted match without blinking.

'I thought we had an understanding back there at the hospital,' he said.

'It wasn't something I planned. I just have a bad way of letting the burner get too hot until something starts to melt at the wrong moment.'

He took a piece of tobacco off his lip and made a sound in his throat. There were drops of perspiration in his eyebrows. Buddy took the plates inside, and I heard him work the iron pump in the sink.

'I guess I had you called wrong. I didn't have you figured for this,' he said.

I looked away from him, took a cigarette out of my pack, and thought, Jesus Christ, what is this?

'Then, I never figured that my own boy would spend five years in a penitentiary,' he said.

'Sometimes you can't call what people will do,' I said.

'Is that the kind of observation you make on human conduct after you're in jail?'

'I don't know if I learned it in jail or not, but my own feeling is that people will do what's inside them and there's not much way to change that.'

'That must be a strange philosophy to live with, especially if what you do ruins most of your life.'

'I thought I had my dues paid, Mr Riordan, and I was going to live cool for as long as I could after that. But maybe you have to keep paying dues all the way down the line and there's no such thing as living cool.'

'I won't try to argue with your experience and what you've shaped out of it. But the world isn't a jail. We just make our own sometimes. Does that make any sense to you?'

I drew in on my cigarette and looked off at the green-yellow haze on the meadow. The field hands were bucking bales on the back of a wagon, and the short pines at the base of the mountain were bent at the tops in the wind.

'I'm sorry I dragged some trouble on your place,' I said, 'and I appreciate your willingness to go bond for me. Otherwise, I'm not sure what to tell you. I'll probably be moving into town in a day or so.'

'I didn't ask you to do that. I just ask you to think a little bit about what I said.'

'You want a beer, Frank?' Buddy called from inside.

'Bring two out, son.' Then to me, 'You probably can't do much with that arm around the place, but I'll pay you to help me with the nutrias. I'm going to introduce them into a couple of beaver ponds up Lost Horse Creek this weekend.'

'You shouldn't ever let those things loose in Montana,' I said.

'I'm afraid you're more conservative than you think, Iry.'

My check from Ace was in the mail the next day, and I treated everyone to a beerbust and picnic at Flathead Lake. We loaded up in two cars, with children's heads sticking out the windows, goggle masks already strapped on their faces, and I bought two cases of Great Falls with cracked ice spread among the bottles and a wicker basket of sausage, cheese, smoked ham, and French bread. It was my first trip up to the Flathead country, and I realized that I hadn't yet seen the most beautiful part of Montana. We began to climb higher north of Missoula, the mountains blue on each side of us, the air thin and cool, and then we were rolling through the Salish Indian reservation, across the Jocko River that was now low and flowing a clear Jell-O green over the smooth bed of rocks with the short grass waving in the current along the banks. Buddy had the Plymouth screwed down to the floor, and he was drinking a beer with one hand, his shoulder against the door like a 1950s hood, and laughing into the wind and talking about the three-point-two weed that grows wild in Montana, while Beth kept one frightened eye on the speedometer and a nervous cigarette between her fingers.

'Look at those buffalo,' he said. 'You know those cats can run at forty-five miles an hour? A chain fence doesn't even slow them down. They got gristle and hair on their chests like armor plate. And they stay in rut like rabbits. So I asked this park ranger once why the government didn't just turn them out and let them reproduce all over the country. And he says, now dig this, man, just imagine some Nebraska wheat farmer going to bed dreaming of a thousand acres of cereal out there, and then he hears this long rumble and looks out the window in the morning and there's nothing but torn ground and thousands of buffalo turds.'

When we stopped for gas, Beth asked me to drive, and Buddy sat against the passenger's door and lit a reefer. The Mission Mountains were the most beautiful range I had ever seen. They were jagged and snow-covered against the sky, with long, white waterfalls running from under the snowpack, and Kicking Horse Lake lay at the bottom like a great blue teardrop. My head was reeling with the thin air and the two beers that I had drunk, the wind and the shouts of the children in the backseat, and I felt Beth's thigh against mine and I wondered if a person could ever hold on permanently to an experience like this.

I slowed the car as we neared Polson, and then I saw Flathead Lake, with the cherry trees along the shores, the huge expanse of blue water, the ring of mountains around it, the cliffs of stone that rose from the middle of its brilliant, quiet surface. It looked like the Pacific Ocean; it was so large that you simply lost conception of your geographical place. Boats with red sails tacked in the thin breeze, their bows white and glistening with sunlight, and the sandy stretches of beach were shaded by pine trees. We drove along the shore toward Big Fork, the water winking through the trees, and I watched the cherry pickers on their stepladders lean heavily into the leaves, their hands working methodically, while the cherries rained like blood drops into their baskets.

It was a wonderful day. We ate poor-boy sandwiches on the beach, drank beer in the sun until our eyes became weak in the glare, then dove into the water and swam out breathlessly into the cold. I rented a small outboard, and we took turns taking the kids out to an island that was covered with Indian cuttings in the rock. Then Melvin bought some large cutthroat trout from a fisherman, and we barbecued them inside foil with tomato sauce. We were all tired and happy when we drove back toward Missoula. Before we got to town, Buddy went to sleep in the backseat with the children, and Beth laid her head against my shoulder and put her hand on my knee. I couldn't tell if it was deliberate or if she was just in that type of dreamy exhaustion that gives women an aura in their sleep. But it made me ache a little, that and the absence of a wife and family at age thirty-one and the probability that I would never have either one.

The next week went by, and each morning I could see the Indian summer steal more heavily across the mountains. The trees were turning more rapidly, flashes of red and yellow among the leaves where there had been none yesterday, and the sky became a harder blue, and there was more pine smoke from the chimneys in the false dawn before the sun broke across the top of the Bitterroots. I helped Mr Riordan introduce his nutrias into Lost Horse Creek and worked a couple of afternoons in the aviary, but I spent most of each day sitting on the front porch, either drinking beer and playing the Gibson with an open tuning (which can be done with one hand if you use a bottle neck along the frets as you would use a bar on a steel or a Dobro) or trying to forget the awful itch and stench of medicine and sweat inside my cast. On some days when I drank too much beer and fell into an afternoon delirium on top of my bed, I imagined that white ants that had never seen light were eating their way into my blood veins.

But altogether I felt quiet inside, and I had a strange notion that if I stayed in one place for a while and didn't do anything extravagant, my scene at the pulp mill would disappear, and my personal war with the locals would be filed away in a can somewhere.

I was cleaning some brook trout in a pan of water on the porch when I saw the sheriff's car turn through the cattle guard and roll along the road in a cloud of dust. I put my hands in the red water and wiped them on my blue jeans and lit a cigarette before he stopped in front of the cabin. He saw that I wasn't going to get up from the porch, so he turned his wheel toward the steps and drove to within four feet parallel of me. There was a bead in his corpulent face, and his arm on the window looked like a fat bread roll. He took his cigar out of the ashtray, puffed on its splayed end, with the red stone of his Mason's ring glinting in the sunlight, and then opened the door part way to release his weight from under the steering wheel.

'You should have been a little more careful, son,' he said.

'How's that, Sheriff?'

'I told you that some of my men are a little dumb and it takes us a while to get there. It took me a while to figure out where you were shooting from, too. You picked them all up from that clip except this one. It was under the pine needles right beside the tree you sat against.'

He held up a small plastic bag, wrapped at the top with a rubber band. Inside was a spent brass cartridge.

'I understand that a print will burn right into a shell after it's fired,' he said. 'You can't scrub it off with sandpaper.'

'I couldn't tell you.'

'Well, you hang around here. I'll let you know what I find after I take it over to the FBI man in Helena.'

# chapter eight

I couldn't sleep that night. I smoked cigarettes in bed, then went out on the porch with a half glass of Four Roses, sat in the chill, and watched a herd of deer graze their way across the meadow toward the canyon. They were sculptured in the moonlight and the wet grass, and when an automobile passed out on the highway, I could see a brown glass eye flash at me from the darkness. Through the pines the wide expanse of the Bitterroot River was dripping with a blue shimmer. I drank the whiskey and tried to keep the shell casing in the plastic bag out of my mind, but I couldn't. I was angry at my carelessness, my failure to count the hulls as they had ejected from the chamber, and the fact that an inconsequential thing, a spent cartridge, could put me back in prison for years.

I don't know when I fell asleep in the chair, but I smelled the smoke just before the false dawn. In my whiskey dream I thought it was pine wood burning from a chimney, but then I heard the horses whinnying and rearing and crashing inside the stalls. The flames were already up one side of the barn, the sparks whipping across the shingled roof, and the loft was framed in a bright square of yellow light from inside. On the dirt road I heard a truck clank hard into gear and thunder across the cattle guard. I ran barefoot into the cabin and shook Buddy by the shoulders in bed.

'What the hell's going on, man?'

'Your barn's on fire.'

We started running across the field just as a single flame cut through the roof and caught the air and sucked a large hole downward in a shower of sparks. Lights were going on all over the main house, and I saw Mr Riordan run off the front porch without a shirt on. The hay bales that had been stacked against one wall of the barn were turning into boxes of flame, and the aviary was filled with flickering yellow light and shadows and the wild beating of birds' wings in the cages.

'The horses,' Mr Riordan shouted.

Their screams were terrible. I could hear their hooves slashing into the wood, and even in the smoke and the heated absence of air I could smell the singed hair.

The rope pulley on the loft caught fire from the heat alone and burned away like a solitary thread of flame. Buddy's three younger brothers ran into the lot behind their father in their pajamas, their eyes wide with fear and uncertainty, the skin of their faces red with the glowing heat.

'Soak blankets and bring them running, boys,' Mr Riordan said, then started through the barn door.

'Get out of there, Frank,' Buddy yelled.

The cinders and ash fell across Mr Riordan's bare shoulders and back as he walked toward the stalls with his forearm held across his eyes.

'That crazy old son of a bitch,' Buddy said.

I don't know why – maybe because I didn't think about it – but I went in behind him. The heat was like the inside of a furnace. The loft door was dripping fire through the cracks, and all the tack was popping in black leathery blisters. The air was so hot it scalded my lungs, and before I had gone five feet, I could feel the smoke getting to my brain. Mr Riordan had opened two of the stalls of the Appaloosas, and one bolted through the door to the outside, but the other had pitched his forelegs over the stall wall and was rearing and cutting his head against an upright post.

'Let him go. You won't get him out,' I said.

'The Arabian,' he said.

The stall was at the back of the barn, which hadn't yet caught fire but was smoking at every joint and crack and seam. The Arabian had kicked half the stall down, and one of his shoes hung twisted off a broken hoof. His eyes stuck out with fright, and he had used his nose to try to break the latch on his door. I threw the bolt and he started out toward the main door, then reared and crashed sideways into a row of stalls that were etched with fire. He rose on his knees, with sparks in his mane and tail, and pawed at the flames that had already consumed the first Appaloosa's stall. The front of the barn was starting to sink, and burning shingles were raining across the doorway, and the smoke was now so thick that I could no longer see Mr Riordan or the other horses. I worked my shirt off my shoulders with one hand and waited for the Arabian to back away from the flames and turn in another circle. Then I hit him running and jumped with my stomach across his back and pulled both knees high up into his shoulders. He kicked backward into a post and some tack and I hit him behind the ear with my cast and got my shirt around his eyes. Then I gave it to him with both heels close under the flanks and bent low on his neck with the shirt pulled tight in both hands, and we bolted through the flames and exploding bales of green hay into the sudden coolness of the blue dawn outside.

His head went up when he smelled the air and the river, and he cut sideways and threw me on my back in the middle of the lot. Then I saw Mr Riordan come out of the huge collapsing square of fire with a soaked blanket wrapped around the thoroughbred's nose and eyes and a trouser belt pulled tight around his neck.

The boards in the walls snapped and curled as the wind blew the flames up through the roof and burst the remaining support timbers apart in arching cascades of sparks. The dark pines at the base of the canyon behind the house wavered in the light from the fire, and the birds in the aviary stood out in the reflection like ugly phoenixes with their wings extended. There were red welts all over my feet, and I could feel small holes on my shoulders like deep cigarette burns. The gauze bandages around my back were black and smelled of the boiled ointment inside, and when I pushed my hand through my hair, it felt as stiff and sharp as wire.

'Hey, man, are you all right?' Buddy said. He stood above me, looking down out of the dawn. Then his father and three brothers were beside him.

'Hey, Iry,' he said. He was kneeling beside me, and he rubbed his hand back and forth over my hair. 'Hey, get out of it, man. We got them all out except one.'

Then Mr Riordan's face was close into mine. He was squatted on his haunches with his hand around my arm. The matted grey hair on his shoulders was burned down to the skin like pig bristles. There was a long red burn along his cheek and through part of his lip that was already swelling into water.

'Let's go up to the house, son,' he said.

'Where in the hell are your neighbors?' I said.

'They'll be here. It just takes them a while.'

A half hour later the volunteer fire truck from Stevensville came up the front lane, followed by two pickup trucks from neighboring ranches. The early sun had climbed above the lip of the mountains, and there were long, cool shadows across the porch, where we sat and watched the firemen spray the burnt timbers and piles of ash. I wore one of Mr Riordan's soft wool shirts over the butter that his wife had spread on my shoulders.

'How fast do these guys get out here when your house is burning down?' I said.

'It ain't what you're thinking,' Buddy said. 'They have to come twenty miles, and before they can do anything else, they have to drag people out of bed all over the valley. They don't like us, but they won't turn away from you in an emergency.'

'Somehow you don't convince me, Zeno.'

'You don't understand Montana people. They'll hate your ass and treat you like sheep dip, but they come through when you're in trouble. Wait and see what happens if you bust an axle back on a log road or get lost deer hunting.'

I lit a cigarette and poured another cup of coffee from the pot Mrs Riordan had brought out on the porch. The tops of my bare feet looked like they had been boiled in water.

'I don't know if you want to see this, Frank, but you better look at it,' one of the firemen said. He had a scorched gasoline can impaled on the end of his fire ax. 'It was against the south wall, and there's a long burn back through the grass where somebody strung out the gasoline.'

'Just put it there,' Mr Riordan said.

The fireman shook the can off the hook and looked away at the smoking timbers. Water dripped off his yellow slicker, and his face was powdered with ash.

'How many did you lose in there?' he said, squinting his eyes without looking back at us.

'One Appaloosa.'

'I'm sorry about this, Frank. You know it just takes a few sons of bitches to make you think that everybody is one.'

'Tell the others to come on up for coffee,' Mr Riordan said. 'Joe, go into the cabinet for me.'

Buddy's little brother went into the house and

came back with a quart of Jack Daniel's while Mrs Riordan poured out cups of coffee with both hands from a huge pot. The firemen and the neighbors in the pickup trucks sat on the steps and the porch railing, mixing whiskey in their cups and smoking hand-rolled cigarettes. Their politeness and quiet manner and the cool blue morning reminded me of scenes in Louisiana on our back porch before we went hunting in the fall, but there was an unrelieved tension here in the averted eyes, the concentration on rolling a cigarette, or the casual sip of whiskey from the bottom of a cup.

The bottle went around a second time, and Mrs Riordan brought out a tray of biscuits that she had heated from the night before.

'When the hell are you going to lay off it, Frank?' It was one of the neighbors, a big man in a blue-jean jacket with patched corduroy pants pulled over his long underwear, and work boots that laced halfway up his thick calves. He didn't look at Mr Riordan, but took a bite off a plug of Brown Mule and worked it against his cheekbone.

'When I close it down, just like we all should have done when they first came in here,' Mr Riordan said.

'I'll be go-to-hell if I should have done any such thing,' the neighbor said. He spit off the porch and put the tobacco plug in his jacket. 'What they do up in Missoula ain't my business. Maybe it smells like a hog farm, but we ain't breathing it and that's them people's jobs up there. If they want to shut it down, let them do it.'

'Do you remember what Missoula was like when you could drive down the Clark without that smoke plume hanging over the water?' Mr Riordan said. 'Do you ever fish that stretch of river today? What are you going to do when you have something like it right here in the Bitterroot?'

'Nobody's going to argue that with you, Frank,' the fireman said. 'But, damn, those people can't go anywhere else for work. Anaconda ain't going to hire them, and that don't even count the gyppos that are going to be losing their tractors and everything else.'

'All they have to do is put in a purification system,' Mr Riordan said. 'Don't you realize that they didn't come here as a favor to us? They're here for profit and they destroy the air and make you like them for it.'

It was silent a moment; then one of the firemen set his cup in the saucer, nodded, and walked back to the truck. The other men smoked their cigarettes, deliberately looking out across the fields and up the canyon, where the sun was now breaking against the cliff walls and tops of the pines. Then one by one they casually stripped their cigarettes along the seam and let the tobacco blow away dryly in the breeze, or placed their cups and saucers quietly on the steps, and walked back across the lawn, pulling their gloves from their back pockets and slapping them across their palms, yawning and arching their backs as though they were thinking profoundly of the day's work ahead of them.

'I'm going to report this to the sheriff's office as

arson,' the fireman who had found the gasoline can said. 'That won't put anybody in jail, but he can scare two or three sons of bitches out of trying to come back here again.'

'They won't be back.'

'Frank, this is a hell of a thing, and I want you to know what I think.'

'Okay, Bob.'

The fireman got up in the seat of the volunteer truck and drove down the lane toward the cattle guard with the other firemen sitting against the coiled hoses in a lazy euphoria of sunlight and early-morning whiskey.

'You want another drink, Iry?' Mr Riordan said.

'Sure.'

Then we went inside and had a breakfast of pork chops and eggs. They were a tough family. There was no mention of the fire at the table, though I knew the image of the burned Appaloosa under the collapsed roof was like a piece of metal behind Mr Riordan's brow. Buddy ate his breakfast quietly and left the table first. Through the window I saw him pick up the bottle from the porch and walk back toward the cabin.

When I got back to the cabin, he was sitting at the kitchen table with a tin cup of whiskey and water in his hand. The bottle was almost down to the bottom.

'Pour a shot,' he said.

'I hate to get drunk before nine in the morning.'

'You were belting it pretty heavy on the porch.'

'I don't get fried every day of the week.'

He drank down the cup and picked up a cigarette butt from the ashtray. I threw my pack of Lucky Strikes on the table, but he ignored the gesture and puffed on a match held close to his lips.

'How'd you know the barn was on fire?' he said.

'I couldn't sleep last night. That fat cop put my *cojones* in a skillet when he showed me that spent cartridge.'

'Don't worry about it. He's just sweating you.'

'You got it figured out, do you?'

'What do you think? If he had you nailed, he would have busted you right there. He could have gotten that shell anywhere.'

'I wish I could be that damn sure, considering it's my ass that's on the line.'

'You talk like a fish. Use your gourd a minute. He wants you to jump your parole.'

There was a touch of irritation and meanness in Buddy's voice that I didn't like.

'Maybe I didn't read him right, then,' I said.

'Besides, even if he picked that shell up, he still don't have crap. You could have been target shooting up there two weeks ago. So forget it.' Buddy poured the rest of the bottle into the tin cup.

I sat on the edge of my bunk and rubbed Vaseline over the tops of my blistered feet, then put on a pair of white socks with my loafers.

'What did the old man talk about after I left?' Buddy said.

'Nothing, except finishing the fence line down by the slough.'

196

'That's all. Nothing about the weather or the goddamn cows or cleaning out the birdcages?'

'He didn't say anything.'

'You all just sat in silence and chewed on your porkchop bones.'

'I don't know what you're pushing at, Buddy.'

'Not a thing, Zeno. Open a beer. Let's get high.'

'I told you I've had it.'

'You look great.' He went to the icebox and came back with an opened can.

'I have to go to the hospital this morning to get my arm checked,' I said.

'That's cool, because you can drive me somewhere else afterwards.'

I sipped off the beer and looked at him. His eyes were red, and he rubbed the nicotine-stained ends of his fingers together. I knew Buddy too well to intrude on whatever strange things were beating inside his crazy head, but something bad was loose and it was ugly as well.

'What do you have to do at the hospital?' he asked.

'I want to find out when I can get this cast off so I can start playing again. I feel like worms are crawling inside the plaster.'

He wasn't listening to me. He knocked the chair over in getting up from the table and went in the back room to change clothes. He came back out dressed in a pair of sharkskin slacks, a blue sports shirt, half-topped boots, and a grey windbreaker. He pumped some water in the sink and washed his face and combed his hair back in ducktails on the sides.

'What are we doing?' I said.

'Getting your arm back into gear, Zeno. Don't worry about it.' He opened the icebox and took out a saucer that had the torn corner of an ink blotter on it.

'Hey, man, let that stuff slide today,' I said.

'There's enough for two. You ought to get up after charging the flames and doing that Korean War–Bronze Star scene.'

'Come on, Buddy.'

He put the blotter in his mouth and bit down easily on it.

'I was talking with this guy in Missoula who's been sending acid into Deer Lodge under postage stamps,' he said. 'All a guy has to do is take one lick and he's flying for the rest of the day.'

We drove through the Bitterroot toward Missoula, and Buddy was snapping to the music on the radio and lighting one cigarette off another while he kept a can of beer between his thighs. I couldn't tell exactly when the acid took him, because he already had enough whiskey in his system to make him irrational and feverish in the eyes. But by the time we reached Lolo he was talking incoherently and punching me on the shoulder with two fingers to illustrate something and each time he touched me a ripple of pain danced across my blistered skin. I shouldn't have left the cabin with him. I looked up the highway that led off the junction at Lolo over the pass into Idaho and thought of driving up somewhere high in the lodgepole pines to let him get his head straight again, but he read me.

'Keep it straight into Missoula, Zeno. We want to get your arm flattened out so you can get into the shitkicker scene again. Then we'll go over to Idaho later.'

I went on through the light at the junction and took the can of beer from between his legs.

'That's what you don't understand about acid, Iry,' he said. 'You can look into people's thoughts with it. Right on down into their ovaries.'

I parked the car in the shade of some elm trees by Saint Patrick's Hospital and left Buddy outside. As I walked up toward the entrance in the bright fall air and spangle of sunshine, I turned around and saw Buddy's half-topped boots resting casually over the edge of the driver's window. The Irish nun who had been a friend to me before changed the dressings on my back with her cool fingers and then took me over to the X-ray room, where I was told that the crack in my arm had knitted well and I probably could have the cast sawed off in another week.

When I got back to the car, Buddy was sitting behind the wheel, drinking a hot beer and listening to a hillbilly radio station. His eyes were swimming with color.

'The heat came around and told me to get my feet out of the window,' he said. 'They said it don't look good around the hospital.'

'Let's go to the Oxford. I'll buy you a steak,' I said.

'They must have told you something good in there.'

'I get my cast off next week.'

He slipped across the seat when I opened the car door. I pulled out on the street and started to drive toward the Oxford. We crossed the bridge over the Clark Fork, and I looked away at the wide curve of green water and the white rocks engraved with the skeletons of dead insects along the banks. It was going to be a good day after all, with no thoughts of cops or parole violation or FBI fingerprint men in Helena. Buddy was probably right, I thought. The sheriff just wanted to spook me into jumping my parole so he could have me violated back to Angola, and if I kept my head on straight, I could probably walk out of the thing at the mill.

'Let's get the steak later,' Buddy said.

'I'm flush and I don't do this often,' I said. 'A couple of T-bones and then we'll have a few drinks with your photographer friend over at Eddie's.'

'Just head on down the highway and I'll give you the directions. You ain't seen Idaho yet.'

'Why don't we keep it solid today, Buddy, and just booze around a little bit this afternoon and fish the river tonight?'

'It's my car, ain't it? Head it down the road, and I'll tell you when to stop at this 1860 bar with bullet holes in the walls.'

'I don't think this is cool. The rods knock on the highway like somebody put glass in the crankcase.'

'Turn left at the light or let me drive.'

We drove west along the river through the high canyons toward the Idaho line. When we climbed a grade toward a long span of bridge and looked down, the river shone blue and full of light, and the moss waved on the smooth boulders below the current. Just before the state line there was an old bar set back from the road against the base of a mountain. The rambling back part of the building was half collapsed, the windows were boarded, and a section of tin roof was torn up from the cave. But the bar itself was made of mahogany and scarred in a half-dozen places by pistol balls, with a long brass rail and a huge, yellow-stained baroque mirror that covered the entire wall.

Buddy ordered two whiskey sours before I could stop him, then dropped a quarter into the jukebox, which was located right next to a table where three workingmen were playing cards. They were annoyed, and they looked at him briefly before they moved to a table in back.

'They built this place when the railroad came through,' Buddy said. 'The back of the building was all cribs. Up on the side of the mountain there's about twenty graves of men that were shot right here.'

One of the cardplayers got up and turned the jukebox down.

'Hey, Zeno, you're messing with my song,' Buddy called out.

I asked the bartender for two paper cups, poured our whiskey sours into them, and walked toward the door. Buddy had to follow me or drink by himself.

'What are you doing, man?' he said outside. 'You can't walk away every time some guy puts his thumb in your eye.'

201

'You want to bet?' I said.

The light was hard and bright, and the blue and green of the trees seemed to recede infinitely across the roll of mountains against the sky. Without looking at Buddy, I casually turned the car around the gas pump toward Missoula. His hand went out and caught the wheel, his forearm as stiff and determined as a piece of pipe.

'No, man, I got to deliver you to this other scene,' he said.

'All right, what kind of caper are we on to?'

'We're going to a cathouse.'

'I don't believe this.'

'Does that rub against some Catholic corner of your soul?'

'Aren't we over the hill for that kind of stuff? I mean, don't you feel a little silly sitting in a hot-pillow joint with a bunch of college boys and drunk loggers?'

'Well, you righteous son of a bitch. You eyeball everything that looks vaguely female, you get drunk and try to make out with some Indian guy's wife, and then you got moral statements to make about your partner's sex life. Some people might just call you a big bullshitter, Zeno.'

We crossed the state line and began to drop down into the mining area of eastern Idaho, a torn and gouged section of the state where everything that hadn't been ruined by stripping had been blighted and stunted by the yellow haze that drifted off the smokestacks of the smelter plants. It was Indian summer in the rest of the northern Rockies, but here the acrid smoke made your head ache and your eyes wince, and the second growth on top of the destroyed mountains was the color of urine. At the bottom of the grade was Wallace, and beyond that, Smelterville, towns that were put together in the nineteenth century out of board, tin, crushed rock for streets, and some type of design on making the earth a gravel pit. The buildings in Wallace looked caved in, grimed with dirt and smoke from the smelters, and their windows were cracked and yellowed. Even the sidewalks sagged in the middle of the streets as though some oppressive weight were on top of them.

'You can really pick them, Buddy,' I said.

'Drive on up the hill to that big two-story wood house.'

The house sat up on a high, weed-filled lawn, with a wide sagging front porch and a blue lightbulb over the door. The white paint was dirty and peeling, and crushed beer cans were strewn along the path to the steps.

'I'll wait for you,' I said.

'None of that stuff. You're not going to pull your Catholic action on your old partner.'

'I'm going to pass. This isn't my scene.'

'You see that car at the bottom of the hill? That's the deputy sheriff who watches this place, and if we keep fooling around he's going to be up here and you can talk to him.'

'I'm telling you, Buddy, you better not get our ass worked over again.'

'Have a beer in the living room. Talk to the

bouncer. He's a real interesting guy. He has an iron bolt through both temples.'

'I'll listen to the radio till you come out,' I said. I smiled at him and lit a cigarette, but there was nothing pleasant in his face.

He walked up the path and knocked on the torn screen door. A girl in blue jeans and a halter opened it, her face expressionless, the eyes indifferent except for a momentary glance, almost like curiosity, in my direction; then she latched the screen again without any show of recognition that a human being had walked past her.

Fifteen minutes later I heard people yelling inside, and then I heard Buddy's voice: 'You go for that sap and you're going to be pulling a shank out of your throat with your fingernails.'

I walked quickly up the path, focused my eyes through the screen, and saw him facing an enormous, bull-necked man in the middle of the living room. The braided leather tip of a blackjack stuck out of the big man's back pocket. Buddy's face was white from drinking, his shirt was ripped and pulled down on one shoulder, and a full whiskey bottle hung from his right hand.

'Turn around and walk out the door and you're out of Indian country,' the bouncer said.

I put my hand through the torn screen, unlatched the door, and stepped inside. All the windows were drawn with yellow roll shades that must have been left over from the 1940s. An old jukebox with a cracked plastic casing stood against one wall, the colored lights inside rippling up and down against the gloom. A hallway separated by a curtain led back from the living room, and there was a garbage can in one corner that was filled with beer cans and whiskey bottles. In the half-light, mill workers and drunks left over from last night's bars sat with the whores on stuffed couches and chairs that seemed to exude a mixture of dust, age, and stale beer. Their faces were pinched with a mean dislike for Buddy, for me, and even for each other. I wondered at my own passivity in allowing Buddy to lead us into this dirty little corner of the universe.

The bouncer's face was as round as a skillet. He smiled with a look of pleasant anticipation.

'Well, I guess it's guys like you that keep me honest and make me earn my pay,' he said. 'But I'm afraid it's a bad day at Black Rock for you boys.'

'Wait a minute, mister. We're leaving,' I said.

'So leave. But if you bring your pet asshole back here again, we'll have to whip some big bumps on him. Give him some real mean hurt. Take his mind off his tallywhacker so he don't have to come here no more.'

'You notice how these guys have a quick turn for everything?' Buddy said. 'They memorize all kinds of hep phrases for every life situation. But they put rock 'n' roll on their jukeboxes and pay their money to the cops and hand out blow jobs to the Kiwanis Club. Look at Mad Man Muntz here. He got his brains at the junkyard, he probably makes a buck an hour, but he comes on like the poet laureate of the brooder house.'

I walked over to Buddy and took him by the arm.

'Our bus is leaving,' I said.

'So long, you lovely people, and remember the reason you're here,' he said. 'You're losers, you got one gear and it's in neutral, and you hire this big clown to keep you safe from all your failures.'

I pulled hard on his arm and pushed him toward the door. The bouncer lifted his finger at him.

'You ought to go to church, boy. You got somebody looking over you,' he said.

The screen slammed behind us, and we walked down the path in the sunlight. The sharpness of the afternoon seemed disjointed and strange after the gloom and anger and bilious view of humanity in the whorehouse.

'I bought a bottle at the bar and was drinking a shot out of it when I saw the guy next to me buying drinks for him and his girl out of my change,' Buddy said as we drove down the hill toward the highway out of town. 'I couldn't believe it. Then he called me a pimp and put his cigarette ashes in my glass. The next thing I knew, his girl was trying to tear my shirt off my back. Man, I thought I saw people do some wild action in the joint, but that's the bottom of the bucket, ain't it?'

I drove without answering and wondered what had really taken place. We passed the town limits, and I stepped on the accelerator as we began the climb up the slope toward the blue tumble of mountains on the Montana line. In the rearview mirror the ugly sprawl of that devastated mining area and stunted town disappeared behind us.

'Yeah, that was a real geek show,' he said.

'Well, how the hell did you get there?' I said righteously, but I was angry at his irresponsibility and the physical danger he had put both of us in again. 'They didn't send out invitations to Florence, Montana. That's their action every day back there, and you go on their rules when you walk through the door.'

I could feel his eyes on the side of my face; then I heard him take a drink out of the whiskey bottle. He didn't speak for another five minutes, and the whistle of air through the window and my cigarette ashes flaking on my trousers began to feel more and more uncomfortable in the silence. I just couldn't stay mad at Buddy for very long.

'How much did they hook you for the bottle?' I said.

'Twelve bucks. You want a shot?'

I drank out of the neck and handed it back to him. The warm bourbon made me wince and my arms tingle.

'Look, Zeno, what's this lecture crap about?' he said.

'Jesus Christ, I just don't want to get busted up again.'

'You could have canceled out early. You didn't have to drive us up there.'

I didn't have an answer for that one.

'You knew what type of scene we were floating into,' he said. 'You better run the film backwards in your own gourd. You were clicking around about maybe improving your love life yourself.'

We dropped over the Montana line, and I really

opened up the Plymouth. The front end was badly out of alignment, at least two bearings were tapping like tack hammers, and the oil smoke was blowing out the frayed exhaust in a long black spiral. The car frame shook and rattled, the doors vibrated on the jambs, and when I had to shift into second to pull a grade, the heat needle moved into the red area on the gauge and the radiator began to sing. Buddy pulled on the bottle and lit a cigarette. But before he did, he split a paper match with his thumbnail, as fast as anyone could pull one from a cover, and flipped the other half on the dashboard in front of me.

'That's pretty good, ain't it, Zeno?' he said. 'I once beat a guy out of a whole deck of cigarettes by splitting thirty in fifty seconds.'

'Why don't you forget all that prison shit?'

'Why don't you forget about destroying my car because you're pissed off?'

I let the Plymouth slow, and I heard Buddy drag off the bottle again. The sun had moved behind the edge of the mountains, and the yellow leaves on the cottonwoods along the river looked like hammered brass over the flow of the current. The blue shadows fell out in front of us on the highway, and the short pines at the base of the hills were already turning dark against the white slide of rocks behind them. The air became cool in minutes, the wind off the river in the canyon seemed sharper, and the banks of clouds on the mountains ahead took on the pink glow of a new rose above the trees.

Buddy pulled steadily on the bottle until he sank

back against the door and the seat with an opened can of hot beer between his thighs.

It was almost dark when I saw the lights of Missoula in the distance. The last purple twilight hung on the high, brown hills above the valley, and a solitary airplane with its landing lights on moved coldly above the city toward the airport. The city seemed so quiet and well ordered in its soft glow and neat pattern of streets and homes and lines of elm and maple trees that I wondered how any community of people could organize anything that secure against the coming of the night and the morrow. For just a moment I let it get away inside of me, and I wondered, with a little sense of envy and loss, about all the straight people in those homes: the men with families and ordinary jobs and ordinary lives, the men who pulled the green chain at the mill and carried lunch pails and never sweated parole officers, cops, jail tanks, the dirty knowledge of the criminal world that sometimes you would like to cut out with a knife, all the ten years' roaring memory of bleeding hangovers, whorehouses, and beer-glass brawls.

But this type of reflection was one that I couldn't afford. Otherwise I would have to put an X through a decade and admit that my brother Ace was right, and the parole office, the psychologist in the joint, the army, everybody who had told me that I had a little screw in the back of my head turned a few degrees off center.

Buddy came out of his whiskey-acid stupor just before we reached the edge of town. His glazed eyes stared at the lights for a moment, then focused on me and brightened in a way that I didn't like. He popped the hot beer open, and the foam showered against the windshield.

'Man, I feel like a dragon,' he said. 'I think I'll go see the wife-o.'

'I think you better not,' I said.

'Just save your counseling and tool on down by the university, Zeno.'

'You're not serious?'

He drank out of the whiskey bottle, chased it with the beer, and then hit it again.

'That's a little better,' he said. 'I could just feel the first snakes getting out of the basket.'

I drove without speaking until I got to the turnoff that would take us back into the Bitterroots.

'Where the hell are you going? I said I wanted to go to Beth's.'

'Let it slide, Buddy.'

'She's my old lady, man.'

'That's the last thing you want to do now.'

'Let Professor Riordan worry about that. Just get it on over there.'

'Where's your head? How do you think she's going to feel when you waltz up to the door like a liquor truck?'

'You should have gone into the priesthood, Iry. You can really deliver the advice about somebody else's life.'

'All right, you've been telling me you want to go back with her. Pull a scene like this and you'll disconnect from her permanently.'

'I guess all this crap comes out of the new Bronze Star you won this morning.'

'What are you talking about?' I said.

'You charged the hill again, didn't you? Shot the heads off all them sixteen-year-old gooks in the trench. Went through the barn door after my old man when I couldn't move.'

'Don't drink any more.'

'You told me about it, right? You went up the hill when everybody else froze and dumped a BAR in their faces, and when you turned them over, you said they looked like children.'

'Put your bag of needles back in your pocket, Buddy. I'm not up to it.'

'No, man. It was the same scene. You saw I was froze, and you followed the old man into the fire. You didn't do it because of him. You knew I was nailed, and your heart started beating. Because you're scared shitless of fire, baby, but you had a chance to make me look like a piece of shit.'

I could feel the anger tighten across my chest and swell into my throat and head until I wanted to hit Buddy as hard as I could with my fist. I took a cigarette off the dashboard and lit it and drew in deeply on the smoke.

'You want to go to Beth's?' I said.

'I told you that, Zeno.'

*OK, son of a bitch*, I thought, and drove toward the university district through the dark, tree-lined streets and past the quiet lawns of all those ordinary people I had wondered about with a sense of envy just a few minutes before.

211

Later, reflecting on the events that were to follow, I would sometimes feel that a human being's life is not shaped so much by what he is or what he pretends to be or even by the compulsions that he tries to root out and burn away; instead it can be just a matter of a wrong turn in an angry moment and a disregard for its consequences. But I didn't know then that I would betray a friend and once more become involved in someone's death.

# chapter nine

I parked in the dark shadow of the maple tree in front of Beth's house.

'You want me to wait or catch air?' I said.

'Come on in. She's got some beer in the icebox.'

'This is your caper, daddy-o. I'm going to rain-check this one.'

He walked across the lawn and the dead leaves onto the wood porch. Under the door light, his body looked small and white. He had to lean against the wall for balance when he knocked again.

I guess I wanted to see Buddy ruin himself with Beth, but as I looked at him there, dissipated, his head crawling with snakes, the unfulfilled rut still in his loins, I wished I could get him back in the car and home again.

Beth opened the door, and I heard Buddy's voice in its strained and careful attempt to sound sober. But the words came too fast, as though they had been rehearsed and pulled out like a piece of tape.

'Somebody burned out the old man's barn this morning, and we were cruising around and decided to drop by.'

She didn't open the screen, and there was a quiet moment while she said something to him, and then his arms went up in the air and he started to rock on both feet in the shadowy light.

'They're my boys, too, ain't they?' he said, and his voice became louder after a few seconds of silence. 'I mean what the hell they have to go to bed so early for, anyway?' Then another pause while Beth spoke.

'You keep listening to that goddamn psychologist and they're going to grow up in Warm Springs.' Another pause.

'I'll roll out the whole fucking neighborhood if I want to. We'll give all these straight cats something to talk about over their breakfast cereal for a week.'

I saw Beth open the screen, then latch it and turn off the porch light. I waited fifteen minutes in the darkness of the maple tree and listened to a hillbilly radio station in Spokane, then decided to go to the Oxford for a chicken-fried steak and a cup of coffee and leave Buddy to his self-flagellation.

But then the light came on again, and Beth stepped out on the porch in a pair of blue jeans and a denim shirt bleached almost white with Clorox. Her blue-black hair hung in a tangle on her shoulders, and her bare feet looked as cold as ivory in the light. She motioned at me, a gentle gesture of the fingers as though she were saying good-bye to someone, and I walked across the dry, stiff grass and dead leaves toward her with a quickening in my heart and emptiness in my legs that confirmed altogether too quickly what had been in my mind all day while I had let Buddy tear his chemistry apart with whiskey and guilt.

'Help me put him upstairs. I don't want the children to see him,' she said.

Buddy was leaned back against the couch in the lamplight, his knees wide apart; his head rolled about on his shoulders like a balloon that wanted to break its string. He was talking at the far wall as though there were someone standing in front of him.

I tried to lift him by one arm, and he slapped at me with his hand, his hair over his eyes and ears.

'What the shit you doing, man?' he said. 'You trying to get me kicked out of two places in one day?'

'We got to go to bed. Your old man wants us to finish the fence line by the slough tomorrow,' I said, though I should have known better than to patronize a drunk, particularly Buddy.

'Well, cool. Louisiana Zeno is looking out for the old man's Angus after he went through the flames.' He tried to raise his head and focus on my face, but the effort was too much.

'What did he take today?' Beth said.

'Just a lot of booze.'

'No, he's been using dope again, hasn't he?'

I heard the boys' voices shouting in the backyard. Beth shook him again by the shoulder.

'Get up,' she said. 'Straighten up your head and stand.'

Buddy fell sideways against the arm of the couch, with one wrist bent back against his thigh. His face was as bloodless and empty as a child's. The back screen slammed, and Beth walked hurriedly into the kitchen and told the children to stay outside. She returned with a wet towel in her hand and pressed it into Buddy's face.

'Goddamn,' he said, his head rolling back.

'Walk to the stairs,' she said. 'Lean forward and hold on to my arm. Damn you, Buddy, they're not going to see you like this.'

'Come on, partner, let's get up,' I said, and wondered at my pretence toward friendship.

We stood him up between us, like a collapsing gargoyle, and walked him toward the staircase. His head hit the banister once, his knees knocked like wood into the steps, and I had to grab his belt and pull with all my weight to keep him from rolling backward down to the first floor.

As I got him over the last step onto the safety of the carpet, my lungs breathless and my good arm weak with strain, I had a quick lesson about the way we as sane and sober people treat the drunk and hopelessly deranged. Considering the amount of acid and booze in his system, and the pathetic behavior in front of his wife on the couch, I had believed that his brain, at that moment, was as soft as yesterday's ice cream, and as a result I had helped drag him upstairs with the care and dignity that you would show a bag of dirty laundry. But when I stood up for a breath before the last haul into the bedroom, he fixed one dilated, bloodshot eye on me from the floor, the other closed in the angry squint of a prizefighter who has just received a murderous leathery shot, and said:

'You really go for the balls when you win, Zeno.'

I put him face down on the bed with his head slightly over the edge so the blood would stay in his brain and he wouldn't become sick. Downstairs, a moment later I heard him hit the floor.

'There's nothing you can do for him,' Beth said.

'I'll get him back on the bed.'

'If he wakes up, he'll wake up fighting. I know Buddy when he's like this. He chooses the people closest to him to help him destroy himself. Take a beer out of the icebox while I get the boys ready for bed.'

'I'd better go.'

'Stay. I want to talk with you.'

The boys came in from the backyard, their faces flushed with cold and play, and drank glasses of powdered milk at the kitchen table. Then they went up the stairs with their eyes fixed curiously on me.

'I bet you still don't believe I used to pitch against Marty Marion,' I said.

'My daddy says you're a guitar player that was in jail with him,' the younger boy said over the banister.

Learn one day not to try to con kids, Paret, I thought.

'Upstairs, and I don't want to hear any feet walking around,' Beth said.

The boys trudged up to their room as though they were being sent to a firing squad.

'What's this about Frank's barn?' Beth said.

'Somebody set fire to it this morning and burned it to the ground.'

217

'Was anyone hurt?'

'We couldn't get one of the Appaloosas out.'

'Does Frank know who it was?'

'He might, but I don't think he would tell anyone if he does. He seems to play a pretty solitary game.'

'Yes, and it's the type that eventually damages everybody around him.'

'That hasn't been my impression about him.'

'He draws an imaginary line that nobody else knows about, and when someone steps over it, you'd better watch out for Frank Riordan.'

'How long did you and Buddy live with him?'

I didn't know that they had, but at this point I simply guessed it as an obvious fact.

'Long enough for Buddy to have to make choices between his own family and his father,' she said.

I avoided the flash in her eyes and looked blankly around at the worn furniture and wondered how I got into this subject. I could think of nothing to say.

'Why did he use dope today?' she asked.

'I guess the fire set off some strange things in his head. I don't know. Sometimes people see the same thing differently.'

'What do you mean?'

'He got wiped out after I followed his old man into the barn and he stayed outside. So I guess he thinks he froze and so he's a coward. After anything like that, you go back over it in your head and try to understand what you did or didn't do, but he doesn't have the experience to see it for what it was.'

She didn't understand what I was saying, and I wished I hadn't started to explain.

'Buddy's not a coward,' I said. 'I've seen him go up against yard bullies at Angola that would have cut him to pieces in the shower if they had sensed any fear in him. He laid it on pretty heavy in the car this afternoon about the Bronze Star I got in Korea, but what he doesn't understand is that you go in one direction or the other, or just stand still, for the same reason – you're too scared to do anything else. It doesn't have anything to do with what you are.

'Look, I shouldn't have brought him here. It's not his fault. He just fried his head today. And I think I better cut.'

'No, I have more beer and some sandwiches in the icebox. Just a minute.'

She walked toward the kitchen with a cigarette in her hand, her thighs and smooth rear end tight against her jeans, and her uncombed hair tangled with light. She came back with a tray and sat on the couch next to me with one bare foot pulled under her leg.

'How did you stay sober while you were carrying around the mad man of Ravalli County?' she said, and laughed, and all the anger with Buddy and Frank Riordan was gone.

'I got some good news about my arm this morning. They're going to saw the cast off next week. I'll probably have to play finger exercises like a kid for a few days, but I ought to have my act back in gear at the beer joint if that fat sheriff doesn't nail me and get me violated in the meantime.'

'Have you run into Pat Floyd again?'

'He eased himself out to the ranch yesterday

219

afternoon to show me a spent shell he said he picked up across the river from the pulp mill. I might have my signature burned right into it.'

Her eyes passed over mine with a gathering concern, then lowered to the ashtray, where she picked up her cigarette.

'Can you go back to prison?' she said.

'If I left that shell and my print is on it. It might not get me time here, but it could be enough for my P.O. to have me sent back to Louisiana.'

When I saw her expression and realized the casual tone of my voice, I also realized something about the impropriety of speaking out of one's own cynical experience to people who are not prepared for it.

'Buddy thinks he's just trying to turn on the butane and get me to jump,' I said.

'Pat Floyd will put you away,' she said.

The seriousness of her voice made something drop inside me.

'Well, you said he wasn't a hillbilly cop.' But the detachment that I wanted to show in my voice wasn't there.

'What do you plan to do?'

'Nothing. What the hell can I do? I can sweat this fat man or run, and if I run, I have another three to pull in Angola for sure. I figure I'll hang around and let Gordo Deficado do his worst.'

'He can do it, Iry.'

'I've known some bad men, too.'

She poured some of her beer into my glass and lit another cigarette from my pack.

'I've got to roll, kiddo. I've burned up too much of your evening,' I said.

'Buddy will need a ride home tomorrow. There's no point in making two trips.' She looked away from me, and I saw the nervous touch of her finger on the cigarette.

'I don't want to cause an inconvenience.'

'Oh, shit,' she said, and stood up from the couch and turned off the lamp on the table. In the darkness, she paused momentarily, listening for a sound from upstairs, then began to undress. She unsnapped her blue jeans and pushed them to her ankles, then pulled off her denim shirt and tried to reach for the back of her bra. In her hurried movement, with the glow of the kitchen light against her white stomach, she looked like an embarrassed contortionist in front of an audience of dolts.

My heart was beating, and I felt the heat come into my face when I looked at her bare legs, her white line of swollen stomach above the elastic of her panties, and her wonderful soft breasts pressing against her bra. I looked up the stairs, where my friend was asleep after his day of dissipation, and before I could reflect on whether my quick glance was a matter of concern for Buddy or personal caution for myself, I looked back at Beth again and felt all the weak ache of two years stiffen into an erection.

I rose uncomfortably from the couch in a bent position and unfastened her bra, and she turned toward me and put her arms around my neck as though she wanted to hide her huge white breasts. I

221

pulled her close, with my face in her hair, and kissed her ear and ran both my hands over the small of her back, down inside her panties and over her butt and thighs. I felt like a gorilla bent in an ugly position over a pale statue. I smelled her blue-black hair, her perfume, the dried perspiration on her neck, her breath, and I felt the backs of my thighs start to shake.

She took her arms away and slipped her panties down over her thighs, then stepped out of them.

'Sit on the couch,' she said.

Her body was silhouetted like a soft white sculpture in the glow of light from the kitchen. I undressed and sat back on the couch, and then she moved over me. She moaned once in her woman's fecund way, her eyes widened, and she spread her fingers across my back.

Then I felt it grow inside of me, too early and beyond any attempt at control, and when it burst away in that heart-twisting moment, she leaned forward and held my head to her breasts as she might a child's.

In the morning we all had breakfast at the kitchen table, and the sky outside was blue and clear over the elm and maple trees, and the sun shone brightly through the window. The two boys were talking happily about a football game at school, and Beth turned the hashbrowns and eggs in the skillet as though she were fixing breakfast on any ordinary morning. But I could feel the tension in her whenever she looked toward me and Buddy at once.

He was badly hung over, his hand shaking on his cigarette, the eyes puffed and dim and still focused inward on some barrel of snakes out of yesterday. His plate went cold in front of him, and finally he dropped his cigarette in his coffee and rested his forehead on the palm of his hand.

'Boy, I really got one this time,' he said.

I didn't want to look at him, because I not only felt an awful guilt toward him but also that sense of primitive victory in making a cuckold out of a rival, particularly one who was coming apart while you had it all intact.

'Try some tomato juice,' Beth said.

'You got any ups? Or some of those diet pills will do it,' he said.

'Don't take anything else,' she said.

He remained with his head in his palm and breathed irregularly.

'Do you have a hangover, Daddy?' the younger boy said.

Buddy got up from the table without answering and walked duckfooted to the icebox. He opened a can of beer and then began looking through the cabinets.

'Where the hell is that bottle of sherry you keep?' he said.

'Don't do it, Buddy,' she said. 'Just let it work out your system and you'll be all right this afternoon.'

'Give me the sherry and don't tell me how to survive the morning.'

She took the bottle from under the sink, and he poured a glass half full of it and then filled the rest with beer and broke two raw eggs into it. He sipped the glass slowly at the table, with his head bent over, holding the glass with both hands. Five minutes later the color began to come back into his face, and his hands stopped shaking.

'Man, that's a little better,' he said. 'That whiskey must have had shellac in it. I haven't had an eggbeater in my head like that since I sniffed some transmission fluid in the joint.' He looked up at Beth, then shook his head. 'OK, I know, wrong reference. But, man, somebody must have stuck an enema bag full of piss in my ear last night.'

That's great, Buddy, I thought.

Beth told the boys to put on their coats and go outside.

'All right, all right, I got a speech defect about bad language,' he said. 'But they hear all that shit at school. You don't have to put earmuffs on them when they're in the house.'

The table was silent, and Beth made a point of not looking directly at either one of us.

'How did I get upstairs last night? You must have dragged me up there by my heels.'

'You floated up there like a balloon,' I said.

'I feel like somebody worked me over with a slapjack. What did you do to me, partner?' He fixed one watery blue eye on me over his cigarette, and I flinched inside.

'I had to use force on you a little bit after you started taking off your clothes in the street. That wasn't too bad in itself, but after you threw those flowerpots through the neighbor's window, I had to do something to keep both of us out of the bag.'

His face tensed momentarily with hangover fear and disbelief. Then he drank from the sherry and beer and stared back hard at me with his cigarette between his lips.

'Son, you are a dirty bastard to put your hung-over partner on like that,' he said, and I saw Beth's hand relax on her coffee cup.

But I couldn't quite forget his lingering, watery blue eye and the probe that it had made. Buddy had a way of knowing things that it was impossible for him to know, and I never was sure if the gift came from the fact that possibly he was crazy or if in his cynicism about human behavior he simply intuited, with a great deal of accuracy, what bad things some people would do in certain circumstances.

He finished the glass and took another beer from the icebox.

'Let's get it down the road,' he said. 'Didn't you say the old man wants us to finish the fence line down to the slough?'

I blinked inside again, because he remembered exactly, almost to the word, what I had told him before we carried him up to bed.

'Well, damn, Zeno, get it in gear,' he said.

We walked out on the front porch, and the yellow and red leaves were blowing across the grass in the sunlight, and the mountains behind the university were sharp and clear against the blue Montana sky. The crack of the fall air was like a cool burn against my face. I wanted to say something, anything, alone

225

to Beth before we left, but I couldn't, and so I just smiled as I would at a casual friend and said good-bye.

We drove back into the long, blue-green stretch of the Bitterroots and stopped at Lolo for a drink because Buddy's nervous system was starting to become unwired again. In the bar I drank a cup of coffee while he began on his second vodka collins. I had a hard time looking at him directly in the eyes.

'You're a quiet bastard this morning, ain't you?' he said.

'I got burnt out yesterday. No more Idaho excursions.'

'Right. Bad scene. I ain't going to let you lead me over there anymore. I feel like somebody stuck thumbtacks all over my head. Come on, let's get out of here and put down those fence posts so I can stop thinking about my problems with ex-wives and kids.'

At the ranch we went back to work on the fence line, though I could do little more than unload the posts off the wagon with one arm and hold them steady in the hole while Buddy shoveled in the dirt. Then he would have to go to work on the next one with the posthole digger, the sweat and booze running off his face and neck into his flannel shirt. We spoke little. He was too hung over, and I was too preoccupied with the latest thing I had gotten myself into. I didn't know what to do about either Beth or Buddy, and any of the answers I could think of were bad ones. Maybe I should just drop it on him, I thought, because I was going to see her again, and eventually he would find out about it if he didn't already have his finger on the edge of it. I slept with your wife last night. What do you think about that? Oh, you don't mind? That's cool, because I thought the shit might hit the fan.

He started to clean the posthole digger in the bucket of water, his face pale with fatigue, then dropped the wood handles and let the whole thing fall to the ground. He wiped his face slick with his sleeve.

'Shit on this. We can do it this evening,' he said. 'Man, I'm going to quit that damn drinking once and for all.'

He walked away alone toward the cabin, his shoulders bent slightly and his back shaking with a cigarette cough.

Buddy slept through the rest of the morning, and I sat on the porch in the cool wind and tried to read from an old paperback copy of *The Old Man and the Sea*. I had read it once in college and again in Angola, and it was my favorite of Ernest Hemingway's books. But I couldn't concentrate on the words; my attention would slip off the page, across the meadow of grazing Angus to the pile of ash and blackened boards where the barn had been.

So where do you go now, I thought. You can move out and try to explain to him why you have to, or you can let things keep falling one onto another without any plan at all until something even worse happens. Under other circumstances I would have just checked it on down the road, maybe up to Vancouver or out to San Fran, but the parole office had a nail through my foot, and the only type of transfer I could get would be back to Louisiana, and that was like going back to first base after you had knocked the ball out of the park.

But if I thought I had great problems to resolve there in the solitude of the porch and a windy sun-filled afternoon, I realized with a glance at the sheriff's car turning in the front cattle guard that the complexities of my day were just beginning. Pat Floyd pulled the car off the dirt road onto the grass and put the gearshift in neutral with the engine still running, which meant we were going somewhere together.

I closed the paperback and set it beside me and looked at him without speaking. At first I'd had no feelings about him; he was just another dick, a member of that vast army who play out their roles and games with their sets of keys and paper forms and intricate rules of human behavior. But I was learning to dislike this fat man. I had the feeling that he was taking a special interest in me, one that went beyond the prosecution of a drunk ex-convict who shot up the local toilet paper factory. I was an outsider, a rounder with a cornpone mystique, a glib troublemaker who had been kicked off his own turf and was using the locals for a doormat.

'Let's take a ride,' he said.

'You got a paper on me, Sheriff?'

'This ain't an arrest. And I wouldn't need a warrant to make one, either, son.'

'Hey, Buddy,' I called back through the screen door.

228

'You don't need him. Just get in, and we're going to talk a minute.'

'I just want to tell him we'll be back soon. We're going fishing shortly.'

I opened the screen and spoke into the dim shadows of the cabin. Buddy was on my bunk with the pillow and quilt over his head, his body deep in the mattress with sleep.

'I'll be out with Sheriff Floyd a few minutes. OK?'

I got in the passenger side of the car and lit a cigarette, and we started up the road toward the cattle guard.

'You're a pretty sharp boy,' he said.

'How's that, Sheriff?'

'You thought I might take you out, beat the shit out of you with a billy, and leave you in a ditch, didn't you?'

'It didn't cross my mind.'

'We don't do it that way up here. In fact, we don't hardly have any crime here to speak of. On Saturday night a few boys might try to break up each other in a bar, and I have to lock them up till Sunday morning, but that's all we get. People around here obey the law most of the time.'

We turned out on the highway, and he reached over with his huge weight and popped open the glove compartment. Inside was a half-pint of whiskey in a paper bag twisted around the neck. He unscrewed the cap with his thumb and took a drink, then set the bottle between his swollen khaki thighs.

'Actually, being a sheriff around here is easy,' he said. 'A lot of times people take care of the law by themselves. A few years ago one of those California motorcycle gangs rode into Virginia City on a Saturday afternoon and said they were taking over the town. By that night every sheepherder and cowboy in the county was in town. They broke arms and heads and legs, beat them till they got down on their knees, and left just enough of that crowd intact to drive the others out of town. That's the way it gets done out here sometimes.'

'What's all this about?'

'Not too much. I just want to tell you a couple of things.' We passed the Sweeny Creek grocery store, a small wood building set back from the blacktop in the trees, and turned onto a rock road that led back toward the mountains. I puffed on my cigarette and looked at him from the side of my eye. He wasn't carrying a billy on his hip, and I hadn't seen one in the glove compartment, but maybe it was under the seat or lying within a second's reach against the doorjamb.

I had never been beaten in prison, or even mistreated for that matter, but I could never forget the time I saw what a Negro could look like after he had been sweated with a garden hose three nights in isolation. He was serving peas in the chow line for the free people, and when one of the hacks told him, 'You better start ladling out them peas a little faster, boy,' he replied, 'You ladle them out yourself, boss.' Three hacks cuffed him in the serving line and took him down to the hole. When he came out his eyes were swollen shut, and the striped bruises on his stomach and back looked like a black deformity.

The sheriff parked the car close into the shade of the pines along the creek and cut the engine. He took another drink out of the whiskey and offered the bottle to me.

'Go ahead. You ain't going to get trench mouth out of it.' He laughed and took a cigar from his pocket. 'You know, you've got a shit pot full of good luck. The FBI man couldn't find a thing on that shell casing. Either you must have wiped all them hulls clean before you put them in the magazine or a deer walked over and took a good, solid piss right on top of it.'

He bit off the tip of the cigar and spit it through the window, then wet the end as though he were rolling a stick around in his mouth.

'Do you think you got pretty good luck?' he said.

'You tell me.'

He struck a match on the horn button and lit the cigar.

'I don't think your luck is too good at all,' he said. 'But that's another matter. I wanted to drive up here today mainly because it's my day off and this is where I always come the first day of deer season. You see where that saddle begins right after the first mountain, where the meadow opens up in the trees? I get two whitetail there opening day every year. I got an elk cow there last year, too, right up the nose with this .357 magnum from forty yards. I was using a shotgun with deer slugs, and I got some snow in the barrel and blew it all apart firing at a doe. Then the elk walked into the meadow with the wind behind her and never smelled a thing. I put it in her snout and tore her ass all over the snow. Those steel jackets will go through an automobile block, and they don't even slow down when they gut an animal.'

I handed his whiskey back to him and looked out the passenger's window.

'You're not a hunter, are you?' he said.

'I gave it up in the army.'

He had started to take a drink, but he lowered the bottle and looked hard at me. I tried to keep my gaze on his face, but it was too much. His anger toward me and what I represented in some vague place in his mind or memory – some abstraction from a childhood difficulty, a sexual argument with his wife, a fear of the mayor or the town councilmen or himself – was too much to contend with in a stare contest, even though he was trying to pull my life into pieces.

'Let me tell you something before we drive back,' he said. 'I don't like you. I probably can't get you for shooting up the mill right now, but I'm going to make you as unwelcome as I can in Missoula County. I'll put you in jail for spitting on the street, throwing a cigarette wrapper down, walking in public with beer on your breath. I'll have you in jail every time I see you or any of my department does. I have the feeling that if I lock you up enough and call your parole officer each time I do it, you'll get your sack lunch and bus ticket back to Louisiana. Which means you better keep your ass out of my sight.'

'Is that it?'

'You better believe it, son.'

232

I opened the door and stepped out on the short grass. My head was light, and the wind blowing through the pines along the creek bed was cold against the perspiration in my hair.

'Where the hell do you think you're going?' he said.

'I'll hitch a ride back to the Riordans'.'

The sun's rays struck through his windshield, revealing in his face all his anger, all his doubt about leaving me to find my way home (and the possible recriminations later), and the most serious question – whether he had struck the fear of God into me with a burning poker.

I walked up the rock road toward the blacktop, smoking a cigarette, and he drove along beside me in first gear with his fat arm over the window, the doubt and anger still stamped in his face, and I was glad no one could see this sad comedy of two grown men acting out a ludicrous exercise in a mountain wilderness so that one of them could go home with a piece of scalp lock to keep his pride intact.

The sheriff floored the car in front of me, fishtailing off the grass that was already turning wet with dew, and spun a shower of rocks off the back tires when he hit second. He threw the whiskey bottle out the window into the gravel as he turned onto the blacktop, then roared away toward Missoula with both exhausts throbbing, his arm like a ham on the window.

By the time I had hitched a ride back to the ranch, the sunlight was drawing away over the mountains in a pink haze, and Buddy was sitting on the porch steps in a sheep-lined jacket, tying tapered leader on his fly line.

'Where you been, man?' he said.

'I went for a ride with that fat dick.'

He looked up from his concentration on the leader and waited.

'That shell casing was clean, but he says he's going to make my life interesting every time he catches me in Missoula,' I said.

'Just stay out of his way. It'll be cool after a while.'

'What am I supposed to do in the meantime? Live out here like a hermit?'

'You want to go fishing?'

'Yeah.'

We took the car down to the river and fished two deep holes in the twilight with wet flies. As the moon began to rise over the mountains, they started hitting. I saw my line straighten out quickly below the surface of the pool; then there was that hard-locking tension when the brown really hung into it, and the split-bamboo rod arched toward the water and the backup line started to strip off the automatic reel. I held the rod high over my head at an angle and walked with him through the shallows until he started to weaken and I could back him into the cattails at the head of the pool. I couldn't manage the rod and the net at the same time because of my cast, and Buddy came up under him slowly with his net, the sandy bottom clouding as the dorsal and tail fins broke the water, and then he was heavy and thick and dripping inside the net, his brown-and-gold color and red spots wet with moonlight.

We cooked the fish with lemons, onions, and butter sauce, and it was warm and fine inside the cabin with the heat from the wood stove and the smell of burning pine chunks and the wind blowing through the trees on the creek. But I couldn't eat or even finish my coffee. Paret, you wrecker of dreams, I thought. How did you do it?

During the week I helped Buddy's father feed the birds and clean the cages in the aviary. We finished the fence line down to the slough, and much against all my instincts and previous experiences with nutrias in Louisiana, I went with him and Buddy up Lost Horse Creek to release two pairs of males and females. At the time I rationalized that it would be two or three years before the damage was felt on a large scale in the area, and I would be safely gone when a mob of commercial trappers, gyppo loggers, and fishermen tore the Riordan home apart board and nail.

I resolved in a vague way to leave Beth alone, but like an alcoholic who goes through one day dry and has to count all the others on the calendar, I knew it was just a matter of which day I would call her or suggest to Buddy that we drive into Missoula.

As it turned out, it was neither. I drove to town on Thursday morning with Melvin to check in with my parole officer, though my appointment wasn't until the following week. He dropped me off by the university library, since I told him that I had three hours to waste before I saw my P.O., and then I walked the four blocks to Beth's house.

She was scraping leaves into huge piles in her front yard with a cane rake. She wore a pair of faded corduroy jeans and a wool shirt buttoned at the throat and rolled over her elbows. Each time she scraped the rake and flattened it across the dry grass, more leaves blew in cold eddies off the piles.

'Do you want to go eat lunch at that German restaurant?' I said.

She turned around, surprised, then stood erect with both of her hands folded on the rake handle. She blew her hair away from the corner of her mouth, her cheeks spotted with color in the coldness of the shade, and smiled in a way that made me go weak inside.

'Let me put on another shirt and get the leaves and twigs out of my hair,' she said.

We went in her car to the Heidelhaus, which inside was like a fine German place in the Black Forest, with big wood beams on the ceiling, checker-cloth table, candles melted in wine bottles, and a large stone fireplace over which was skewered a roasting pig. We drank Tuborg on tap and ate sausage-and-melted-cheese sandwiches, and then the waitress, in a Tyrolean dress, served us slices of the roasted pork in hot mustard. It was so pleasant inside, with the warmth of the fireplace, the buttered-rum drinks after dinner, the college kids in varsity sweaters at the bar, and the candlelight on her happy face, that the threats of the sheriff and my other problems lapsed away in a kind of autumnal euphoria. Her eyes were bright with the alcohol, and when her knee brushed mine under the table, we both felt the same recognition and expectation about the rest of the afternoon.

We went back to her house and made love in her bed upstairs for almost two hours. I heard the screen slam downstairs and jerked upward involuntarily, but she simply smiled and put her finger to my lips and opened the bedroom door slightly to tell the boys to play outside. She walked back to the bed, her body soft and white and her huge breasts almost like a memory from my prison fantasies. Then she sat on me and bit my lip softly, her hair covering my face, and I felt it rise again deep inside of her until my loins were burning, and the weak light outside seemed to gather and fade from my vision in her rhythmic breathing against my cheek.

That Saturday I had my cast cut off at the hospital. The electric saw hummed along the cast and shaled off the plaster, and then the whole thing cracked free like a foul and corroded shell and exposed my puckered, hairless white arm. The skin felt dead and rubbery when I touched it, as though it wasn't a part of me, and when I closed my fist, the muscle in the forearm swelled like an obscene piece of whale fat. But it felt good to have two arms again. While I put on my shirt and buttoned it easily with two hands, I recalled something I had thought about when I was in the hospital in Japan after I had been hit: that everybody who thinks war is an interesting national excursion should give up the use of an arm, an eye, or a leg for one day.

I practiced chord configurations on the guitar for three days to bring back the coordination in my left hand. I had lost the calluses on my fingertips, and the strings burned the skin on the first day and raised tiny water blisters close to the nails, and the back of my hand wouldn't work properly when I ran an E chord up the neck in 'Steel Guitar Rag.' But by Tuesday I could feel the resilience and confidence back in my fingers, the easy slides and runs over the frets, and the natural movements I made without thinking.

It was twilight, and I was alone in the cabin, slightly drunk on a half-pint of Jim Beam and my own music and its memory of the rural South. The glow from the wood stove was warm against my back, and I could feel the chords in the guitar go through the sound box into my chest. A freight-train whistle blew coldly between the mountains, and though I couldn't see that train, I knew that it was covered with the last red light of the dying sun and in the cab there was an engineer named Daddy Claxton, highballing for Dixie like the Georgia Mail.

I put my thumb picks on and played every railroad song I knew, double picking like A. P. Carter and Mother Maybelle, moving on with Hank Snow, running from Lynchburg to Danville on the Ole 97, the tortoiseshell picks flashing over the silver strings, the rumble and scream of mile-long legendary trains as real in that moment as when they ran with overheated fireboxes and sweating Negro coal shovelers and engineers who would give their lives just to make up lost time.

Buddy never understood why I made my living as a country musician when I probably could have worked steady with hotel dance bands in New Orleans or tried the jazz scene on the West Coast, where I might have made it at least as a rhythm guitarist. But what he didn't understand, and what most northerners don't, is that rural southern music is an attitude, a withdrawal into myths and an early agrarian dream about the promise of the new republic. And regardless of its vague quality, its false sense of romance, its restructuring of the reality of our history, it is nevertheless as true to a young boy in southern Louisiana listening to the Grand Ole Opry or the Louisiana Hayride on Saturday night as his grandfather's story, which the grandfather had heard from *his* father, about the Federals burning the courthouse in New Iberia and pulling the bonnets off white women and carrying them on their bayonets. It was true because the boy had been told it was, and he would have no more questioned the veracity of the story than he would have the fact of his birth.

I was deep into my southern reverie and the last inch of Jim Beam when Buddy walked through the door, his eyes watery with the wind.

'I heard you across the field. It sounds very good, young Zeno,' he said. 'For a minute, I thought I heard that colored blues player on Camp A. What was his name?'

'Guitar-git-it-and-go Welch.'

'Man, he was shit on that twelve-string, wasn't he? What the hell were you doing with Beth at the Heidelhaus?'

I poured the rest of the Beam in my tin cup and picked up my cigarette from the edge of the table. The stove was hot against my back, and I felt a drop of perspiration slip down from my hairline.

'You want a drink?' I said.

'No, man. I want to know what you were doing with my old lady.'

'Having lunch. What the hell do you normally do in a restaurant?'

'What other kind of lunch did you have?'

'All right on that shit, Buddy.'

'You just happened to bop on down to the university library with Mel and take Beth out and not mention it for a week.'

'I saw my P.O. and had four hours to kill before I met Melvin. I didn't want to hang around town and get picked up by the sheriff again, and I didn't feel like sitting in the library anymore with a bunch of college students. So I asked her to go out for lunch.'

I had done a number of things over the years that were wrong, but lying was not one of them, even in prison, and I don't know if this was because of my father's deep feeling for truth and the habit it established in me or if I had found that the truth is the best pragmatic solution for any complex situation. But I had lied to Buddy and the words burned in my cheeks. I lifted the cup and took a sip out of it, then puffed off the cigarette.

'So why don't you tell somebody about it?' he said. 'I ain't going to cut out your balls in the middle of the night.'

'I thought it wasn't a big deal.'

'Well, it ain't, Zeno. It ain't. Just drop some words on your old partner so I don't feel like a dumb asshole when Mel sends this kind of news across the mashed potatoes. I mean, that cat is all right, but my mother is serving the steak around, and he says, "Was Beth's car still working all right when she took Iry down to the Heidelhaus?"'

He took my cigarette out of my fingers and drew in on the stub.

'What was I supposed to say, Zeno?' he said. 'My sister had gloat in her eyes, and the old man took out his pocket watch like he'd never seen it before. Say, no shit, man, you ain't balling her, are you?'

'No.'

'You want to get high? I got some real good Mexican stuff today.'

'I'd better go to bed early. I want to go up to Bonner tomorrow and see if I can get back on with the band.'

I took the guitar strap off my neck and laid the sound box face down across my thighs. I pulled the picks off my fingers and dropped them in my shirt pocket.

'Come on and get loaded,' he said.

'I better look good tomorrow.'

'That's on the square? You haven't been milking through your partner's fence?'

'I already told you, Buddy.'

241

I wrapped the Gibson in a blanket and went to sleep on my bunk, leaving him to a large kitchen matchbox of green Mexican weed and all the paranoid nightmares he could get out of it.

Friday night I was playing lead guitar again on the platform at the Milltown Union Bar, Cafe and Laundromat. The barstools and the tables were filled with mill workers and loggers and their masculine women, and at nine o'clock I attached the microphone pickup to my sound hole and opened up with Hank's 'Lost Highway,' a lament about a deck of cards, a jug of wine, and a woman's lies. Their faces were quiet in the red-and-purple neon glow off the bar, and by the time I slipped into 'The Wild Side of Life,' they were mine. Then I did a song about gyppo loggers written by our drummer ('the jimmy roaring, the big wheels rolling, the dirt and bark a-flying'), and I could see the words burn with private meaning, with affirmation of their impoverished lives, into all those work-creased faces.

It was good to be working again, to hear the applause, to sit at the bar between sets in a primitive aura and receive the free drinks and the callused handshakes. We played until two in the morning, turning our speakers higher and higher against the noise on the dance floor, the rattle of bottles, and the occasional violent scrape of chairs when a fight broke out. My voice was hoarse, my left arm throbbed, and my fingertips felt like they had been touched with acid, but that was all right. I was playing with that sense of control and quietness inside that came to me only when I was at my best.

After everyone had left, I had a bowl of chili and a cup of coffee at the bar with the drummer, both of us light-headed with alcohol, exhaustion, and the electric echoes of the last five hours. Then I walked out into a sleeting rain and drove the Plymouth back toward Missoula and Beth's house.

# chapter ten

During the night the sleet and wind whipped the trees against the second-story bedroom window, and when the dawn began to grow into the sky, the grass was thick with small hailstones, and the sidewalks looked like they had been powdered with rock candy. I drove back to the ranch as the sun broke coldly over the edge of the Bitterroots, and I saw the snow in the pines high up in the mountains and the drift of white, shimmering light when the wind blew through the trunks. I should have left Beth's house earlier, but in the warmth of her bed and with her woman's heat against me and the wet rake of the maple on the window, I drifted back into sleep until the room was suddenly gray with the false dawn. Now, I worried about Buddy and the lie I would have to tell him if he was awake.

But he was asleep, face down in the bed with his clothes and shoes on, his arms spread out beside him, a dead joint stuck like a flag in a beer can on the floor. It was cold inside the cabin, and I fired the wood stove, fanned the draft until the kindling caught and snapped into the hunks of split pine, and started to undress on the edge of my bunk. Through the side window I could see the snow clouds above the mountaintops turning violet over the dark sheen of the trees. My body was thick with fatigue, and I could still hear the noise of the bar and the electronic amplifiers as though the few hours' interlude with Beth hadn't been there. Then, as I lay back on the pillow with my arm over my eyes and started to sink into the growing warmth of the wood stove and the lessening of my heartbeat, I heard Mr Riordan's boots on the porch and his quiet knock on the screen.

He said he needed one of us to go up Lost Horse Creek with him to turn loose some more nutrias, so I got in the pickup, and we headed down the highway with the wire cages bouncing in the bed. I looked around through the window at the red eyes of the nutrias and their yellow buck teeth and porcupine hair and had to laugh.

'You must find them a great source of humor,' he said. His red-check wool shirt was buttoned at the collar and wrists under his sheep-lined jacket.

'I'm sorry,' I said, still laughing. 'But I can't get over these things being introduced deliberately into an area. One time my father and I had to spend a week cleaning out the irrigation ditches in our rice field after these guys had gone to work.'

'They're that bad, are they?' he said, his face on the road.

'No, sir, they're worse.' I laughed again. It was too ridiculous.

'If these prove that they can acclimate to the

environment and be of commercial value, the beaver in the Northwest might be with us a few more years.'

He was a serious man not given to levity about his work, and I now felt awkward and a bit stupid in not having seen as much. He drove with his forearms against the steering wheel and tried to roll a cigarette between his fingers while the tobacco spilled out both ends of the paper.

'You want a tailor-made?' I said.

'Thank you.' He crumpled the paper and tobacco grains in his palm and dropped them out the wind vane. I had a notion that he could have rolled that cigarette into a tube as slick as spit if he had wanted, but he was a gentleman and had just erased that moment of righteousness that had led to my discomfort.

We turned on the rock road that wound along Lost Horse Creek and started up the long grade through the timber in second gear. As we veered on the corner of the switchbacks and the creek dropped farther below us like a cold blue flash through the tree trunks, I felt the air begin to thin, and the smell of the pines grew heavy in my head. On up the road I could see the first mountain start to crest, and then others rose higher and bluer behind it until they disappeared in the wet mist and the torn edges of snow clouds. We turned up another switchback, and again I looked down below at the creek. It was small and flecked with white water, and the remaining leaves on the cottonwoods looked like pieces of stamped Byzantine bronze. Rocks spilled off the edge of the road and dropped a hundred feet before they struck a treetop.

'We'll pick up the creek again farther on. The height doesn't bother you, does it?'

Hell no, I always light one cigarette off another like this, I thought.

'I just wonder what you might do if you blow out a tire on one of these turns,' I said.

'We probably just wouldn't have to worry about putting the nutrias in a beaver pond today.'

The grade evened off, and the road began to straighten with thick pines on each side of it, and then I saw the creek again, this time no more than fifty yards away through the front window, a white roar of water breaking in a shower between smooth grey rocks that were as big as small houses. Mr Riordan pulled the pickup off the road at an angle into the pines and rolled a cigarette between his thumb and forefinger, licked it, seamed it down, twisted both ends, clicked a match on his thumbnail, and had it smoking in less than a minute, and there weren't three grains of tobacco on his flat palm. He opened the door and laid his sheep-lined jacket on the seat. His bib overalls and buttoned-down, red-check shirt made me think of a southern farmer. We could hear a logging truck up the road as it shifted into low gear for the slow descent down the grade.

'Are you courting Buddy's wife?' he said, the cigarette wet in the corner of his mouth.

I got out the passenger's door and walked around to the tailgate and pulled loose the chain hook. The nutrias had been frightened by the ride over the rock

247

road and the rattle of the chain, and they started to chew against the wire cages with their yellow teeth.

He leaned with one stiff arm against the truck bed and held the cigarette between his thick fingers as he looked away at the fallen trees across the creek.

'Are you courting his wife?' he said. 'Which means, are you sleeping with her?'

'Yes, I am.'

'Have you thought about what he'll do if he decides to stop looking in the other direction?'

'I haven't gotten that far yet.'

'Because frankly I don't know what he'll do. I just know I don't want my boy back in prison again. I think you can understand that.'

'He's not the type to do what you're thinking about,' I said.

'You're pretty damn sure of that, are you? Let me tell you a lesson, son. The man who kills you will be the one at your throat before you ever expect it.'

The wind felt cold on my neck. The thought of Buddy as a murderous enemy seemed as incongruous and awful as a daytime nightmare.

'I won't try to explain any of it to you,' I said, 'but sometimes things just happen of their own accord and it's not easy to revise them.'

'I didn't ask you for an apology. I just want you to think about consequences. For everybody.'

'Is that why we took this ride?'

'No. I figure you already knew what I had to say. And it's probably not going to make any difference anyway.'

'You want me to pull out?'

'You're his guest. That's between you and him. I don't hold anything against you. Beth marked him off a long time ago, but he hasn't come to accept that yet. I'd just hoped that with some time he could come to see things as they are. He's not up to having another big hole dug for him.'

'Maybe he's tougher than you think.'

'It doesn't take "tough" to go to jail and do all five years because you can't stay out of trouble.'

'I don't think you know what kind of special feeling the hacks had for him in there. He was different. He didn't take them seriously, and that bothered them right down in their scrotums.'

'That's blather. Buddy was looking for that jail for years, but there's no point in arguing about it. Let's get these cages down to the pond.' He rubbed out the fire on his cigarette between his fingers and scattered the tobacco in the wind.

We heard the gears of the log truck wind down on the switchback, the air brakes hissing. Then the cab bent around the edge of the mountain with the huge flatbed behind it, and the great snow-covered ponderosa trunks boomed down with chains that cut whitely into the bark. The driver was bent over the wheel, his arm and shoulder working on the gear stick as the weight shifted on the bed; then the brakes hissed again, and he slowed to a stop where the grade evened off. He pulled off his leather gloves and picked up a cigar stub from the dashboard.

'Hey, Riordan,' he said. 'You turning more of them rats loose?'

'What the hell does it look like?'

'Goddamn, if they ain't beautiful,' the driver said, and laughed with the cigar in his teeth. 'I guess if one of them tops a beaver, we'll see animals running around with yellow teeth and porcupine quills growing out their asshole.'

'You're probably late with your load, Carl,' Mr Riordan said.

'Don't worry about that. I want to see you put them things in the creek. Do you have to club them in the head first and carry them down on the end of a shovel?' The driver giggled from the truck window with the cigar stub in the center of his teeth.

'You have a hot dinner waiting for you at home, Carl. Don't make your wife throw it out in the backyard again.'

'You want me to help you with them things, in case they start biting your tires all to pieces?' the driver said.

'Tell him to get fucked,' I said.

Mr Riordan looked at me with a sharp, brief expression, then picked up the two sawed-off broom handles that we used to put through the cages and carry them to the stream.

'Better put them in here, because the creek is dryer than a popcorn fart higher up,' the driver said. 'In fact, I seen a couple of them rats walking up the road carrying a canteen.'

Mr Riordan pushed the broom handles through the first cage, and we lifted it out of the pickup bed and carried it down the incline toward the beaver pond. The truck driver was still giggling behind us; then we heard him turn over his engine and shift into gear. We walked over the pine needles through the short trees, the nutrias tumbling over one another in the cage and gnawing with their buck teeth on the wood handles.

'Why do you take it off them?' I said.

'He's a harmless man. He means nothing by it.'

'I don't know how you define son of a bitch around here, but it seems to me that you have an awful lot of them.'

'They're afraid.'

'Of what, for God's sake?'

'The people who control their livelihood. All the eastern money that gives them a job and tells them at the same time that they're working for themselves and some pioneer independent spirit. They tried to organize unions here during the Depression, and they got locked out until they begged to work. So they think that any change is trouble, and they've told themselves that for so long now that they've come to believe it.'

'You have more tolerance than I do.'

'I imagine that you made the same type of realizations in growing up in the South, or you would have left it a long time ago,' he said.

He set his end of the cage down by the edge of the pond and began to roll a cigarette, his grey eyes focused intently on the quiet swell of water around the pile of dead and polished cottonwoods and pines that had been cut through at the base of the trunks by beavers until they toppled into the center of the creek. The wood had turned bone white from sun and rot, and tree worms had left their intricate

251

designs in the smooth surface after the bark had cracked and shaled away in the current. On each side of the pile, two feet under the current, were burrowed openings where the beavers could enter and then surface into a dry, sheltered domed fortress. Behind the dam, where the gnawed stumps of the cottonwoods protruded from the water and formed a swift eddy against the surface, cutthroat trout, brookies, and Dolly Vardens balanced themselves against the pebble bottom, drifting sideways momentarily when food floated downstream toward them, their color a flash of ivory-tipped fins and gold and gills roaring with fire.

I unhooked the cage door and tilted the cage upward into the pond. At first the nutrias clung to the wire mesh with their strange, webbed feet; then they clattered over one another and splashed into the water, their pelts beaded with light. They turned in circles, their red eyes like hot bbs, then swam toward the log pile.

'I don't think the beavers are going to like these guys,' I said.

'Then one of them will move,' Mr Riordan said.

I looked at him to see if there was a second meaning there. If there was, it didn't show in the rigid profile and the lead-gray eyes that were still focused intently on the pond.

'You see those grouse tracks on the other side?' he said. 'There haven't been grouse up this creek since I was a boy. Two years ago I turned some blues loose about fifty yards from here, and they still water at this hole.'

He dropped the cigarette stub from his fingers into the shallows, as though it were an afterthought, and we got back in the pickup and started down the grade in second gear. Through the pines bordering the road I could see the blue immensity of the valley and the metallic sheen of the Bitterroot River winding through the cottonwoods.

'I'll buy you a steak at the Fort Owen Inn,' he said.

'You don't owe me anything.'

'You better take advantage of it. I don't do this often. Besides, I'll show you the place where the Montana vigilantes hanged old Whiskey Bill Graves.'

'I'll bet some of the locals put a monument up there.'

He cleared his throat and laughed. 'How did you know?'

'I just guessed,' I said.

It was Saturday afternoon, and the Inn was full of families from Stevensville and Corvallis and Hamilton. They sat around the checker-cloth tables like pieces of scrubbed beef, stuffed in their ill-fitting clothes and chewing on celery and radishes out of the salad bowl. A few of the men nodded at Mr Riordan when we walked in, but I had the feeling that we were about as welcome there as cow flop. He slipped his sheep-lined jacket on the back of the chair and ordered two whiskies with draft chasers.

'Are you sure you want to eat here?' I said.

'Why shouldn't we?'

I saw the same type of deliberate nonrecognition

in his face that I used to see in my father's when he refused to accept the most obvious human situation.

'It was just an observation,' I said.

He drank the whiskey neat, his lead-gray eyes blinking only once when he swallowed. He sipped off the top of the beer and set the mug evenly on the tablecloth.

'You don't care for Jim Beam?' he said.

'I have to work tonight. Musicians can get away with almost anything except showing up high.'

His eyes went past me, into the faces of the people at the other tables; then he looked back at me again.

'You have to use that kind of caution in your work, do you?' he said.

I drank out of the beer.

'I have a habit of falling into the whole jug when I get started on bourbon,' I said. I smiled with my excuse, but he wasn't really talking to me anymore.

He took his package of string-cut tobacco out of his pocket and creased a cigarette paper between his thumb and forefinger. His nails were broken back to the cuticle and purple with carpenter's bruises. But even while the tobacco was filling and shaling off the dented paper, before he wadded it all up and dropped it out of his palm into the ashtray, I already saw the dark change of mood, the vulnerable piece in his stoic armor, the brass wheels of disciplined empathy shearing against one another. At all those other tables he was at best a tolerable eccentric (since it was a Saturday afternoon family crowd that would make allowances).

'You want to drink at the bar?' I said.

'That's a good idea.'

We walked between the tables into the small bar that adjoined the dining room, and Mr Riordan told the waitress to serve our steaks in there.

'How are you, Frank?' the bartender said. I recognized him as one of the volunteer firemen who had come to the ranch when the barn burned.

'Pretty good, Slim. Give this man here a beer, and I'll take a Beam with water on the side.'

The bartender set a double-shot glass on the counter and continued to pour to the top.

'Just one,' Mr Riordan said.

'I like to give away other people's whiskey.' The bartender glanced sideways at the empty stools and into the dining room. 'Did you hear anything about who might have had that gasoline can?'

'No.'

'There were some guys drunk in here the other night talking about lighting a fire to somebody's ass.'

Mr Riordan rolled the whiskey back against his throat and swallowed once, deeply, the gray eyes momentarily bright.

'Who were they?' he said.

'I think one of them drives a tractor-trailer out of Lolo.'

'Slim, why in the hell would a truck driver want to burn me out?'

'I don't know. I just told you what I heard them saying.'

'And you don't know this man's name.'

'Like I said, maybe I've seen him pulling out of

255

Lolo a couple of times. I thought I might be of some help to you.'

Mr Riordan clicked his fingernail on the lip of the glass.

'Well, next time call me while they're here, or ask them to leave their name and address.'

The bartender's lips were a tight line while he poured into the glass. He set the bottle down, lit a cigarette, and walked to the rounded end of the bar and leaned against it, with one foot on a beer case and his back to us. Then he squeezed his cigarette in an ashtray and took off his apron.

'I'm going on my break now,' he said. 'Pour what you want out of the bottle, and add it on to your dinner bill.' I could see the color in his neck as he went through the doorway.

I shook my head and laughed.

'Buddy told me you had a private sense of humor,' Mr Riordan said.

'I can't get over the number of people around here who always have a firestorm inside themselves,' I said.

'Oh, Slim's not a bad fellow. Actually, his problem is his wife. Her face would make a train turn left on a dirt road.' He was into his third shot, and the blood was starting to show in his unshaved cheeks. 'One time he came in on a tear from the firemen's picnic, and she sewed his bedsheet down with a sail needle and wore him out with a quirt. He got baptized at the Baptist church the next Sunday.'

When he grinned, his teeth looked purple in the light from the neon beer sign above the bar.

'Do you believe what he said about that man in Lolo?' I said.

'No. But it's not important, anyway.'

'It's pretty damn important when they're setting fire to your home and your animals.'

It was rash, and I hated my impetuosity even before I saw his face fix mine in the mirror behind the bar. The skin was tight against the bone, the eyes even, his red-check wool shirt buttoned like a twisted rose under his neck.

'I think I know who they are,' he said, his voice low and intense. 'I don't know if I could put them in the penitentiary, but I could probably do things to them myself that would make them never want to destroy a fine horse again. But that won't stop others like them, and it won't change the minds of those people in the dining room, either.'

The waitress brought our steaks, thick and swimming in blood and gravy, a piece of butter on the charcoaled center, surrounded with boiled carrots and Idaho potatoes. The meat was so tender and good that the steak knife clicked against the plate as soon as you cut into it.

Mr Riordan finished his bourbon, then began to cut at the steak, his back rigid and his elbows at an angle. The steak slipped sideways on the plate and knocked potatoes and gravy all over the bar.

'Well,' he said, and picked up the bartender's towel. He had a good edge on, and I could feel him deciding something inside himself. He pushed the plate away with his fingertips, rolled a cigarette slowly, and poured again from the bottle of Jim

Beam. 'Go ahead and eat. Remind me in the future to stay away from morning whiskey.'

It was colder when we walked outside, and the snow clouds had covered the sun. The wind bit into my face and made my eyes water. A few early mallard ducks were winnowing low over the cotton-woods on the river. Mr Riordan walked across the gravel to the truck as though the earth was about to shift on its axis. He took the keys out of his overalls pocket and paused at the driver's door.

'I think you probably want to drive a truck again,' he said, and put the keys in my hand.

As we rolled along the blacktop toward the ranch, he looked steadily ahead through the windshield, his shoulder sometimes slipping momentarily against the door. He started to roll another cigarette, then gave it up.

'What do you plan to do in the future?' he said, because he felt that he had to say something.

'Finish my parole. Take it easy and cool and slide with it, I guess.'

'You probably have about thirty or forty years ahead of you. Do you think about that?' The movement of the truck made his head nod, and he blinked and widened his eyes.

'I've never gotten around to it.'

'You should. You don't believe you'll be fifty or sixty. Or even middle-aged. But you will.'

I looked over at him, but his eyes were focused on the blacktop. His large, worn hands lay on his thighs like skillets. The back of his left hand was burned with a thick white scar, hairless and slick as a piece of rubber. He cleared his throat, blinked again, and then his eyes faded and closed. He breathed as though he were short of breath.

Buddy had told me about his old man riding for five bucks a show on the Northwestern rodeo circuit during the Depression. In 1934 he couldn't make the mortgage payments for seven months on an eight-hundred-acre spread outside of Billings, and a farm corporation out of Chicago bought it up at twenty dollars an acre. They knocked the two-story wood home flat with an earth grader, bulldozed it up in a broken pile of boards, burned it, and pushed it in a steaming heap into the Yellowstone River. Mr Riordan pulled his children and wife around in a homemade tin trailer on the back of a Ford pickup through Wyoming, Utah, and California, working lettuce, topping carrots and onions, and picking apples at three cents a crate.

He took a job in Idaho on a horse farm by the Clearwater, breaking and training Appaloosas for a man who provided rough stock on the rodeo circuit. In a year and a half of stinting, eating welfare potatoes, and listening to the wind crack off the mountain and blow through the newspaper plugged in the trailer's sides, he put away four hundred dollars in the People's Bank of Missoula. It all went down on the ranch in the Bitterroots. He had no idea of how he could make the first mortgage payment. But nevertheless it went down, and he pulled the tin trailer up to the house, stomped down the chicken-wire fence with his boot, let the kids out of the trailer door into a yard full of pigweed and cow flop, and said, 'This is it. We're going to do it right here.'

He stayed two days at the house and then left Mrs Riordan to clean, scrub, and boil an entire ranch to cleanliness while he followed the circuit through Oregon and Washington and Alberta. He worked as a pickup man and hazer, then rode bulls and broncs for prize money. In Portland he drew a sorrel that had a reputation as an easy rocker, but when the sorrel came out of the chute, he slammed sideways into the gate and then started sunfishing. Mr Riordan stayed on for six seconds, and then he was twisted sideways on the horse's back with his left hand wound in the leather. The pickup men couldn't get the bucking strap off. The leather pinched Mr Riordan's hand into a shriveled monkey's paw, and the bones snapped apart like twigs.

His rodeo career ended six months later at Calgary. He had won forty dollars that afternoon in the calf roping and had enough money for his trip back to Montana and the entry fee in another event. So that night under the lights he entered the bulldogging competition and drew a mucus-eyed, blood-flecked black bull with alabaster horns that had already taken out two riders and ground a clown into a board fence. The rope dropped, and Mr Riordan bent low over the quarter horse and raced even with the bull toward the far end of the arena, the judge's clock ticking inside of him with his own heartbeat and the blood rushing in his head as he leaned out of the saddle, waiting for that right second to come down on the horns with both hands, the weight perfectly balanced, the thighs already flexed like iron for the sudden brake against the earth and the violent twist of the bull's neck against his chest. But he misjudged his distance and pushed the quarter horse too hard. When he left the saddle, one arm went out over the bull's face, the other hand grabbed a horn as though he wanted to do a gymnastic push-up, and his body folded into the horns just as the bull sat on all four legs and brought his head up. He was impaled through the lung in a way that could be equaled only by a medieval executioner. The blood roared from his nose and mouth while he was twisted and whipped like a rag doll on the boss of the horns and the pickup men and clowns tried to pull him free. The bull dipped once, knocking him into the sawdust and horseshit, then trampled over him in a shower of torn sod.

Buddy said he should have been dead three times during his first week in the hospital, and the surgeon who cut out part of his lung told Mrs Riordan that even if he lived, he would probably be an invalid the rest of his life. But four months later he got off the train in Missoula (thirty pounds lighter and as pale as milk, Mrs Riordan said) with a walking cane, a tan western suit on, a gold watch in his vest, and an eight-hundred-dollar cashier's check from the Rodeo Cowboys' Association. While he was on the circuit through all those dusty shitkicker Depression towns, he had put his money together with a rider named Casey Tibbs, who at that time saw the profit to be made in buying rough stock and trained horses for Hollywood films.

I had the heater on in the truck as we bounced along the corrugated road toward the main house, where I planned to let Mr Riordan off, but the cold seemed to gather and swell in all the plastic and metal of the cab, and even the windshield looked blue against the cold sky. The grass along the irrigation ditch was dry and stiff in the wind, or a momentary sear brown when a gust out of the canyon blew it flat against the ground. Flurries of snow were starting to whirl out of the grey sun and click in broken crystals against the glass. It was a good day for pine logs burning and snapping and bursting into resinous flames in a stone hearth, with mulled buttered rum in flagons and tin plates full of venison stew and French bread.

'It's early this year,' Mr Riordan said.

'Sir?' I said, because I had thought he was still asleep.

'It's early for snow.' His eyes were squinted at the canyon behind his house. 'The deer will be down early this year. As soon as a snow pack forms on that first rise, they'll move down to feed along the drainage just the other side of my fence. The grouse move down about the same time.' He straightened himself in the seat and opened the window slightly to let the wind blow into his face. 'Where are you going?'

'To your house.'

'Let yourself off at the cabin and I'll take the truck home.'

'I can walk across the field.'

'Son, just do what I tell you. Besides, Buddy is

probably wondering where we've been.' His breath was heavy with whiskey.

I backed the truck around in the center of the road and drove back to the Y fork that divided off toward Buddy's cabin. I could see Buddy on the front porch in a red wool shirt and a pair of corduroys with a white coffee cup in his hand.

'I don't guess there's a need to take up our conversation with him, is there?' Mr Riordan said.

I didn't want to answer him or even acknowledge his presumption. But he was still drunk, his gray eyes staring as flatly at me as though he were looking down a rifle barrel.

'No, sir, I don't guess there is,' I said.

I got out of the truck, and he slipped behind the wheel, clanked the transmission into first with the clutch partially depressed, the gears shearing into one another like broken Coke bottles, then popped the pedal loose and bounced forward across the field toward his house. I heard him shift into second, and the transmission whined as though there were a file caught in it.

Buddy walked toward me off the porch with his cup of coffee in his hand. His face was pinched in the wind.

'What happened to the old man?' he said.

'He got the sun in his eyes.'

'I don't believe it. The old man really drunk? He don't get drunk.'

'He had some bad stuff working in him back there in the restaurant.'

'What?'

'He wants to believe in his friends.'

'What are you talking about, man?'

'All those shit-hog people who call themselves neighbors.'

'You smell like you put your head in the jug, too.'

'Tell me how you live around these bastards. They treat your old man like sheep-dip.'

'What set you off?'

We closed the cabin door behind us, and I felt the sudden warmth of the room in my face and hands.

'I really don't understand it,' I said. 'Your father's a decent man, and he puts up with a gyppo logger giggling on a cigar like a gargoyle, and these guys in the restaurant acted like somebody held up a bedpan to their nostrils when we walked in.'

'Are you sure you weren't into my blotter when you left here this morning?'

I pulled off my coat and took a beer out of the icebox. Two elk steaks covered with mushrooms and slices of onion were simmering in the skillet on the stove.

'Man, you're a righteous son of a bitch today,' Buddy said. 'You're genuinely pissed because people can act as bad here as where you come from. And remember, Zeno, that's where redneck and stump-jumper was first patented.'

'You're wrong there, podna. I didn't grow up around a bunch of thugs that would beat the hell out of you or burn you out because they didn't like you. They might sniff at you a little bit, but you have your own variety of sons of bitches here.'

I picked up the guitar and put the strap around

my neck. I tuned the big E down and did a run from Lightning Hopkins' 'Mojo Hand.' Buddy took a cigarette out of my shirt pocket and lit it. I could feel him looking down at me. He flicked the paper match at the stove.

'Are you playing tonight?' he said quietly.

'Yeah, at nine.'

'Are you looking for company?'

'Come along. It's the same old gig. A bunch of Saturday-night drunks from the mill getting loaded enough to forget what their wives look like.'

'You've really got some strong shit in your blood today, babe,' he said. 'I'm going to walk down and fish the river for a couple of hours. Move the skillet to the edge of the fire in about thirty minutes.'

I nodded at him and began tuning my treble strings with the plectrum. I heard him open the door and pause as the wind blew coldly against my back.

'You want to come along?' he asked.

'Go ahead. I better sleep this afternoon,' I said.

I had another beer and played the guitar in my sullen mood while the sky outside became grayer with the snow clouds that rolled slowly over the peaks of the Bitterroots. But even in my strange depression, which must have been brought on by lack of sleep and early morning booze, I felt a tranquillity and freedom in Buddy's absence, the way one would after his wife has left him temporarily.

Still, it was a dark day, and no matter how much I played on the guitar, I couldn't get rid of that heavy feeling in my breast. Normally, I could work out anything on the frets and the tinny shine of sound from my plectrum against the strings, but the blues wouldn't work for me (because you have to be a Negro or a dying Jimmie Rodgers to play them right, I thought).

And I still couldn't get my song 'The Lost Get-Back Boogie' into place, and I wondered even more deeply about everything that I was doing. I was betraying a friend, living among people who were as foreign to me as if I had been born in another dimension, and constantly scraping through the junk pile of my past, which had as much meaning as my father's farm after Ace surveyed it into lots and covered it with cement. And I was thirty-one now, playing in the same beer joints for fifteen dollars a night, justifying what I did in a romantic abstraction about the music of the rural South.

The reality of that music was otherwise. The most cynical kind of exploitation of poverty, social decay, ignorance of medicine, cultural paranoia, racial hatred, and finally, hick stupidity were all involved in it. And the irony was that those who best served this vulgar, cynical world often in turn became its victims. I remembered when Hank Williams died at age twenty-nine, rejected by the Opry, his alcoholic life a nightmare. They put his body on the stage of the Montgomery city auditorium, and somebody sang 'The Great Speckled Bird' while thousands of people slobbered into their handkerchiefs.

I put the guitar down and moved the skillet of elk steaks to the edge of the fire, then lay down on my bunk with my arm across my eyes. For a few minutes I heard the wind outside and the scrape of the pines against the cabin roof, and then I dropped down into the warmth of the blanket and the gray afternoon inside my head.

I dreamed I was in Korea again. It was hot, and three of us were sitting in the shade of a burnt-out tank with our shirts off, drinking warm beer out of cans that I had punched open with my bayonet. The twisted cloth straps of the bandoliers crisscrossed over my chest were dark with perspiration, and the metal side of the tank scorched my back every time I leaned against it. A couple of miles out from the beach, in the Sea of Japan, a British destroyer escort was throwing it into two MiGs that banked up high into the burning sky each time they made a strafing pass. I hadn't seen Communist planes this far south before, except Bedcheck Charlie in his Piper Cub when he used to drop potato mashers on us, and it was fun to be a spectator, in the shade of the tank, with a lazy cigarette in my mouth and a wet can of beer between my thighs. The sea was flat and slate green, and the tracers from the pom-poms streaked away infinitely into the vast blueness of the sky. Then suddenly one of the MiGs burst apart in an explosion of yellow flame and flying metal that spun dizzily in trails of smoke toward the water.

The man next to me, Vern Benbow, an ex-ballplayer from the Texas bush, belched and held up his beer can in a toast. There were grains of sand in his damp hair, and his pale blue, hillbilly eyes were red around the edges.

'May you find peace, motherfucker,' he said.

267

Then the scene changed. It was night, and Vern and I were in a wet hole fifteen yards behind our concertina wire, and the dark outline of a ridge loomed up into a darker sky that was occasionally violated with the falling halos of pistol flares. I was shaking with the malaria that I had picked up in the Philippines, and I thought I could hear mosquitoes buzzing inside my head. Every time a flare ripped upward into the blackness and popped into its ghostly phosphorescence, I felt another series of chills crawl like worms through every blood vein in my body.

'I think I got it figured out why they blow those goddamn bugles,' Vern said. 'They're dumb. That's why they're here. Nobody in his right mind would fight for a piece of shit like this.'

My rifle was leaned against the side of the hole with a tin can over the end of the barrel. I tried to straighten the poncho under me to keep the water from seeping along my spine.

'What the hell do we want that hill for?' Vern said. 'Let the gooks have it. They deserve it. They can sit up there and play their bugles with their assholes. You couldn't grow weeds here if you wanted to.'

His young face and the anxiety in it about tomorrow and the barrage that came in every day at exactly three o'clock was lighted momentarily by the pale glow of a descending flare. He took his package of Red Man chewing tobacco out of his pocket, filled his fingers with the loose strands, and put them in his mouth along with the slick lump that was already in his jaw. Out in the darkness, we saw the sergeant walking along the line of holes with his Thompson held in one hand.

'I guess I'll go out tonight,' Vern said.

'You went out last night,' I said.

'You pulled mine two days ago. Besides, your teeth are clicking.'

I raised myself on one elbow, unbuttoned my shirt pocket, and took out the pair of red dice that I had carried with me since the Philippines.

'Snake eyes or boxcars?' I said.

'Texas people is always high rollers. Even you coonasses ought to know that.'

I rattled the dice once in my hand and threw them on the edge of his muddy blanket.

'Little Joe. You son of a buck,' he said. He put his pot on, picked up his rifle, slipped a bandolier over his shoulder, and lifted himself out of the hole. His back and seat were caked with mud.

That was the last time I saw him. He and fifteen others were caught halfway up the hill between two machine-gun emplacements that the Chinese had established on our side of Heartbreak Ridge during the night.

I heard the screen door slam on the edge of my dream and Buddy pulling off his heavy jacket. His hair was powdered with wet snow, and his trousers were damp up to the thighs from the brush along the riverbank. He rubbed his hands on his red cheeks.

'It's too damn cold to fish,' he said. 'I had one brown on and almost froze my hand when I stuck it in the water.'

'Where's the brown?'

'Very clever,' he said.

'It was just a question, since I was trying to sleep and you came in like gangbusters.'

'Go back to sleep, then. I'm going to eat.' He unlaced the leather string on one boot and kicked it toward the wall. 'You want some elk?'

'Go ahead. I'm not hungry.'

'You're not anything these days, Zeno.'

'What am I supposed to do with that, Buddy?'

'Not a goddamn thing.'

'You want to just say it? If it's on your mind, if it's in some real bad place?'

'I don't have nothing to say. I didn't mean to piss you off because I woke you up. Or maybe you're just pissed in general about something that don't have anything to do with you and me.'

I sat up on the bunk and lit a cigarette. Outside, the snow was swirling in small flakes into the wet pines next to the cabin. The clouds had moved down low on the mountains until the timberline had disappeared. I wanted to push him into it, some final verbal recognition between the two of us about what I was doing with Beth and to him, my friend, so I wouldn't have to keep contending with that dark feeling of deceit and betrayal that caught like a nail in my throat every time I looked at him. But I couldn't push it over the edge, and he wouldn't accept it either. I blinked into the cigarette smoke and took another deep puff, as though there were something philosophical in smoking a cigarette.

'I got pretty drunk last night, and it didn't help to

get half loaded again this morning,' I said. 'I think I ought to hang up my drinking act for a while.'

'When you do that, Zeno, the Salvation Army is going to pass out free booze on Bourbon Street.'

'I believe that would be a commendable way to celebrate my sobriety.'

'Man, you are a clever son of a bitch. You sound like you went to one of those colored business colleges. You remember that psychotic preacher back in A that used to start hollering when the captain clanged the bell for evening count? His eyes were always busting out of his head after he'd been drinking julep in the cane all day, and he'd scream out all this stuff about standing up before Jesus that he'd memorized from one of those Baptist pamphlets, but he could never get all the words right. He'd stand there in the sun, still shouting, until the captain led him into the dormitory by the arm.'

In a moment Buddy had been back into our common prison experience, which I didn't care to relive anymore, and I suddenly realized that maybe this was the only thing we shared: an abnormal period in our lives, since neither of us was a criminal by nature, that contained nothing but degradation, hopelessness, mindless cruelty (newborn kittens flushed down the commodes by the hacks), suicides bailing off the top tier, a shank in the spleen on the way to the dining hall, or the unbearable sexual heat that made your life a misery. I just didn't feel any more humor in it, but Buddy's face was flushed with laughter and anticipation of my own. I drew in on

271

my cigarette and blew out the smoke without looking at him.

'What's all that noise out there?' I said.

'What noise?' he said, his face coming back to composure.

'It sounds like a fox got into somebody's hen house.'

He stood up from the kitchen chair and looked through the front window. He held the curtain in his hand a moment and then dropped it, almost flinging it at the window glass.

'What's the old man doing?' he said. 'He must have lost his mind.' He sat on the chair and pulled his wet boots back on without lacing them.

I looked out the window and saw Mr Riordan walking off balance through the rows of birdcages in the aviary, the snow swirling softly around him in a dim halo. He had a canvas birdfeed sack looped over one shoulder, and he was pulling back the tarps on the cages, unlatching the wire doors, and slinging seed on the ground.

'I'll go with you,' I said.

'I'll take care of it.'

'I was the one that got him drunk.'

'Nobody gets the old man drunk, Zeno.'

We walked hurriedly across the wet, cold field to the main house. Mrs Riordan and Buddy's sister had come out on the front porch and were standing silently by the rail with the wind in their faces. I could see a bottle of whiskey on top of one of the cages.

Birds were everywhere, like chickens all over a

roost when an egg-sucking dog gets inside ruffed grouse, Canada geese, greenhead mallards, ground owls, gulls, bobwhites, ring-necked pheasants, an eagle, egrets, pintails, blue herons, and two turkey buzzards. Most of them seemed as though they didn't know what to do, but then a mallard hen took off, circled once overhead, and winnowed toward the river. Buddy started latching the doors on the birds that hadn't yet jumped out after the seed.

'Frank, what in the hell are you doing?' Buddy said.

Mr Riordan's back was to us, his shoulders bent, as he sowed the seed from side to side like a farmer walking a fallow field.

'Don't let any more of them out,' Buddy said. 'It'll take us a week to get them back.'

Mr Riordan turned and saw us for the first time. The bill of his fur cap was pulled low over his eyes.

'Hello, boys. What are you doing here?' he said.

'Let's go inside,' Buddy said, and slipped the heavy sack of feed off his father's shoulder. The pupils in Mr Riordan's eyes had contracted until there was nothing left but a frosted greyness that seemed to look through us.

He walked with us toward the porch, then as an afterthought picked up the bottle of whiskey by the neck. I thought he was going to drink from it, but I should have known better. He was not the type of man who would be seen drinking straight out of a bottle, particularly when drunk, in front of his family.

273

'Put it away for today, Frank,' Buddy said.

'Go get us three cups and the coffeepot that's on the stove,' he said.

'I don't think that's good,' Buddy said.

He looked at Buddy from under the bill of his cap. There was no command in his expression, not even a hint of older authority, just the gray flatness of those eyes and maybe somewhere behind them a question mark.

'All right,' Buddy said. 'But those birds are going to be spread all over the Bitterroot by tonight.'

He went inside with his mother and sister and a moment later came back with three cups hooked on his fingers and the metal coffeepot with a napkin wrapped around the handle.

We sat on the steps and leaned against the wood railing, with the snow blowing under the eave into our faces, and drank coffee and whiskey for a half hour. Occasionally, I heard movement inside the house, and when I would turn, I would see the disappearing face of Mrs Riordan or Pearl in the window. The snow was starting to fall more heavily now, with the wind blowing from behind us out of Idaho, and I watched the mountains on the far side of the valley gradually disappear in the white haze, then the stripped cottonwoods along the river, and finally our cabin across the field.

Mr Riordan was talking about his grandfather, who had owned half of a mine and the camp that went with it at Confederate Gulch during the 1870s.

'He was a part-time preacher, and he wouldn't allow a saloon or a racetrack in town unless they contributed to his church,' he said. 'He used to say there was nothing the devil hated worse than to have his own money used against him. Once, two of Henry Plummer's old gang tried to hoorah the main street when they were drunk. He locked them in a stone powder house for two days and wouldn't give them anything to drink but castor oil and busthead Indian whiskey. Then he made them wash in the creek, and took them home and fed them and gave them jobs in his mine.'

'It's starting to come in heavy, Frank,' Buddy said. 'We better get the birds back in and the tarps on.'

Mr Riordan poured the whiskey and coffee out of his cup into the saucer to cool it.

'You should take Iry to a couple of the places around here,' he said. 'There's a whole city called Granite up eight thousand feet on the mountain outside of Philipsburg. Miners were making twelve-dollars-a-day wage, seven days a week, in the 1880s. They had an opry house, a union hall, a two-story hospital, one street filled with saloons and floozy houses, and the day the vein played out you couldn't count ten people in that town. They left their food in plates right on the table.'

He was enjoying his recounting of Montana history to me, not so much for its quality of strangeness and fascination to an outsider, but because it was a very great part of the sequence that he still saw in time.

'I told you about where they hanged Whiskey Bill Graves,' he said, rolling a cigarette out of his string tobacco, 'but before they got to him, they bounced

Frank Parrish and four others off a beam in Virginia City. You can still see the rope burns on the rafter today. When they hoisted Parrish up on the ladder with the rope around his neck and asked him for his last words, he hollered out, 'Hurray for Jefferson Davis! Let her rip, boys!' and he jumped right into eternity.'

'I'm going to get the canvas gloves,' Buddy said.

'What?' Mr Riordan said.

'Those damn birds.'

Buddy went inside again, knocking the heavy wood door shut when it wouldn't close easily the first time. Mr Riordan smoked his rolled cigarette down to a thin stub between his fingers, his elbows propped on his knees, his face looking out into the blowing snow that covered the whole ranch. The bib of his overalls had come unbuttoned and hung down on his stomach like a miniature and incongruous apron. I felt sorry for him, but I didn't know why.

'I guess we'd better go inside,' I said.

'Yes, that's probably right,' he answered.

By that time Buddy had come out on the porch with the thick, canvas elbow-length gloves for handling the birds. Mr Riordan started to rise, then had to grab the banister for support. I put one hand under his arm, as innocuously as I could, and helped him turn toward the door. The whiskey and blood drained out of his face from the exertion. His weight tipped sideways away from my hand. He breathed deeply, with a phlegmy tick in his throat.

'I believe I'm going to have to leave it with you, boys,' he said.

Buddy and I walked him upstairs to bed, then went outside and set about trying to put three dozen confused birds back in their cages. After an hour of chasing them in a whir of wings and cacophony of noise, we still hadn't caught half of them.

'Shit on it,' Buddy said. There were two blood-flecked welts on one cheek. 'The ducks won't go any farther than the slough, and the rest of these assholes will put themselves back in when they're ready.'

I went inside the house with him to return the canvas gloves. His sister sat by the burning fireplace with a magazine folded back in her hands. When Buddy walked into the back of the house and left us alone, I could feel her resentment, like an aura around her, in the silence. I stood in the center of the room with an unlit cigarette in my mouth, the melted snow dripping out of my hair.

'You really leave your mark when you stay at somebody's place, don't you?' she said, without looking up.

'How's that?' I said. I really didn't want an exchange with her, but it looked like it was inevitable, and I was damned if I was going to lose to someone's idle attempt at insult.

'Oh, I think we both know that you have a way of letting everybody know you're around.'

'Yeah, I guess I led your father into a bottle of whiskey, and I got Buddy those five years in the joint. They must be pretty susceptible to what a part-time guitar picker can do to them.'

Her curly head looked up from the magazine, the light from the fireplace bright on the sunburned ends of her hair.

'You are a bastard, aren't you?'

'A genuine southern badass.'

'It must be nice to have that awareness about yourself,' she said.

No more tilting, babe, because you're an amateur, I thought. I had gotten to her, but I should have known then that she was going to pull out that arrow point later and give it back to me, in a form that I wouldn't recognize until it was too late.

Buddy and I walked back to the cabin in the gray light. Most of the afternoon was gone, and there wasn't enough time to take a nap before I would have to get ready to work that night. I hadn't realized how tired I was. The lack of sleep from last night, unloading the nutrias with Mr Riordan, an hour of fighting birds that pecked and defecated all over you, and two excursions into drinking in one day all came down on me like a wood club on the back of the neck.

I got into the tin shower and turned on the hot water, and just as I was thinking of a way to coast through the evening (no booze on the bandstand, long breaks between sets, letting the steel man do the lead and the drummer most of the vocals) until I could be back at Beth's after we closed, Buddy decided that everyone should go to Milltown with me. The water drummed against the tin sides of the shower, and I tried to think of some reasonable way to dissuade him, but I knew that Beth was in the center of his mind and there was nothing I could say that wouldn't sound like a door kicked shut in his face.

So while I dressed, he went back to the main house and talked to Melvin, who needed little encouragement for any kind of adventure, and a half hour later they were sitting in the front room of the cabin with a bottle of vodka that Melvin had been working on through the afternoon. Pearl evidently had argued about going, because Buddy and her husband kept making reassuring remarks to her in the way obtuse or drunk people would to a child. Actually, I couldn't believe it. Neither one of them saw how angry she was or how much she disliked herself for being in any proximity to me.

Then Buddy went one better. While I was wrapping the guitar in a blanket, he took a blotter of acid out of the icebox and convinced Melvin to eat some with him. Pearl looked out the window like an angry piece of stone.

'Take a hit, Iry,' Melvin said.

'I've got too many snakes in my head already.'

'Zeno has to do his Buck Owens progressions tonight,' Buddy said.

'Why don't you join them?' Pearl said, her face still turned toward the window.

'I'm afraid I can't handle it.'

'It's all them big slides on the guitar neck,' Buddy said. 'There's three chords in every one of those shitkicker songs, and Zeno has to stay sharp.'

Buddy's voice had a mean edge to it, and I knew that no matter what I did, we were headed into a bad one.

I drove the Plymouth to Missoula while Buddy sat beside me, giggling and passing the quart bottle of vodka to Melvin in the backseat. The wind was blowing strong off the river, and the melted snow on the highway had glazed in long, slick patches. The Plymouth's tires were bald, and every time I hit ice, I had to shift into second and slow gradually, holding my breath, because the brakes would have sent us spinning sideways off the shoulder.

We stopped at Beth's house, and Buddy banged on the door as though there were a fire inside. The porch light went on, and I could see Beth in silhouette and the children behind her. I felt awful. I wished I could tell her in some way that this wasn't my plan, wasn't something that was born out of a day's drinking and dropped on her doorstep to contend with. But I knew that I wouldn't get to talk with her alone during the evening, and there would be no visit at her house after the bar closed, and she would be trapped four or five hours at a soiled table while Buddy and Melvin got deeper and deeper into a liquor-soaked, acid delirium.

We drove along the Clark through Hellgate Canyon to the bar, with the snow blowing out of the dark pines into the headlights. There was no easy way to coast through the evening. The building was already crowded when we got there, the steel man had cut off one of his fingers with a chain saw that afternoon, and the drummer, who I thought could take the vocal, had four opened beers sitting in a row on the rail next to his traps.

I got up on the platform, slipped the guitar strap around my neck, and tripped the purple and orange lights with my foot. In the glare of light against my eyes I saw Buddy walk with his arm around Beth's shoulders to a table by the edge of the dance floor. I put on my thumb pick, screwed the guitar into D, and kicked it off with 'Poison Love.' I didn't have a mandolin to back me up, and my fingers still felt stiff from the cold outside, but Johnny and Jack or Bill and Charlie Monroe never did it better. Then I rolled into Moon Mulligan's 'Ragged but Right' and knocked out four others in a row with no pause except for the bridge into the next key. The cellophane-covered lights were hot against my face, and my eyes were starting to water in the drifting clouds of cigarette smoke. The dance floor and the tables were lost somewhere behind the rail of the platform and the violent glitter and rattle of bottles and glasses. I felt the sweat roll down off my face and hit on my hand, and when I went into the last song, I heard the drummer miss a beat and clatter a stick against the metal edge of the trap.

'Hey, man, save some for later,' he said.

After the set I went to the table, which was now wet with spilled beer and scorched with cigarettes that Buddy had mashed out on the cloth. Beth's face was almost white.

'Give me the keys,' he said.

'What for?' I said.

'Because they're my keys. And because it's my

goddamn car, and that's my goddamn wife. You understand that's my wife, don't you?'

Everyone looked momentarily into the center of the table.

'Don't go driving anywhere now, man,' I said.

'I ain't. And you didn't answer my question.'

'Take the keys. Get into the stock-car derby if you like,' I said.

'Just answer me. Without all that southern bull-shit you put out.'

'I got to get back on the bandstand.'

'No, man, you answer something straight for the first time in your fucking insignificant life.'

'He just wants the keys to get in the trunk,' Melvin said. 'He bought a couple of lids from some university kids.'

'They're right there,' I said. I rose from the chair and started back toward the platform. Out of the corner of my eye I saw Beth lean forward and place her forehead against her fingertips.

I couldn't get between two tables because a fat man had fallen over backward like a beer barrel in his chair. Up on the stand, the drummer was draining the last foam from a bottle, and our bass man was slipping his velvet glove back on his hand. I felt Melvin's arm on my shoulder and his sour liquor breath along the side of my cheek.

'Take a walk with me into the head,' he said.

I followed him inside the yellow glare of the men's room and leaned against the stall with him.

'Look, he just ate too much acid, and maybe we ought to get out of here early tonight,' he said.

**282**

I looked at him, with his tailored attempt at some romantic western ethic, and wondered if his rebellion was against a mother or father who owned a candy factory in Connecticut.

'I work here,' I said. 'If I leave, I don't get paid. Also, I probably get fired. What happened at the table with Beth?'

'What do you mean?' He looked at the garish color of the wall in front of him, as though he had seen it for the first time.

'She looked sick.'

'Buddy was trying to feel her up under the table.'

'Man, I don't believe it,' I said.

'That's what I said. We should leave early tonight.'

I left him leaning over the trough and went back to the platform just as the rhythm guitarist was starting to fake his way through 'Folsom Prison Blues' by humping the microphone and roaring it out with enough amplification to blow the front windows into the parking lot.

I cut it short at one-thirty in the morning, and normally there would have been a protest from the crowd. But the temperature was dropping steadily, and the little plastic radio behind the bar said that a storm that had already torn through Calgary and southern Alberta would hit the Missoula area tomorrow.

The bar emptied out while we put away our instruments on the bandstand, and after I tripped off the purple and orange lights with my foot, I could see Buddy at the table with his arms folded under his head. Melvin was leaned back in the chair, his tie pulled loose and a dead cigarette in his grinning mouth, his arms hooked back over the chair's supports like a man who had been crucified by comical accident.

There were no keys to the Plymouth. No one was sure what happened to them. Buddy possibly broke one off in the trunk and lost the other one while wandering around in the snow after all his reefer blew away in the wind. I said good-night to Harold, the owner, took a glass of Jim Beam with me, and while Melvin, Buddy, and Pearl slept in a pile in the backseat Beth held the flashlight for me under the dashboard and I used a piece of chewing tobacco tinfoil to wrap together the wires behind the ignition.

She sat close to me on the drive back to Missoula, with her hand inside my coat, and each time the draft would come up through the floorboard, she would press her thigh against mine and hold a little tighter with her arm. I forgot about Buddy in the backseat and what he would think later. I just wanted to be with her again upstairs in her house with the tree raking against the window. She knew it, too, as we came through the Hellgate into Missoula, with the water starting to freeze into white plates on the edge of the Clark. She leaned her breasts into my arm and kissed me with her tongue against my neck, and I knew everything was going to be all right when I came around the last curve on the mountain into Missoula.

The sheriff's car pulled out even with the Plymouth from the gravel turnaround, the bubble-gum light revolving in a lazy blue-and-orange arc. His souped-up V-8 motor gunned once when he went past us on a slick stretch of ice. He braked to the side of the road and got out with a flashlight in his hand, the collar of his mackinaw turned up into the brim of his Stetson to protect his ears. He walked back to the Plymouth against the wind, as though his own weight was more than he could bear, and opened the door with the flashlight in my face.

'Don't kick over that glass trying to hide it with your foot, son,' he said. 'You don't want to spill whiskey all over the car. Now what's those wires doing hanging under the dashboard with tinfoil around them?'

I took a cigarette from the pack inside my coat and tried to pop a damp kitchen match on my thumbnail, but it broke across my finger. He clicked off the light and pulled back the door a little wider for me to get out.

'Sometimes you get caught by the short hairs, Paret. You ought to look out for that,' he said.

# chapter eleven

Fifteen days. I thought I would get out of it with a fine when I went to guilty court the next day, but the sheriff put in a few words for me with the judge to make sure that would not be the case. (He mentioned, as a casual aside, that I was an out-of-state parolee.)

They put me in a whitewashed eight-man cell on the second floor with the usual collection of county prisoners: habitual drunks, petty check writers, drifters, barroom brawlers, and hapless souls in for nonsupport. There was no window in the cell, the white walls were an insult on the eyes, and we got out only one hour a day for showers. It was going to be a long fifteen days.

I was angry with myself for getting busted on a punk charge like driving with an open container, but I realized that the particular charge didn't make any difference. That fat cop was going to nail me one way or another; it was just a choice of time and place.

Buddy came to see me during the visiting hours that afternoon. I didn't want to talk with him after the scene in the bar, and in fact I wasn't in a mood to talk with anyone. The men in that crowded cell were generally a luckless and pathetic lot, but nevertheless each of their movements (their knee bends and push-ups) and attempts at conversation to relieve their boredom were irritating, eye-crossing reminders of all the wasted nights and days and the impaired, lost people I had known in Angola.

The hack unlocked the cell door and took me downstairs to the visitors' room by the arm.

'You want some cigarettes from the machine while we're down?' he said.

I gave him some change from my pocket and sat on one side of the long board table across from Buddy. There were still grains of ice on his mackinaw, which hung on the back of his chair. His face was white with hangover, and his hand with the cigarette shook slightly on top of his folded arm.

'You have thunder in your eyes, Zeno,' he said.

'Room service was bad today.'

'I'm sorry, man. That's a bad deal. I thought they'd just lighten your wallet a little bit.'

'It could have been worse. They might have tried for drunk driving.'

He paused and looked away.

'You want a butt?' he said.

'The screw's bringing me a pack.'

'Hey, man, I didn't mean to go over the edge last night.' His eyes came back into mine.

'Everybody was drunk. That stuff's always comedy, anyway.'

'You want the guitar? The jailer said you can have it up there.'

'I better not. A couple of those characters would probably try to screw it,' I said.

'Look, I feel like a piece of shit about it.'

'Forget it. I'm going to take up yoga.'

'No, I mean getting it on about Beth.'

The guard put the package of Lucky Strikes in front of me, and I peeled away the cellophane from the top.

'I wouldn't have brought it out like that unless my head was soaking in acid and booze. Shit, I know I can't make up back time with her. What you do is between you and her, Zeno.'

I felt my face flush, and I didn't want to look at his self-abasement.

'I haven't been thinking about any of that,' I said.

'Man, I can read you. I know what you're going to think before a spark even flashes across that guilt-ridden spot in the center of your brain. You're going to tango out of here after your fifteen days, move out of the cabin, and start being a family man in Missoula with some bullshit guilt about old friends hung on your shirt like a Purple Heart.'

'You've got it figured a lot better than I do, then,' I said.

'Because I know you.'

'You don't know diddly-squat, Buddy. The only thing I've got in mind is living two weeks upstairs with some question about what my parole officer is going to do with this. After that scene at the pulp mill, this could be the nut that violates me back to Angola.'

'Yeah,' he said, quietly mumbling, with the backs of his fingers against his mouth. 'I hadn't thought about that. That geek would probably do it, too. I didn't tell you I went to high school with him. He has the IQ of a moth, a real pocket-pool artist. He would probably put you in the toilet just to close the file on you.'

Buddy had a fine way of making you feel better about the future.

'Maybe we can bring a little pressure to bear,' he said, his eyes still introspective. 'My sister says he hangs around with a bunch of faggots in East Missoula.'

'I'd appreciate it if you wouldn't do these things for me.' I could see the color coming back into Buddy's face as his fantasy became more intense and the memory of last night and his discomfort in front of me started to fade into an ordinary day that he could live with.

'We always have alternatives, Zeno,' he said. 'You can't sit on a bunk all that time and worry about Louisiana and moving your baggage around and all this marital crap.'

I heard the hack light a cigar behind me and scrape his chair. Buddy looked past my shoulder, then put his pack of cigarettes on the table with four books of matches.

'I better roll, babe,' he said. 'I'll bring some candy bars and magazines tomorrow.'

'You don't have to do that.'

'Become popular with your bunkies. But look, man, the cabin's yours when you get out. None of this moving into town because you think you got to do something. Besides, the old man wants you to stay there.'

'When did he say this?'

'This morning.' He answered me in a matter-of-fact way, then looked at me with a new attention. 'Why?'

'I just wondered. I thought I might have burned my welcome.' But it didn't work.

His eyes studied mine for even the hint of some private relationship between his father and me, and I was probably not good in concealing it.

'Keep the butts and the matches,' he said. 'You never did learn how to split them, did you?'

He put on his mackinaw and walked down the hall toward the front door of the courthouse, that square of brilliant natural light with the snow blowing behind it, and the trees along the street hung with ice, rattling and clicking in the wind, and the people in overcoats and scarfs, their shoes squeaking on the sidewalks while they walked toward homes and fireplaces and families. I put Buddy's cigarettes, along with my own and the books of matches, into my denim shirt pocket and waited for the hack to put his hand around my arm for the walk upstairs.

The days passed slowly in the cell, with the endless card games and meaningless conversation and the constant hiss of the radiator. Beth visited me every afternoon, and I almost asked her to stop coming, because I wanted her so badly each time after she left. At night I lay on the bunk and tried not to think of being in bed with her, but when I drifted into sleep, my sexual heat embraced wild erotic dreams that made my loins ache for release. Then I would awake, my mattress damp with sweat, draw up my knees before me like an adolescent child suddenly beset with puberty, and debate the morality of masturbation.

I didn't think it was going to be so hard to pull fifteen days. But after nine days I would have volunteered to pull thirty on a road gang to get away from my seven cell mates, their explosions into the toilet, their latent homosexuality (which they disguised as grab-assing), and finally a definite hum that was beginning in the center of my brain.

I noticed it at the end of the first week when I was sitting on my bunk, with my back against the wall and staring at nothing in particular. Then I saw a plastic Benzedrex inhaler on the concrete floor, and the hum started like a tuning fork beginning to vibrate. It was like that dream you have as a child when you pick up something small and inconsequential off the ground, and suddenly it grows in your hand until it covers the whole earth, and you know you are into a nightmare that seems to have no origin.

Somebody in the cell had gotten hold of some inhalers and was chewing the cotton rings from inside, which was good for a high that would knock the head off King Kong. But for some reason my glance on that split-open plastic tube brought back all the listless hours in my cell at Angola and all the visions I had there about madness in myself and madness all over the world. My mother had killed herself and my sister Fran in the house fire, even though my father always pretended that it was an accident, and as I grew up, I always wondered if she had left some terrible seed in me. But in Korea I believed truly for the first time that I was all right, because I realized that insanity was not a matter of individual illness; it was abroad in all men, and its definition was a very relative matter. I even took a perverse pride in the fact that I *knew* the lieutenant was lying when he said we couldn't take six gook prisoners back to the rear and we had to blow them all over a ditch. Four members of the patrol did it and enjoyed it, but they never admitted later that it was anything but necessary.

Even my father had the same strange dualism about war and people at their worst in the middle of an inferno, and their failure to recognize it later for what it was. He went all the way across France in the Great War, as he called it, a seventeen-year-old marine who would be hit twice and gassed once before his next birthday. But he refused to talk about it in even the most vague or general way. I often wondered what awful thing he carried back with him from France, something that must have lain inside him like a piece of rusted barbed wire.

But he was working an oil job at Texas City when it blew up in 1947 and killed over five hundred people, many of them roughnecks whom he had known for years. A ship carrying fertilizer was burning out in the harbor, and while people watched from the docks and a tug tried to pull it out to the Gulf, the fire dripped into the hold and then the ship exploded in a mushroom flame that rained onto the refineries and chemical plants along the shore. The town went up almost at once – the gas storage tanks, the derricks, the entire Monsanto plant – and blew out store windows as far away as Houston. The men caught in the oil field, where blown wellheads fired geysers of flame into the sky under thousands of pounds of pressure, were burned with heat so great that their ashes or even their scorched bones couldn't be separated from the debris.

A year later my father and I were cane fishing for bream in some tanks on a stretch of bald prairie about six miles from Texas City, and we walked around a huge, scalloped hole in the earth where a sheet of twisted boiler plate, the size of a garage door, had spun out of the sky like a stray, ugly monument to all that agony back there in the flames. The hole had filled partially with water, tadpoles hovered under the lip of the rusted metal, and salt grass had begun to grow down the eroded banks.

My father rolled a cigarette from his package of Virginia Extra and looked out toward a windmill ginning in the breeze off the Gulf.

'I lost some of the best friends I ever had in that thing, Son,' he said. 'There wasn't any reason for it either. They could have gotten that fertilizer ship out of there or shut them rigs down and taken everybody out. Those boys didn't have to die.'

So the madness in war was an area that was sacrosanct, not even to be recognized, and there was no correlation between that and the death of your best friends because of corporate stupidity.

But I lost my point, with that description of the hum in my head back in Angola, that distant echo of a bugle that went even farther back to a hole in Korea. The Benzedrex inhaler had conjured up my old cell in the Block, on a languid Louisiana summer afternoon, with the humidity damp on the walls and the bars, and my cell mate W. J. Posey across from me, wiping the sweat off his naked, tattooed body with a washcloth. We were both stoned on Benzedrex and the paregoric that he had stolen from the infirmary.

'So you killed the son of a bitch,' W. J. said. 'A punk like that has it coming. You iced people in Korea that didn't do nothing to you.'

'He broke the shank off in him when he went down. He bled on the bandstand like an elephant.'

'You're breaking my knob off. You got two years. Take another drag on ole Sneaky Pete.'

I got out of jail on Tuesday. Buddy was waiting for me at the possessions desk with a crazy grin on his face.

'How did you know what time I was coming out?' I said.

'They always flush you wineheads out about ten in the morning.'

I had hoped Beth would be there, and he must have seen it in my face.

'She couldn't leave the house,' he said. 'Both of the kids swoll up with mumps yesterday.'

'Are you putting me on?' I picked up the brown envelope with my belt, shoestrings, and wallet inside.

'I know you never had them, Zeno. I wouldn't put you on like that.'

Damn, I thought.

'Figure it this way,' he said. 'You could have gone over there one day earlier and had your rocks swell up like a pair of basketballs.'

The woman behind the desk looked up with her mouth open.

'Let's get out of here,' I said.

'There you go, babe. Let's boogie on down the street, because your daddy is about to get into a gig again.'

We walked outside into the cold, sunlit day, and the sharp air cut into my lungs. The green trees on the mountains were heavy with snow, and the sky was so clear and deeply blue that I thought I would become lost in it.

'Let's walk to this place,' Buddy said. 'My tires are so bald you can see the air showing through. I didn't park the car at that angle. It slid sideways through the intersection.'

'What's this gig?'

'I thought I might clean up my act and get back in the business. A guy I know runs this college joint up in the next block, and he wants to try a piano player to bring in all those fraternity cats and their sweet young girls. Somebody with class, such as myself. Someone to keep them plugged into magic sounds so they won't bust up the place every night and puke all over his crapper.'

'That sounds good, man.'

'Well, he's not real sure about me. Thinks I'm crazy. Undependable. I might show up with a hype hanging out of my forehead. Anyway, he asked me to come down this morning and play a few because his wife will be there, and she knows music. Now dig this, man. I used to know her in high school when she was in the band, and she couldn't tell the difference between a C chord and a snare drum. She was so awful that the bandleader put the tubas in front of her to blow her back into the wall. She used to wear Oxford therapeutic shoes and these glasses that looked like they were made out of the bottoms of Coke bottles. She also had gas all the time. Every two minutes you could hear her burping through her alto sax.'

I was shaking my head and laughing.

'Zeno, you don't believe anything anybody tells you,' he said.

'Because nobody in the world ever had experiences or knew people like these.'

'All right, you'll see, partner. Just be prepared to meet humanity's answer to the goldfish.'

I never did know why Buddy boozed and doped. He could get high in minutes on just himself.

The bar was a beer-and-pizza place with checker-cloth table covers and rows of fraternity steins on the shelves. The contraceptive machine in the men's room had long since been destroyed, and young, virile Americans had punched out big, ragged holes in the fiberboard partitions. I sat at the bar and had a sandwich and a beer while Buddy played the piano for the owner and his wife, who looked exactly as Buddy had described her. (This is why I could never tell whether he was lying, fantasizing, or telling the truth.) She stared at him a few moments with those huge orbs of color behind her glasses, then began washing glasses in a tin sink.

I watched Buddy play. I had forgotten how really good he was. He started out with 'I Found a New Baby,' and he played it the way Mel Powell used to at the Lighthouse in California: a slow, delicate, almost conventional entrance into the melody, then building, the bass growing louder, his right hand working on a fine counterpoint, and finally he was way inside himself and all the wild sounds around him. He didn't even look the same when he played. A strange physical transformation took over him, the kind you see in people who are always partly out of cadence with the rest of the world until they do the one thing that they're good at. As I looked at him, with his shoulders bent, his arms working, the eyes flat and withdrawn, I would have never made him for the Buddy I knew the rest of the time.

Later the owner bought us a beer and told Buddy to come to work the next night. He wanted to hide it, but I could see he was truly happy. He hadn't worked as a musician since he went to jail, and that was six years ago.

'Let's make it,' I said.

'One more beer. I have to ease the effect of joining the work force again. It really blows my self-image.'

'One, damn it, and that's it. I'm not getting into any more of your bloody capers.'

'Oo, oo, oo, oo,' he said, his face in a feminine pout. 'Dig who's coming on about capers. The mad fire bomber of Missoula.'

'Hey, man,' I said, hoarsely.

'Anyway, I wanted to tell you this story, since it just rolled into my gourd while I was into that 1950 Lighthouse shot. I never told you about the Legend of the Gigantic Fart, did I?'

'Put the beer in a paper bag. Let's get it on the road.'

'No, man, this story became a legend and is still told in the high schools around the county. You see, it was at the junior prom, a very big deal with hoop dresses and everybody drinking sloe gin and R.C. Cola outside in the cars. Now, this is strictly a class occasion if you live in a shitkicker town. Anyway, we'd been slopping down the beer all afternoon and eating pintobean salad and these greasy fried fish before we got to the dance. So it was the third number, and I took Betty Hoggenback out on the floor and was doing wonderful, tilting her back like Fred Astaire doing Ginger Rogers. Then I felt this wet fart start to grow inside me. It was like a brown rat trying to get outside. I tried to leak it off one shot at a time and keep dancing away from it, but I must have left a cloud behind that would take the varnish off the gym floor. Then one guy says, "Man, I don't believe it!" People were walking off the floor, holding their noses and saying, "Pew, who cut it?" Then the saxophone player on the bandstand threw up into the piano. Later, guys were shaking my hand and buying me drinks, and a guy on the varsity came up and said that was the greatest fart he'd ever seen. It destroyed the whole prom. The saxophone player had urp all over his summer tux, and they must have had to burn the smell out of that piano with a blowtorch.'

Buddy was laughing so hard at his own story that tears ran down his cheeks. He caught his breath, drank out of the beer glass, then started laughing again. The woman behind the bar was looking at him as though a lunatic had just walked into the normalcy of her life.

We drove back to the ranch, and later in the afternoon I walked up the gravel road to the general store on the blacktop and used the pay phone to call Beth. I told her that I had never had the mumps and couldn't come to the house because I didn't feel like becoming sterile; then I waited with my hand tight on the receiver during a long, heart-beating pause. She said she didn't have anyone to stay with the boys and couldn't leave them for any period of time anyway, and that was the end of that. So that meant another two weeks on the shelf, I thought, as I walked back down the road in the cold air between the rows of pine trees.

During the next week I helped Mr Riordan feed the birds in the aviary and start work on a new barn, but I couldn't go to sleep at night, even though

I was physically exhausted, until I had sat at the kitchen table alone for two hours with a bottle of Jim Beam. I was back with the band on the weekend, and one night I went into town with Buddy to the pizza place and called Beth again in a beer fog, hoping that she would say, *Yes yes yes. Check into the Florence. I'll be there in a few minutes*. However, like most drunken wishes, it didn't have much to do with reality. I liked to hear Buddy play, but I couldn't sit long in the middle of that college crowd.

I don't know why they bothered me. It wasn't their loud and bullish behavior that came after three beers, or even their curiosity about my foreign presence which was like the appearance of a dinosaur among them. They reached down and touched something else in me that I couldn't articulate. Maybe it was just the fact that they were young and still standing on first base with all the confidence and expectation of stealing second. There was no such thing as a clock in the universe, and all of them knew that they would never die. I walked down the street to the Oxford in the light snow and sat on one of the high wood chairs in the side room and watched the strange collection of late-night characters play cards until Buddy got off.

Monday afternoon we caught part of a storm that blew over the mountains from Idaho, and my hands got so cold hammering nails into the side of the barn that I could hardly feel the blow when I missed once and came down on my thumb. My ears felt like iron inside the hood of my coat, and when the light started to fail, I waited for Mr Riordan to stick his hammer through the loop of his overalls; but instead he kicked a bunch of scrap boards into a pile, poured gasoline over it, paused long enough to relight his cigarette in his cupped hands, and dropped the match into the pile. We finished the side frame in the light of the fire, which flared into a cone of flame and then flattened into a white circle of heat each time the wind sucked under the boards.

When we got back to the cabin, Buddy took off his clothes, dropped them on the floor, and turned the hot water on in the tin shower just long enough to bring the feeling back into his body. He stood naked by the wood stove and dried himself with a towel. His ribs drew tight against his sides each time he breathed. There was a tattoo of a pair of dice showing a six and a five inside one thigh.

'Wow, I'm tired,' he said, rubbing the towel into his face and hair. 'And I'm late, and my fingers feel like balloons, and I didn't press a shirt this morning, and I don't feel like making that gig, Zeno.'

'Do it,' I said. I sat at the table, with my wet clothes dripping on the floor and a damp cigarette in my fingers. I had poured a glass of neat whiskey, but I hadn't had the strength yet to pick it up.

'That's very cool. While I entertain these college cats, you'll be sitting home by the fire digging on some whiskey dream about southern freight trains. So I have a suggestion. Why don't you zip on my Uncle Zeno suit and try filling in for me. If you think playing for a bunch of shitkickers is a zoo scene, do a shot with the junior lettermen that ask you to play

"Happy Birthday" for a chick they're going to assault in the backseat that night.'

'Go to work, Buddy.'

He went into his bedroom and came back with his suit on the hanger, his underwear, and the soiled shirt that he had worn last night. He dressed by the stove, his body thin and yellow in the light of the electric bulb overhead. I took a drink out of the whiskey, and I felt the first warmth come back into my lungs.

'Where did you get that tattoo?' I said.

'Before I got nailed, I used to live with this mulatto girl that played sometimes at Pat O'Brien's. I sat down at the piano once with her, and she thought I was her Mister Cool, the best thing since Brubeck, Monk, Mel Powell, or anybody. Except she liked shooting craps better than playing jazz. She made me take her to a couple of those upstairs games on Rampart, and she'd fade every bet on the board. When we got cleaned out, she'd bust up the apartment and call up some Baptist preacher in Mississippi and promise never to hang around white musicians again.'

'How did you get the tattoo?'

'I just told you.'

'Buddy, you are a dislodged madman. I think the hacks were right. That glue got to you a long time ago.'

'That's because you got all your wiring tuned in to another radio set,' he said. 'And speaking of that, while your high-rolling daddy is about to move it down the road and do his act for the sweater girls and their Howdy Doody boyfriends, let me click on the radio so we can listen to that fine jazz station in Spokane and dig on Shorty's flügelhorn.'

Buddy turned on the radio that was set in the kitchen window, his trousers unzipped, one-half of his shirt hanging off his back. The tubes warmed in the old plastic box, the static cracked, and when the sound sharpened through the speaker, Shorty Rogers and Shelly Mann were actually playing.

Buddy put his arm through the other sleeve, as though he had been in suspension, and then began jiggling all over in rhythm to the music while he buttoned his shirt in his bare feet.

'Tell me, truthfully,' he said. 'Were you ever tempted when you were inside? I mean, to just quit fighting it and let the girl have her way?'

Without rising from the chair, I reached over and turned up the radio to full volume and finished the whiskey in my glass. A few minutes later I heard Buddy grind the starter on the Plymouth outside.

After I had showered and put on a soft wool shirt and clean pair of khakis, I saw the pickup truck stop in front of the porch. I opened the door and looked through the screen at Pearl in the blowing snow. She wore a man's mackinaw with a scarf tied around her head, and her face was red with cold.

'Tell Buddy that –'

'Come in before you turn into a snowman,' I said.

'Just tell him that Frank –'

I opened the screen for her.

'Come in if you want to talk with me. You might not mind freezing, but I do,' I said.

She stepped inside, and I closed the wood door behind her.

'Frank'll pick him up at six-thirty in the morning to go into Hamilton for some lumber,' she said.

'Oh, he'll like that.'

'You can do it for him.'

'All right. No problem in that.' I could see she had on only a light shirt under the mackinaw, and she was shaking with the sudden warmth of the room. 'You want a cup of coffee?'

'I have to get a loaf of bread up at the store before it closes.'

I took an unopened loaf from the bread box in the cupboard and set it on the table.

'Sit down. A cup of coffee won't ruin your general feelings toward me.' I washed a cup under the iron pump and filled it from the pot on the stove.

She untied her scarf and shook her hair loose. It was wet with snow on the ends. She picked up the cup with both hands and sipped at the edge.

'Put a little iron in it,' I said, and tipped a capful of whiskey into her coffee. 'Where's Mel tonight?'

'He's at a faculty meeting.'

'Is he serious about that revolution business?'

'In his way, yes, I guess he is.'

'What do you mean "in his way"?'

'You wouldn't understand,' she said.

'I've had some experience with people who are always trying to right the world by wiping out large portions of it. They all have the same idea about sacrifices, but it's always somebody else's ass that gets burned.'

'Mel's a good man,' she said, and looked at me flatly.

'I didn't say he wasn't. I didn't say anything about him. I just asked a question.'

'He believes in idealistic things. He wasn't in a war like you, and he doesn't have your cynicism about things.'

I took a good hit out of the bottle on that one.

'You know, I think you're a crazy woman and you belong in a crazy house,' I said. 'The next time I get drafted into one of Uncle Sam's shooting capers, I'll write the draft board and tell them I'd rather opt out because I don't want to come home with any cynical feelings.'

'Let me ask you a question. Do you feel anything at all about taking from everything around you no matter what it costs other people who have nothing to do with your life?'

I walked in my socks to the stove and poured more coffee and a flash of whiskey in her cup and sat back down. She had pulled back her mackinaw, and her breasts were stiff against her shirt as she breathed. Her full thighs were tight inside her blue jeans and spread open indifferently on the corner of the chair. I had to hold the anger down in my chest, and at the same time she disturbed me sexually.

'Let me hang this one on you, Pearl, and you can do with it what you want to,' I said. 'I didn't take anything from anybody, and any problem they have isn't of my making. It was already there.'

She moved herself slightly in the chair, just

305

enough so that her thighs widened an inch and her buttocks flattened.

'That must be a convenient way to think,' she said.

'It's better than that. It's the truth. And I don't like anyone trying to make me take somebody else's fall.'

'That must be some of your prison terminology.'

'You better believe it is. I paid my dues, and straight people don't con a con.' I felt my heart beating and my words start to run away with themselves.

'Maybe all people don't behave toward one another with a frame of reference they learned in jail.'

'Well, the next time you want to talk about people's problems, come down here again and I'll help you solve a couple of yours.'

She didn't say anything. She just buttoned up her mackinaw, tied her scarf around her damp hair with the remote manner of a lady leaving a distasteful situation, and walked out the door to the truck. She left the door open, and the wind drove the snow into the room.

I didn't even bother to shut it for ten minutes. I felt a red anger at myself for my loss of control that left me trembling. Talk about a con not being conned, I thought. You are a fish who just got conned into thinking he was a con who could not be conned. And for somebody who thought he had touched all the bases over the years, this was no mean thing to consider.

The two weeks finally passed, and it was a bright, cold day with the snow banked high on the lawns in Missoula when I knocked on Beth's door. The boys were at school, and we made love on the couch, in her bed, and finally, in a last heated moment, on the floor. Her soft stomach and large, white breasts seemed to burn with her blood, and when she pressed her hands into the small of my back, I felt the fifteen days in jail and the two weeks of aching early morning hours drain away as in a dream.

Each morning I helped Mr Riordan put in the stall partitions in the barn and feed the birds in the aviary; then after lunch I hitched a ride or flagged down the bus into Missoula. Beth and I whitefished in the broken ice along the banks of the Clark, a fire of driftwood roaring in the wind with the coffeepot set among the coals. We ate bleeding steaks by the stone fireplace in the German restaurant and explored ghost towns and mining camps up logging roads and drainages where the trees rang with the tangle of ice in their limbs. I had forgotten how fine it was to simply be with someone you love.

We drove up a graded log road off Rock Creek, high up the side of the mountain, to a mining camp that had been abandoned in the 1870s. The cabins were still there along the frozen creek, where they used to mine placer gold that washed down from the mother lode, and the old sluices and rocker boxes were covered with undergrowth, the rusted square nails and bits of chain encased in ice. But if you blinked for just a minute, and let your imagination have its way, you could almost see those old-timers of a century ago bent sweatily into their futile dream of a Comstock or Alder Gulch or Tombstone. They always knew that wealth and the fulfillment of American promise was in that next shovel-load of sand.

'What are you thinking so hard about?' Beth said, her face bright with the cold wind that blew down the drainage.

'Those old-timers must have really believed in it. Can you imagine what it was like to pull the winter up here in the 1870s when they had to haul everything up the side of the mountain on mules? Before they could even go to work, they had to do something minor, like build those cabins. I bet they didn't even think about it. They just did it. And I bet you couldn't tear those logs apart with a prizing bar.'

She put her hands inside my arm and pressed against my coat.

'You're a strange mixture of men,' she said.

'Well, none of that analysis crap. You see that house down there with the elk droppings by the door? Think of some veteran from Cold Harbor in there, drunk every night on whiskey just to stay warm until the next day, and not sure that an Indian wouldn't set his place afire after he passed out. Those must have been pretty formidable people.'

She pulled the bill of my fur cap and laughed and squeezed herself against my arm.

'I thought you believed Montana people were barbarians,' she said.

'Only those who burn up trucks and guitars that belong to me.'

'I guess destroying half of a parking lot at the mill doesn't count,' she said, and laughed again.

I built a fire in the snow and boiled a can of stew on a piece of tin from one of the cabins, and as the snow melted away in a widening circle from the heat, I looked over at her and wanted her again. We went into her car and made love on the backseat, with the doors open and the wind blowing snow in the sunlight and the distant sound of a gyppo logger's truck grinding up the next hill.

We went grouse hunting up Rattlesnake Creek for blues and ruffs with an old dogleg twenty-gauge that I borrowed from Buddy's little brother, and we knocked six down in a stand of pines on the lip of a huge canyon and cooked them at her house in wine sauce, onion, and wild mushrooms. The next day I bought a resident deer tag, and we drove into the Swan Valley which was so white and blinding under the sun that you had to look at the green of the timberline to keep from losing the horizon. We crossed two hills of lodge pine in deep snow, pulling her boys' sled in blue tracks behind us, our lungs aching in the thin air, her Enfield rifle slung by its leather strap on my shoulder.

We found a place on the edge of the trees that overlooked a long valley where they would probably cross at sunset. I took the folded tarpaulin off the sled, spread it in the snow between the pine trunks, and set down the big coffee thermos and ham-and-turkey sandwiches. The air was clean and sharp,

309

with the sweet scent of the pines, and the far side of the valley seemed to grow and recede in the sunlight over the mountain. I unscrewed the thermos top, and the steam and the smell of the coffee blew around us in the wind.

I hadn't hunted for deer, or any animal for that matter, since I was discharged from the army. At home after the war, I had shot ducks and certainly fished a lot, but I wouldn't go out with my father any more after coons or shoot deer with him in east Texas. Once, he asked me why I would take the lives of fish and knock birds out of the air with a double-barrel when I wouldn't drop an animal running across the ground. I didn't have an answer for him, because I had thought until his question that it was just a general reaction to killing things, and he said: 'You don't want to bust something living on the land because it's just like you. You know it hurts him just like it does a man.'

Regardless of my father's explanation about the lack of ethical difference in taking the lives of wild things, I wasn't up to busting a deer or an elk that might work down through that snowfield in the sun's last red rays over the mountains. Also, I had hunted enough deer at home to know that anything that came out of that distant stand of pine on the far side of the valley would be either a doe or an elk cow, because the males always kicked them out into the open before they would cross themselves.

However, Beth had no such reservations. She was a real Montana girl. While I was holding an unlit cigarette and cup of coffee in my hands and thinking about striking a match (my dead army friend from Texas, Vern Benbow, used to say that a deer can see you fart from six miles), Beth slipped the sling of the Enfield up her left arm, eased the buckle tight, pushed a shell into the chamber, and lay on the tarp in a prone position. The sun had started to dip behind the line of trees on the next ridge, and the light fell out in long bands of scarlet on the valley floor.

'You know how to use iron sights at a distance like that?' I said.

'Be quiet. They're coming down in a minute,' she said. The hood of her coat was back on her shoulders, and her black hair was covered with snow crystals.

'You're frightening, woman.' But she wasn't listening. She was aimed into the other side of the valley, her white hands numb with cold, those wonderful breasts as hard as ice against the ground.

I leaned back against a pine trunk and drank out of the coffee and ate a ham-and-turkey sandwich. Before the last Indian wars of the 1860s and 1870s, the Blackfoot and the Salish used to pass through this valley on their way to the Clark in their timeless migrations across their sacred earth. As I set my coffee down in the snow and felt the sandwich bread turn stiff in my jaw, I looked into that dying sunset on the snowfield and thought of how those count-less people who had been here for thousands of years were decimated and removed without trace in one generation. I wondered if in spring, when the snow melted and mountain flowers burst from the wet ground, there wouldn't be some scratch of them there – a rose-quartz arrowhead, a woman's broken grinding bowl, a child's foolish carving on a stone.

My reverie was broken by the explosion of the Enfield. Two doe had started down out of the pines on the opposite side of the valley, their tracks sharp and deep behind them, and Beth had fired high and popped snow into the air off of a wind-polished drift. She ejected the brass casing, slammed another shell into the chamber, and fired again. I saw her cant the rifle before she squeezed off. The deer turned in a run and headed for the far end of the valley.

'You better hold it straight and lower your sights,' I said, quietly. 'We're higher than they are, and that bullet's not dropping.'

She worked the bolt and pushed it home, pulled the rifle tight against its sling, and let off another one. The doe in the rear bucked forward on her knees as though she had been struck by an invisible hammer. She struggled in the snow, the hooves tearing long scratches and divots in the incline as she tried to get to her feet. Then she stumbled forward, with a single trail of bright red drops behind her.

'Damn, you gut-shot her,' I said. 'Bust her again.'

Beth's hands were shaking, and when she pulled the bolt, it hung halfway back, and the spent shell caught in the chamber. The doe was pumping hard for the cover of the trees, the blood flying in the wind between her flanks. I pulled the sling of the Enfield free from Beth's arm, banged the heel of my hand against the magazine until the brass casing dislodged, shoved another shell into the chamber, and locked the bolt down. I didn't have time to use the sling or get into a prone position. I steadied the Enfield against a pine trunk, aimed the iron sights just ahead of the deer, let my breath out slowly, and squeezed off. The bark shaled off the pine from the recoil, and my right ear was momentarily wooden from the explosion. I hit the doe right behind the neck, and I knew that with the downward angle the soft-nosed bullet must have torn through her heart and lungs like a lead tennis ball.

Beth sat up on the tarpaulin and shook the snow out of her hair with her hands. She tried to find a cigarette inside her coat, but it was as though all of her pockets were sewn together. I set the rifle down and handed her my pack.

'That was a wonderful shot,' she said, but her voice was uneven with an unnatural pitch to it in the quietness.

'Where did you learn to hunt deer?' I said.

Her hands were still shaking when she lit the cigarette.

'Why?'

'Because you never take a shot from a distance like that without a telescope.'

'Should I apologize?'

'Don't be defensive about it. Hell, you know you were wrong.'

She picked up my coffee cup from the snow and drank out of it, then took a deep drag on the cigarette.

'Buddy told me you could be righteous sometimes,' she said.

'Well, shit, you let off on something that you can only hit with luck, and she wanders around for two days before she dies.'

We didn't speak for a moment, and I ejected the spent shell from the Enfield and slipped out the unused cartridges from the magazine. She looked out over the valley, where the last light was starting to glow in a rim of fire on the mountain's edge.

'You didn't want to shoot anything and you did,' she said. 'You want me to walk home with my mad money?'

I pulled the hood of her coat up on her head and tied the strings under her chin. Her cheeks were red, and there was still a brush of snow in the black hair over her eyes. I pushed her hair back with my hand and stuck one stiff finger in her ribs.

'We'd better get her on the sled before they send the search-and-rescue in after us,' I said.

She looked away, still angry and unwilling to give up, then kicked me gently in the calf with her boot and turned her fine woman's face into mine.

The snow was already starting to freeze as we pulled the sled across the valley floor. Our boots crunched through the surface, then sank in the soft snow underneath, so that by the time we reached the doe, we were sweating inside our clothes, and the moon had come up in a clear sky and turned the whole valley into a blue-white, tree-lined place on the top of the world that made you fear time and mortality. I gutted the deer and threw the steaming

314

entrails on the ground and we tied down the frozen carcass on the sled and worked our way back up toward the dark border of pines. The sleeves of my coat were splattered with blood, my head was dizzy from the thin air and the effort of pulling the sled up the hill behind me, but I felt a quiet exhilaration in the long day and its completion. We roped the doe on the fender of the car and drove back out of the moon-drenched mountains of the Swan Valley toward Missoula, and as I steered down that blacktop highway with those huge, dark shapes on each side of me, I understood why men like Jim Bridger, Jediah Johnson, and Jim Beckworth came here. There was simply no other place better, anywhere.

The next week Frank Riordan got his way with the state of Montana, the Anaconda Company, and in fact the whole lumber industry and anybody else who had anything to do with polluting the air. He and an environmental group got a temporary injunction from the court in Helena to shut down every pulp mill and tepee burner in western Montana. It was one of those things that nobody believed. A court decided on an abstraction that had nothing to do with economics, jobs, or clean air and water. It was just a matter of law. A judge's signature went on the injunction, and suddenly the plume of smoke blowing down the Clark thinned and disappeared, and the tepee burners smoldering with sawdust crumpled slowly into ash and were covered by snow.

But other things happened, too. The workers at the plywood mill got a pink slip with their next check, the men who planed boards and pulled the green chain at the lumber companies were told to come around again in a month or so, the Anaconda Company was shut down at Bonner, and the gyppo loggers (the independents who owned their own tractors) had to either haul pine to a market in Idaho or Washington or go out of business.

Beth had told me once what a lumber town could be like when the mills shut down and the paychecks stopped and families had to line up at the federal food-surplus center. Except in this case there was no workingman's strike involved, no collective anger directed at management or unions, no depression to be blamed on federal bureaucrats and New York sharpers. Every unemployed man in Missoula County and the Bitterroot Valley knew there was only one reason for the deprivation of his family, his humiliation at accepting welfare and food commodities, and his daily visits to the state employment office for the chance of a casual labor job with the Forest Service: Frank Riordan.

Their mood was mean and dirty. It took on different forms that ran the gamut from an insult in the face to the failure of a neighbor to wave out of his truck cab, but it was all the same thing. I can't say that they hated him, because they didn't; it was more a matter of outrage and disbelief that one of their own kind would betray them and join forces with college people and slick lawyers to cause so much trouble in their lives.

316

I stopped going to the Oxford in Missoula for steak dinners after I sat at the corner and heard the loud and pointed remarks from the poker table behind me, and Eddie's Club across the street was no place to have a beer in the afternoon when there were three or four drunk men against the bar who would happily bust your head open with a pool cue. One day I walked up to the small grocery store on the blacktop for a loaf of bread and a quart of milk, and the woman behind the counter looked through me like smoky glass while she counted out each hot coin in my palm.

The irony is that my job was also affected when the mills shut down. Our band was fired at the Milltown Union Bar, Cafe and Laundromat. On Saturday night, the first week after the injunction came down, there was a crowd of five people in the bar, and all of them were drinking on the tab. We played loyally to them until one in the morning, which was like singing into a neon-lighted cave, and the owner paid us off, gave us free bowls of chili and a fifth of Cutty Sark, and said to come back when the mills opened.

I could do without the job financially, because I had money in the bank, but our steel man and bass player got loaded on the bottle of Scotch in their truck before they drove home. Both of them had been laid off at the sawmill in Seeley Lake, and they had been cleaning furnaces three and four days a week to make enough, along with their three nights' work at the bar, to keep from going on welfare until the mills reopened.

Now I had no job, except for my work on the ranch, and no place really to go. I lived with a man whom I had made a cuckold out of. I slept with his wife every evening I could get into Missoula, and without embarrassment he and I fished each afternoon through the ice on the Bitterroot, which was shameful in itself. On the nights I couldn't be with Beth (because of her boys or her temporary job waiting tables at the bus depot) and when Buddy went off to play at the college pizza place, I stayed alone in the cabin and drank neat whiskey and looked out the window at the fields of snow under the moon and the glistening sides of the canyon behind the Riordan house.

I worked on my song, the one I had never finished while I was in the penitentiary. The strange thing was that I could play lead on almost any country song that I had ever heard, and I could imitate Hank Williams, Jimmie Rodgers, and Woody Guthrie in a way that left a southern or Okie audience banging their tables with beer bottles when I finished. But I couldn't write a song myself. As I sat there with the three tortoiseshell picks on my fingers and the Gibson across my knee, I was reminded of an old Negro preacher who did odd jobs for my father. His son had been given five years on Sugarland Farm in Texas, and when the old man was told of the sentence, he said, 'I tried to keep him out the juke joint. But he just like a mockingbird. He know every song but his own.'

I had most of my song, but the rest wouldn't come. Maybe that was just because when you try to catch all of something, particularly something very good, it must always elude you in part so that it retains its original magic and mystery. I remembered when my cousin Andre and I found an Indian canoe submerged in four feet of water back in the swamp. The canoe was made of cypress and had stayed intact for over a century. The bow and sides were etched against the silt bottom with green moss, and we slid through the water quietly so as not to cloud it, our hearts tripping inside our wet shirts. We caught the canoe by each end and tried to lift it slowly, and when it wouldn't rise, we pulled harder and our hands slipped on the moss, and the silt swelled out in a black balloon from the bottom. Then I ducked under the surface again and jerked on the bow with all my strength. It ripped away like wet newspaper in my hands. I felt heartsick, and with each of our hurried, young efforts to salvage what was left, we tore the canoe into dozens of pieces until finally we had only a pile of rotted cypress wood, like any other in the swamp, to take home in the bottom of my pirogue.

I heard a shotgun go off across the meadow, and before I could set down the guitar and walk to the window, there were three more reports and then a chain of five cracks in a row that must have come from an automatic without a plug in it. I threw open the door and the snow blew in my face, but I could see the individual flashes of the guns in the aviary, a lick of flame and sparks against the darkness of the mountain beyond. There was a pause while they must have reloaded, and then another roar of noise and streaks of fire that looked like a distant night scene from the war.

*Jesus God*, I thought.

I could hear the birds crying in their cages and the splatter of shot against the wire and wood sides. The only gun in the cabin had been the Springfield, which Buddy had buried, and as I stood there with my coat half on, I felt suddenly impotent to do anything about the terror that was going on in the aviary. But I went anyway, running across the dry grass that protruded through the snow, my chest beating with a fear that I hadn't felt since Heartbreak Ridge. The cold air cut like a razor in the dryness of my mouth and throat, and in my feeling of nakedness in that bare field under the moon I prayed desperately that something would happen before I got there.

All the lights were on in the house now; there was a brief silence while the shots echoed away into the canyon, then one more solitary crack, and then I saw three men in silhouette running like stick figures with their guns for their truck, which they had parked on the far side of the house. They roared off with the cab doors still open, the tire chains ripping snow and frozen mud into the air.

I saw Pearl under the porch light, wearing only a brassiere and a pair of blue jeans, with a Winchester lever-action in her hands.

'You goddamn dirty bastards!' she yelled, and at the same time let off the round in the chamber. Then she worked the action and fired one round after another at the diminishing dark outline of the truck.

320

But she got home with one, because a moment after the explosion from the barrel I heard the bullet whang into the metal like a ball peen hammer.

When I got to the porch, she was trying to pump free a spent cartridge that was crimped in the slide. Just as it ejected and she shoved another cartridge home, a pair of headlights came down the gravel road and bounced across the cattle guard, illuminating the truck that was headed out at a good fifty miles an hour.

Pearl aimed the Winchester against the porch post, her breath steaming in the air, the white skin of her shoulder already red from the recoil of the rifle. I slapped at the barrel and knocked it at the downward angle, and her face, which had been filled with murderous intent, suddenly went blank and looked at me as a surprised girl's would have.

'That's Buddy's Plymouth,' I said.

# chapter twelve

The three men did a thorough job in the few minutes that they unloaded on the aviary. We could see the freezing tracks of their boots where they had walked to the fence and fired, and the empty shotgun shells that had melted with their own heat deep in the snow. They had loaded with precision to take care of everything living in the yard: their shells ranged from deer slugs and buckshot to bbs. They had laid down a pattern to kill, blind, or cripple every animal and bird within thirty yards. The deer slugs and buckshot had blown the cages into splinters, and the blood dripped through the floor wire in thick, congealing drops. The birds that had only been wounded twisted on their broken wings or quivered like balls of feathers in the snow. The bald eagle had been shot right through the beak, and he lay with his great reach of wings in a tangle of wire and birdseed.

The nutrias were at the far end of the yard. None of the birdshot had gotten through the other cages to them, but those twelve-gauge deer slugs, which were as thick as a man's thumb, had flattened against the board side of their pen and hit them like canister. Their heads were torn away, their blue entrails hung in ropes out of their stomachs, and their large, yellow teeth were bitten into their tongues.

Mr Riordan had on only his overalls and long-sleeved underwear with the bib hanging loose in front and the straps by his sides. He had put on a pair of unlaced leather boots without socks, and the snow and water squeezed over his ankles with each step as he walked back and forth through the aviary with a terrible rage on his face.

'That's unbelievable,' Buddy said.

Mr Riordan methodically knocked one huge fist against his thigh, and I was sure at that moment that he would have torn the lives out of those three men with his bare hands. His face was livid, his throat was lined with veins, and his grey eyes were so hot in the moonlight that I didn't want to look at them. He bent over and picked up one of the wounded nutrias, and the dark drain of blood ran down his forearms before he placed it back in the shattered cage.

'Go back inside, Daddy,' Pearl said.

But he didn't hear her. There was a heat inside his brain that must have made the blood roar in his ears. His chest began to swell up and down, as though his heart were palpitating, and I heard that deep rasp and click in his throat.

'It don't do any good to stay out here now, Frank,' Buddy said.

'You don't tell your father what to do,' Mr Riordan said.

We stood in the silence and looked at him standing among the scattered bodies of the birds and the wet feathers that blew in the wind and stuck against his overalls. His grey hair was like meringue in the wash of moon that shone down over the canyon.

He coughed violently in his chest and bent forward to hawk and spit in the snow, as though he had some terrible obstruction in his throat. The vein in his temple swelled like a piece of blue cord. Then he coughed until he had to lean against one of the remaining cages for support.

'You better get him inside,' I said.

Still, Buddy and his sister and the others on the porch remained motionless.

'You better listen to me unless you want to put him in a box,' I said.

'Let him be,' Buddy said.

'You're crazy. All of you are,' I said, and walked up to Mr Riordan and put my hand under his arm. His long-sleeved underwear was wet with perspiration. He turned with me toward the house, the back of one hand against his mouth and the spittle that he couldn't control. I heard Buddy walk up quickly behind us and take him by the other arm.

We led him up the steps and into the house and laid him on the couch. When Mrs Riordan pulled off his boots, his feet were blue and covered with crystals of ice. The top button on his underwear had twisted loose, and I saw the flat, white scar where a bull's horn had gone deep into his lung. He turned his head sideways on the pillow to let the phlegm drain from his mouth, and his wife pressed a towel into his hand and moved it up so he could hold it close to his face. I heard Pearl on the telephone in the kitchen, calling a doctor in Hamilton.

Buddy wiped the water out of his father's hair with his hand, then began to brush at it with a shawl that was on the back of the couch. But Buddy's hands were trembling, and his face had gone taut and pale. He took the blankets from his mother and spread them awkwardly over Mr Riordan, then took the bottle of whiskey out of the cabinet.

'Don't give him that,' I said.

'He's cold,' Buddy said.

I took the bottle gently, and he released his fingers while he stared into my eyes with an uncomprehending expression.

'Why not?' he said.

'It's just no good for him,' I said.

I looked at Mr Riordan's ashen face, his lips that had turned the purple color of an old woman's, and his great knuckles pinched on the top of the blankets, and wondered at how time and age and events could catch a man so suddenly.

Twenty minutes later we saw the red lights on the ambulance revolving through the fields toward us, the icy trees and snowdrifts momentarily alive with scarlet until they clicked by and disappeared behind the glare of head lamps. The doctor, who was actually an intern at St Patrick's in Missoula, and the volunteer fireman who drove the ambulance strapped Mr Riordan onto a litter and carried him gingerly outside. Buddy pulled open the back door of the ambulance, and they eased the litter up onto the bed without unbuckling the straps. The doctor turned on the oxygen bottle and slipped the elastic band of the mask behind Mr Riordan's head.

'Well, what the hell is it, doc?' Buddy said. 'He got horned in the chest once –'

'I don't know what it is. Shut the door.'

Buddy closed the door, and the ambulance turned around in a wide circle in the yard, cracking over the wood stakes on the edge of Mrs Riordan's vegetable garden, and rolled solidly down the road toward the cattle guard with the red lights swirling out over the snow.

'Why not the whiskey?' Buddy said.

'You just don't give it to somebody sometimes.'

'Don't give me that candy-ass stuff. There ain't anybody else out here now.'

'He's probably had a stroke.'

'Goddamn, I knew that's what you were going to say,' he said, and pushed his snow-filled hair back over his head.

'Take it easy, Buddy.'

The sports clothes he had worn to the pizza place were soaked through. There were bird feathers all over his trousers, and his white wool socks had fallen down over his ankles. The army surplus greatcoat he wore over his sports clothes was eaten with moth rings and hung at a silly angle on his thin shoulders. His eyes were still looking at me, but his mind was far away on something very intense.

326

'Come on, Zeno. Hold it together,' I said.

'They took it all the way down the road this time.'

'Yeah, but, man, you got to –'

He turned away from me and went inside, then came back out with a handful of cartridges that he spilled into the pocket of his greatcoat. He picked up the lever-action Winchester that Pearl had propped beside the door, and headed for his father's pickup truck. His shoes squeaked on the snow in the silence. I caught him by the arm and turned him to face me.

'Don't do something like this,' I said.

'I know who they are. I saw the driver's face in my headlights. I won't have any doubts when I find his truck, either, because Pearl slammed one right along his door.'

'Then call the sheriff.'

'That bastard won't do anything, no more than he did when they burned the barn. They'll just say the truck got hit while they were hunting.'

'You don't know that. Give it a chance. At least until tomorrow.'

'Let go, Iry.'

'All right,' I said. 'Just talk a minute. A minute won't make any difference.'

'Tell my mother I went to the hospital.' He started for the truck again, and I stepped in front of him.

'Look, maybe I'm the last person that should tell anyone about being rational and not going out on a banzai trip to blow somebody away,' I said. 'But, damn it, *think*.'

'That's right. You are the last person that should.

327

Old Zeno, the shank artist of Louisiana and the fire bomber of lumber mills. The saver of horses from the flames. But he's my old man, and maybe they've punched his whole ticket.'

He started around me for the truck, his mouth in a tight line, and I stepped once more in front of him.

'I ain't going to play this game anymore with you, Iry.'

His hands were set on the barrel and stock of the rifle, and his right arm and shoulder were already flexed.

'What are you going to do, bust me in the teeth? You ought to save your killer's energy for those cats you're going to blow all over a barroom wall someplace.'

But it didn't work. He glared into my face, breathing loudly through his nose, his hair wet against his forehead.

'OK, step in your own shit,' I said.

He walked past me and got in the truck, then set the Winchester in the rack against the back glass and started the engine. He turned around and drove slowly past me with his window still down. I began to walk hurriedly along beside the truck, my legs almost comical in their attempt to keep pace with it before Buddy accelerated down the lane.

'Jesus Christ, don't do this,' I said. 'I'll go after them with you in the morning. We'll put their ass in Deer Lodge for ten years –'

He rolled up the window, and his face disappeared into an empty oval behind the frosted glass;

then he hit second gear and the loose tire chains clanked and whipped along the frozen earth.

I started to go back into the house, but I didn't belong there, and there was nothing truthful that I could say to anybody inside. I walked back across the field to the cabin and poured a glass of straight whiskey at the kitchen table and tried to think. I imagined that Mrs Riordan or Pearl or Melvin had already called the sheriff's office, but that wouldn't do any good for Buddy, as none of them knew why he had left in the truck, unless someone had noticed that the Winchester was gone, which they probably hadn't. So that left few alternatives, I thought, and sipped at the whiskey and looked at the crumbling ash in the grate of the stove. I could tell his family about it and let them make their own decisions, or I could call one of the deputies aside in front of the house (and I could already see him talking into the microphone of his car radio, with the door open and one leg sticking out in the snow, telling every cop in Ravalli County to pick up dope-smoking ex-convict Buddy Riordan, who was armed and headed down the Bitterroot highway to gun somebody). Then they could call the intern back to the house to give Mrs Riordan a tranquilizer shot, and in the meantime there would be shitkicker dicks with shotguns behind roadblocks all the way to Missoula who would urinate with pleasure in their khakis if Buddy should try to get past them.

So you can't tell his family, and you don't drop the dime on a friend, I thought, and drank the last of the whiskey from the glass and filled it with water under the pump. And that leaves us where in this Sam Spade process of deduction? Nowhere. He's simply out there someplace on the highway, driving too fast across the ice slicks, his heart beating, the Winchester vibrating in the rack behind his head, his brain a furnace.

Then I thought, That's exactly what he's doing. He's looking at every beer joint on the way back to Missoula, pulling into the gravel parking lot and cruising slowly past the line of parked cars and trucks. Because he is con wise to criminal behavior, and he knows that anyone, except a professional, who pulls a violent job usually does not go back directly to home and normalcy; he stops at what he thinks is the first safe bar to toast his aberrant victory and quiet that surge of blood in his head.

I tied the ignition wires together on the Plymouth and drove down the blacktop toward Missoula. I was guessing about the direction Buddy would have taken as well as the three men in the pickup, but I doubted that the killing of the birds was done by anyone in the south Bitterroot, since there was only one small sawmill south of us, at Darby, which was almost to Idaho, that had been affected by the injunction. I passed the bar at Florence, which would have been too close for them to stop, and looked for Buddy's truck in the parking lots of the two bars at Lolo. The snow was coming down more heavily now, in large, wet flakes that swirled out of my headlights and banked thickly on the windshield wipers that shuddered and scratched across the glass. As I dropped over the hill into the outskirts of

Missoula and again met the river, shining with moonlight and bordered by the dark, bare shapes of the cottonwoods, the wind came up the valley and polished the ice along the road and buffeted the Plymouth from side to side.

I pulled into every bar parking lot on the highway until I reached the center of town. No Buddy, no ambulances, no bubble-gum lights swinging around on the tops of cop cars. Strike three, babe, I thought. So I drove over to Beth's, with the ignition wires swinging and sparking under the dash and the snow piling higher on the hood against the windshield.

The elm and maple trees in her yard were dripping with ice, and the yellow porch light fell out in shadows along the glazed sidewalk. She opened the door partway in her nightgown against the draft of cold air, her mouth in an oval, beginning to smile, then her eyes focused on my face. She closed the door behind me and touched my chest with her hand.

'What happened?'

I told her, in the quietest way I could, keeping the sequence intact and lowering my voice each time I saw the brightness and sudden confusion start to come into her eyes.

'Oh God,' she said.

'He'll probably just drive around until he gets the lightning bolts out of his brain.'

'You don't know him. Not when it comes to his father and all his crazy guilt about failing him.'

'Buddy?' I looked at her with the strange feeling of an outsider who would never know the private moments of confession between them in the quiet darkness of their marital bed.

'He's not a violent man,' I said. 'Even in Angola, the big stripes let him alone. He wasn't a threat to anyone. He was just Buddy, a guy with glue fumes in his head and music in his fingers.'

But I was talking to myself now. Her eyes were looking at the blackness of the window, and she held an unlit cigarette in her lap as though she had forgotten it was there.

'I don't know what else to do, Beth.'

'Call the sheriff's office.'

'You're not thinking.'

'He told you he knew who they were. He's going to kill someone.'

'You weren't listening while I was talking,' I said.

'We'll have to use the phone next door or go to the filling station.'

'Listen a minute. That fat son of a bitch you call a sheriff would love blowing Buddy all over the inside of that truck or welding the door shut on him in Deer Lodge.'

Her eyes were blinking at the darkness beyond the window.

'I'll talk,' she said. 'I'll tell them he's drunk and he tore up my house and I want him arrested.'

'That's no good, kid.'

'Why? What do you offer as an alternative, for God's sake?'

'He won't pull over for any dicks, and it'll get real bad after that.'

She sat back in the chair and rubbed the palm of

her hand against her brow. I took the cigarette out of her fingers and lit it for her.

'I can't sit here,' she said.

I wished I hadn't come. It was selfish, and now I had included her in my own impotence to do anything in an impossible situation.

'Do you have anything to drink?' I asked.

'I think it's in the cabinet.'

I found the half bottle of Old Crow and brought back two glasses. I poured into a glass and put it in her hand. She raised it once to her mouth as though she were going to drink, then set it aside on the table.

'I lied to the children for five years about their father,' she said. 'They're too old to lie to now. They're not going to go through any more because of Frank Riordan and Buddy and all their insane obsessions.'

'Mr Riordan didn't choose this.'

'He's done everything he could for twenty years to leave his stamp on everybody around him. He was never content simply to live. His children always had to know that he wasn't an ordinary man.'

'He wouldn't want Buddy out with a gun. You know that.'

'I'm sorry, but you didn't learn very much living at his place.' That fine strand of wire was starting to tremble in her voice again. 'He never thought about what would happen after he did anything. If he raised children to live in the nineteenth century, and if they ended up neurotic or in jail, it was the world's fault for not recognizing that the Riordans were not only different but right.'

'You've got him down wrong,' I said. 'His ball game is pretty well over, and I think he knows it and doesn't want grief like this for Buddy or anybody else.'

She put her fingers over her eyes, and I saw the wetness begin to gleam on her cheeks.

'Don't let it run away with you,' I said. 'He might have gone to the hospital by now.' I stood up behind her and put my hands on her shoulders. They were shaking, and she kept her face averted so I couldn't see it.

It was a time not to say anything more. I rubbed the back of her neck until I felt her composure start to come back and her shoulders straighten. I picked up my whiskey glass and looked out the window while she got up and went into the bath. Behind me I could hear the water running.

The snow was frozen in broken stars around the edge of the window glass, and the shadows of the trees swept back and forth across the banked lawn. High up on the mountain behind the university I could dimly see the red beacon for the airplanes, pulsating against the infinite softness of the sky.

'I'm sorry,' Beth said, behind me, her face clear now.

'Do you want your drink?'

'I'd rather go to the hospital. You don't mind, do you?'

'No.'

'It'll take me just a minute to dress.'

A few moments later she came back downstairs in a pair of corduroys and a wool shirt with a mackinaw under her arm. Her blue scarf was tied under her chin, and the flush in her face and the strands of black hair on her cheeks gave her the appearance of a young girl on her way to a nighttime ice-skating party.

I closed the door on her side of the Plymouth and put the ignition wires back together to start the engine. Her breath was steaming, and I could see her breasts rise and fall under the heavy mackinaw.

'If Buddy's not at the room, that doesn't mean he hasn't been by and gone back home,' I said as I drove slowly up the street.

'The head sister will know if he's been there.'

'There's another thing to think about, too. He might just talk to the doctor downstairs and go to sleep in the truck out on the street.'

'Just drive us there, Iry.'

We didn't get past the receptionist's desk. Frank Riordan was in intensive care, no one was allowed to see him, and the only persons in his family who had been at the hospital were Melvin and Pearl, and they had gone across the street to the all-night cafe.

'How's he doing?' I said.

'You'll have to ask the doctor when he comes down,' the receptionist said.

'When does he come down?'

'I don't know. Are you a member of the family?'

'Where's that little Irish nun that used to work here?'

'Sir?'

'There was an Irish sister that used to work on the second floor.'

'I don't know who you mean.'

I walked outside with Beth toward the automobile. The snow had stopped blowing, and there was just a hint of blue light beyond the mountains in the east. The thin shale of ice over the gravel in the parking lot cracked under our feet.

'You want to go back home?' I said.

'No. Call Mrs Riordan.'

'I don't think we should do that.'

'She's not sleeping tonight. One of the boys will answer the phone, anyway.'

'Beth, let it slide for tonight.'

'A phone call isn't a lot to ask, is it?'

I put her in the Plymouth, started the engine, turned on the heater, and walked across the street to the cafe to use the public phone outside. My fingers were stiff with cold, and I had trouble dialing the numbers and depositing the coins for a toll call. Through the lighted window of the cafe I could see Melvin and Pearl drinking coffee in front of their empty plates.

Buddy's little brother, Joe, answered the phone and said that Buddy hadn't gotten back yet from the hospital, and no, there was no light on in his cabin, and no, sir, he would have seen the headlights if the pickup had come down the road.

I walked back across the street to the automobile and sat down heavily behind the steering wheel.

'Where do you want to go now, kiddo?' I said.

She shook her head quietly and looked straight

ahead at the dark line of mountains. Her face was drained of emotion now, and her hands lay open in her lap. I put my arm briefly around her shoulders, and we drove back in silence to her house.

She wanted the glass of whiskey now, but I took it out of her hand and walked her upstairs to bed. It was dark in her bedroom, and she turned her head on the pillow toward the opposite wall, but I could see that her eyes were still opened when I covered her.

'I'll be downstairs when you wake up,' I said, and closed the door softly behind me.

I fixed coffee in the kitchen while the blueness of the night began to fade outside and the false dawn rimmed the edge of the mountains. I poured a shot of whiskey into the coffee and smoked cigarettes until my lungs were raw and my fingers and the backs of my legs started to shake with fatigue and strain. I lay back on the couch and closed my eyes, but there were red flashes of color in my head and that persistent hum in my blood that I had felt in jail. I touched my brow, and my fingers were covered with perspiration.

I put on my coat and walked out into the cold, early light and drove to the sheriff's office. The streets were empty, and newspapers in plastic wrappers lay upon the quiet lawns. Some of the kitchens in the houses were lighted, and occasionally I caught a glimpse of a workingman bent over his breakfast.

I walked up the courthouse steps, trying to light a cigarette in the wind. I was sweating inside my clothes, and when I entered the gloom of the hallway and smelled the odor of the spittoons and dead cigars, the hum started to grow louder in my head. Three sheriff's deputies sat on wooden chairs in front of the dispatcher's cage, reading parts of the newspaper and yawning. A drunk who had just bonded out of the tank was accusing the dispatcher of taking money out of his wallet while it was in Possessions.

'You used it to go bail,' the dispatcher said. The other deputies never looked up from their paper. Their faces were tired and had the greenish cast of men who worked all night.

'I had thirty-five goddamn dollars in there,' the drunk said.

'Get the hell out of here before I take you upstairs again,' one of the deputies said from behind his paper.

The dispatcher looked at me from his radio desk.

'Yes, sir?' he said.

I started to speak, but didn't get the chance.

'What are you doing in here?' the sheriff's voice said behind me.

His khaki sleeves were rolled up over his massive fat arms, and the splayed end of his cigar was stuck in the center of his mouth. He clicked his Mason's ring on the clipboard that he carried in one hand.

'Do you have Buddy Riordan in jail?' I said.

'Should I?'

'I don't know.'

'What's he been doing?'

'He didn't come home last night.'

His head tilted slightly, and he narrowed his eyes at me.

'What is this, Paret?'

'I want to know if he's in jail. That's not hard to understand.'

He took the cigar out of his mouth and pushed his tongue into one cheek.

'Did you book Buddy Riordan in here last night?' he said to the dispatcher.

'No, sir.'

The sheriff looked back at me.

'Is that all you want?' he said.

'Sheriff, there's something you might want to know,' the dispatcher said. 'One of the deputies at the Ravalli office called on the mobile unit and said that three guys shot the hell out of Frank Riordan's birds last night.'

The sheriff walked to the spittoon, his head bowed into position as though he were over a toilet, and spit a dripping stream into it.

'What was Buddy driving?' he said.

I wanted to get back out into the cold air again, away from the hissing radiators and the indolent, flat eyes of the men looking at me.

'Forget it,' I said. 'He's probably on a drunk over in Idaho.'

'Don't fool with me, son. I ain't up to it this morning.'

I lit my cigarette and wiped my damp hair back over my head.

'Give me that accident report that come in from Frenchtown,' the sheriff said to the dispatcher. He took his glasses out of his shirt pocket and squinted at the small writing on the paper.

'Was he driving a '55 Ford pickup?' he said, pulling his glasses off his nose.

'Yes.' I felt something drop inside of me.

'Take a ride with me.'

He started walking down the hallway toward the front door, his waist like an inner tube under his shirt. I remained motionless, the cigarette hanging in my mouth, watching his huge silhouette walk toward the square of dawn outside.

'You better go with him, mister,' the dispatcher said.

I caught up with the sheriff outside on the glazed sidewalk. I could feel my shoes slipping on the ice, but his very weight seemed to give him traction on the cement.

'All right, what are we playing?' I said.

'Get in.' But this time his voice was lower and more human.

I got in on the passenger's side and closed the door. The sawed-off twelve-gauge pump clipped vertically against the dashboard knocked against my knees. He flicked on the bubble-gum light without the siren, and we headed west out of town. He was breathing heavily from the fast walk to the car.

'About an hour ago a '55 pickup went off the road on 263 and rolled all the way down to the river,' he said.

My head was swimming.

'So what the hell are we doing?' I said. 'You've

340

got a junked truck in the river. You want me to identify it so you can give Buddy a citation?'

He opened the wind vane and flipped his cigar out. He waited a moment, and I saw his hands tense on the wheel before he turned to me with his pie-plate face.

'The driver's still in there, Paret. It burned.'

We drove down the highway by the side of the Clark and the water was blue and running fast in the middle between the sheets of ice that extended from the banks. The sun came up bright in a clear sky over the mountains, and men were fishing with wet flies and maggots for whitefish on the tips of the sandbars. The thick pines on the sides of the mountains were dark green and bent with the weight of the new snow, and the sunlight on the ice-covered boulders refracted with an iridescence that made your eyes water.

The truck was scorched black, and all the windows had exploded from the heat. There was a large melted area around it in the snow, and the tires had burned away to the rims. I could see the huge scars in the rock incline where the truck had rolled end over end and had come to rest against a cottonwood tree, as though its driver had simply wanted to park there with a high school girl after a dance. The men from the coroner's office had already wrapped the body in a rubber sheet, covered it with canvas, and strapped it on an alpine stretcher that they worked slowly up the incline. A deputy sheriff walked to the car with the melted barrel and torn magazine of a rifle in his hand. The stock had been burned away, and the ejection lever hung down from the trigger.

'Look at this son of a bitch,' he said. 'Every shell in it blew up. He must have had a bunch of them in his clothes, too, because they went off all over him.'

We were outside the car now, standing in the snow, though I didn't remember how we got there. Across the river the sunlight fell on the white mountain as it would on a mirror.

*You don't know it's Buddy,* I thought. *There are ranchers all over this county that drive pickup trucks, and they all carry a lever-action in the deer rack. Every week a drunk cowboy goes off the road in a pickup. And this one just happened to burn.*

'You don't know who he is,' I said, my voice loud even to myself.

The deputy looked at me curiously.

'Did you find anything that says who he was?' the sheriff said.

'No, sir. The tag was burned up, and so was anything in the glove. But like the coroner said, the damnedest thing is the way that guy went out. He must have caught his head inside the steering wheel when he turned over, and the top half of him was burned into a piece of cork. But there wasn't a mark on his legs, except for a tattoo inside his thigh.'

I walked away from the car, along the shoulder of the road and the glistening shine of the snow melting on the asphalt and the yellow grass that protruded through the gravel. I could hear the cottonwoods clatter dryly against one another in the wind along the river, and water was ticking some-where in flat drops off a boulder into a crystalline pool. Then I heard the powerful engine of the sheriff's car next to me, the idle racing, and his voice straining through the half-open passenger's window.

I turned and looked at him as I might at someone from the other side of the moon. He was trying to hold the wheel with one hand and roll down the window completely with the other. His pie-plate face was filled with blood and exertion, and his words came out with a labored wheeze in his chest.

*Get in, Paret.*

*That's all right, Sheriff. I just got to stretch it out a little bit.*

*Get in, son.* Then he pulled the car at an angle to me so I couldn't walk down the road farther, and popped the door handle on the passenger's side.

*Take a drink out of this.*

The steam on the highway sucked away under us, and then we began to pass cars full of families and ranchers in pickups and a few gyppo loggers that were still operating in western Montana. They were all in their ordered place, driving into a yellow, wintry sun, with the confident knowledge that they would never have to correct time when there was none left.

*Take another bite out of that bottle.*

I felt the steady vibration of the engine under my feet, and then I saw the mountains re-form and come back into shape on the horizon, and the river was once more a blue spangle of light coursing through the sheets of ice far below.

*That's better, ain't it?*

*Sure.*

*Damn right, it is.* And he turned up the volume on his mobile unit and drove intently with a fresh purpose.

# epilogue

Frank Riordan was in the hospital four weeks, and by the time he was released, the lawyers for the lumber mills had gotten his injunction lifted. So when they brought him back home in the ambulance, he could look out the window and see the smoke in the valley from the pulp mill and the plumes rising in dirty strings from the tepee burners.

But he didn't seem to care now. His right side was paralyzed from the stroke, his arm was frozen at a crooked angle against his rib cage, and when he talked, his mouth worked as though there were a stitch sewn on the edge of his lips. He stayed in a wheelchair the first two months at home, and then he was able to walk about the house with a cane, but he looked stricken and grey as though a light had been blown out inside him. When the weather started to warm toward the end of March, I took him fishing with me on the Bitterroot, and he could hold the rod stiffly and work the automatic reel with his atrophied hand and take up the slack line with the other. He couldn't wade the stream or false cast, and he had to stay in one position and use wet flies, but when he hooked into a rainbow, I could see a smile come back into his gray eyes again.

Beth and I were married in a Catholic church in Missoula, and I bought twenty acres off Mr Riordan by the base of that blue canyon that cuts back through the mountain into the climbing pines beyond. Twenty acres isn't much in Montana, but it's mine, and it has a small stream and apple trees on it, and at night the deer come down to feed in the grass under an ivory moon. Two of the musicians from the band helped me build a split-log house on it, with a huge stone fireplace and a chimney and a front porch that looks out toward the river, the line of cottonwoods along the banks, and the infinite roll of the mountains beyond the fields.

I finished my song. I didn't get everything into it that I had wanted; but maybe you never do, just like the time my cousin Andre and I tried to raise in our young vanity that dead Indian's canoe from the silt bottom of the swamp. But I got most of it – the bottle trees during the Depression, the smoky green of the Gulf at sunset, the Southern Pacific blowing down the line at night toward Mobile. My parole officer gave me interstate travel privileges, and I drove up to Vancouver with Beth and our bass man and recorded it. It wasn't a big record. It was released only on the West Coast, but it played on the radio and on jukeboxes for a month, and two weeks after I thought it had been melted into slag, a recording studio in Nashville called and asked me to send a tape of anything else I had written.

It's May now, and the runoff from the snowpack

on the mountain behind my house has filled the creek bed in the canyon with a torrent of white water that bursts over the boulders in a rainbow's spray, lighting the pine and fir trees along the bank with a dripping sheen, and then flattens out at the base of the mountain and runs in a brown course through the pasture toward the river. The grass is tall and humming with insects where the water has flowed out into the field, and occasionally I can see the sun flash on the red beaks of mudhens in the reeds. The river is high and yellow, the sandbars and gravel islands have disappeared under the churning surface, and the bottoms of the cottonwoods cut long, trembling Vs in the current. I can feel the spring catching harder each day, and the irrigated fields across the river are a wet, sunlit green against the far mountains and the patches of snow still melting among the pines on the crest.

In the early evening it turns suddenly cool, you can smell wood smoke in the air, and mauve shadows fall across the valley floor as the sun strikes its final spark against the ridge. From my front porch, I can see Buddy's cabin faintly in the gathering dusk. Even after it has dissolved into the darkness and black trees and the laughter of his sons playing in the yard, I can still see it in my mind's eye, lighted, the wood stove lined with fire, and sometimes in that moment I'm caught forever in the sound of a blues piano and the beating of my own heart.